S0-BLY-649

THE DAY
Cinderella
DIED

by
Coll Ela Goetz

Brighid's Pen

Publishing, U.S.A.
1995

The Day *Cinderella* Died

Pulished by
Brighid's Pen Publishing
P.O. Box 7511
Colorado Springs, Colorado,
80933-7511, USA

Copyright © 1995 by Brighid's Pen Publishing, First Edition, First Printing: 1997

All rights reserved by Brighid's Pen Publishing. No part of this book, including cover may be reproduced or transmitted in any form, by any means (electronic, photocopying, recording, or otherwise) without prior written permission of the publisher. Library of Congress Catalog Card No.: 95-80868

ISBN 0-9469154-3-X

Printed in the United States of America

10 9 8 7 6 5 4 3 2

For sales inquiries and special bulk quantity prices, contact Brighid's Pen Publishing,

TEXT TO BE USED AS AN EPIGRAPH from <u>TRAUMA AND RECOVERY</u> by JUDITH LEWIS HERMAN, M.D. Copyright © 1992 by BasicBooks, Division of HarperCollins Publishers Inc. Reprinted by permission of BasicBooks, a subdivision of HarperCollins Inc.

TEXT USED IN CHAPTER 5, PG. 143 from <u>MOTHER WIT: A FEMINIST GUIDE TO PSYCHIC DEVELOPMENT</u> by DIANE MARIEDHILD. Copyright © 1981 by The Crossing Press, Freedom, CA. Reprinted by permission of The Crossing Press.

My deepest gratitude to both.

Author's Disclaimer: Some of this is real.
Some is not

This has been listed as a work of fiction.

This Book is Dedicated to: *To my beautiful daughters; to my sponsor, without whom I would never have been able to begin this book; to my Spirit Sisters without whom I would never have been able to finish this book; to my more recent spirit brother, Walking Crow and his ancestors, whose gentleness permitted me to connect with horror and come out whole; to my perpetrators, I assign you the status of teachers; to those in bondage to their nightmares world wide, there is freedom; to those in recovery from anything,* **Yes You Can!***; to those who assist us on our journey; to my therapist; to those I haven't met yet and those I may never meet in this time/space both outside me and inside me.*

A Special Word to Survivors *who read this book: There are scenes in this book that are graphically detailed traumatic events which might strike a familiar chord paralleling many lives. As my therapist has suggested with me: Please be very sure your memories are your own and distinguish what in my book is only similar to yours. If you have a support system, it may serve you to be in close contact as you read this book. If you do not have a support system, it may serve you well to develop one without procrastination. For those who begin to awaken and connect with traumatic memories long forgotten: There is help.* **Be sure what is yours and what is <u>not</u>.** *Blessings to all, Coll Ela.*

Lastly, the integrated I wish to recognize the woman and man we knew as my mother and my father. Mother, Father: Ann, Edward: We are aware that you loved me in the only ways you could. The integrated I accept the gifts of heritage and strength you gave me (us). The integrated I thank you and forgive you. The integrated I release you. The integrated I love you and bless you. Namaste ` (The ALL in all of me recognizes the ALL in you.)

ACKNOWLEDGMENTS

*I wish to thank my editors and reviewers. A special thanks to Sara Bailey, my Spirit Sisters, and my therapist for critiquing this work to make it readable for the public. I'd like to thank Thaddeus Golas (How many times will you do it again?!) for **Lazy Man's Guide to Enlightenment**- you were my first breakthrough many years ago (1979) and a constant companion for my reconstruction, Judith Lewis Herman, M.D., and her book **Trauma and Recovery** for helping my most recent reconstruction, and her publishers BasicBooks a division of HarperCollins, Diane Mariechild who wrote **Mother Wit: A Feminist Guide to Psychic Development** and her publishers The Crossing Press for some basic guidelines in many areas and being able to use a part of their books in my work. I especially would like to thank my perpetrators: I believe you've taught me well enough I won't have to repeat this ever again and you helped me to create this book, I am honored to be the one to do so... **NAMASTE!!** So many authors, books, lives, and music that gave me something to hang onto while I was finding my light buried in the catacombs beneath the debris of my childhood and the process of maturation and integration once I had enough pieces I could make sense of. One evening, in the summer of 1994 sitting on Fiddlers Green waiting for a concert to start, I wondered what I could possibly do with all this... this stuff, then I heard you Yanni. I heard what you had to say...*

"NO EXCEPTIONS!"...
I heard you. This is my creation.

Thank you. Thank you all.

Epigraph

Trauma and Recovery, Judith Lewis Herman, M.D., Professor of Psychiatry, Harvard University

"The ordinary response to atrocities is to banish them from consciousness. Certain violations of the social compact are too terrible to utter aloud: this is the meaning of the word unspeakable.... The conflict between the will to deny horrible events and the will to proclaim them aloud is the central dialectic of psychological trauma. People who have survived atrocities often tell their stories in a highly emotional, contradictory, and fragmented manner which undermines their credibility and thereby serves the twin imperatives of truth-telling and secrecy."
pp. 1, the Introduction.

They all came to "The Gathering" expecting to be revitalized and renewed as they shared their accomplishments with each other. How did they know... this time, it would be different?

Players at "The Gathering"

1.) **Brighid**: competent mechanic, Wiccan High-Priestess and Witch by the ancient Laws. She'll walk "the other roads" to find an answer.

2.) **Judy**: a psychotherapist, happily married to Mitch. She opens the gates to recovery for survivors and guides them back to wholeness.

3.) **Libby**: a business mogul, woman who has worked her way around the Good Ol' Boy system successfully... until...

4.) **Ollie**: emaciated on all levels. She finds Michael. She desperately wants the relationship to bring a panacea of change. It does.

5.) **Lea**: wants to restore the exciting days of her youth to take away the boredom she feels married to John. She may start her own club.

6.) **Mona**: born poor, worked her way to being one of the richest women in the world. Now she must use her superior intellect differently.

Players at "The Gathering"

7.) **Julie**: leader of the Duke's personal team of attorneys. First, only friend to Kitten, the Duke's wife. Did someone tell the Duke?

8.) **Kitten**: Texas oil magnate's wife, mother of his brood. She can have anything money can buy, but can she keep what she really wants?

9.) **Penny**: forged her way from ghetto life to become artist, poet, writer, entrepreneur able to make a living for her husband and herself.

10) **Dee**: well bred teacher, housewife, and mother, aspiring entrepreneur and writer. Teaching the tools of empowerment to many.

11) **Jo**: diagnosed M.P.D. after being sober and clean in AA for 17 years. Moving from disintegration to wholeness at lightning speed.

12) **Chris**: top charge nurse/health practitioner in OB/ER, one in a 15 year, 7 adult-6 child poly-fidelitous marriage. Much hinges on her skills.

13) **Hazel**: is Hostess for this year's "Gathering" in Colorado Springs. Hazel is well loved around the world as well as by those coming to the "Gathering".

Chapter 1

She was still in bed. Dreaming. Meditating. Half dreaming - half meditating, in the pre dawn space/time, where everything and nothing is real. She went back into visions, back into solutions for problems, back to ideas.

The strange kaleidoscope of events and scenarios blended and wove near believable tales flowing into one another. The air was clean and cool enough to make the images touchable. The bed was soft and enfolded her body. Under the covers, it was warm. She really intended to meditate but her mind swept away, chasing one thought after another like a butterfly flitting to a spring flowers' symphony.

Am I dreaming, then?... Oooh!... It's autumn, my favorite time of the year! When the weather turns cooler, there's something just below my heart that starts to move... I turn and I whirl... and I spin,... and begin The Dance within me. My body leaves the earth... It soars and wheels and fires The Sacred Dance. On a clear, cold day I meld into the wind; the crisp air blows tiny, electric, sparkles through my hair.

Every cell of my skin beckons me to join the current. My insides are light, fluid, transparent, ready to dance with the wind... I feel my dance weave its lace in and around me. I light facing the sun. Its red-yellow brilliance through my eyelids, blazes my insides... the cold tingles first my face... the sun, infuses the cold with luminance... tingling becomes vibration... becomes creation... Becomes... and The Dance begins again...

Bri suspected some of the "Gathering" would call it a spirit dance, Chi concentration, Kundalini energy or whatever. She knew this was herself saying *"Yes!"*, *"Thank You!"*, and *"Count me in!"* to Life, all in one.

She had heard of an athletic training technique where the athletes sit and visualize the feat they want to perform. Every day improving their performance, making corrections where necessary, they see it perfectly, in their minds.

If this was effective, then, each year as the weather cooled, she became liquid motion, spinning and turning and lifting off to music within herself. **Being** became motion, and light, and sound, and form in and around her.

It seemed funny as this happened to her, the people around her seemed to change. She wasn't sure if her perception of people changed the way they responded to her or people had their own dance to which they responded. So, she simply observed the changes in people as they occurred, or both, or neither. Maybe she thought too much and was just nuts or what... but she knew she liked The Dance in her, and the way most of the world around her appeared when she danced.

She also realized she was still in bed. She was going to be late if she didn't continue this in the erect position, getting ready for work. Her body didn't move: her mind went dancing on...

She tried to share this feeling with the "Gathering". A few said they understood and had experienced it different times of the year. A few only thought she was getting stranger and ought to grow up, quit playing fantasy games in her head to escape from real life. The "Gathering" was this year, in a few weeks as a matter of fact. They'd gathered every five years since high-school. She remembered when they first promised each other they would get together every five years. Some of them went on to college and finished, some didn't. Some went on to careers. Some got jobs until they were married, some got married right away. But, they all vowed, they would not die through stagnancy-precipitated brain death the way they had seen their parents and other adults of their time do.

Some of their classmates had already dropped into the *catabolic brain* as the "Gathering" called it. These *catabolic brains* already made up their minds that school was over for them, **for good**. They knew everything they would ever need to know about living... prob'bly learned it in grades one through six. Yep! Anything else could be left for the politicians, scientists or other people. They would remain as their ancestors before them, and, by the way, stay HAPPY.

She wondered how many deaths and births there would be if these people had their TV's and stereos taken away from them, say for ten years. They would almost have to live like their ancestors. She didn't think they would fare as well as their kinsmen.

She chuckled at the thought of ol' Bobby Henderson without his earphones and Walkman. Why, he'd have to listen to someone else besides the Rockman and the voices inside his head. Maybe that's what he was trying to escape from, anyway. *There I go again thinking, thinking, thinking.*

Of course, there were always parents, teachers, and the chronic, perhaps terminal, realists who warned, "Wait till you get out on your own! You won't have time for that nonsense." or "It's tough enough to just try to make a living without worrying about further education." There were always those well meaning people letting you know, "Life will teach you all you need to know." *Oh! Yes! Let's not forget,* "If you take care of the responsibilities you ought to be taking care of, as an adult, you won't have any energy left for all that foolishness!" There were those understanding, tolerant people, too, that just knew it was a matter of time: "When you're older - reach maturity - get married and get busy with a family - you'll settle down, not ask so many questions, and be HAPPY like the rest of us."

Before Bri looked up the definition of commencement, she believed, like most, it meant the grand finale. "Now you're gonna find out what **real** life is all about!", instead of the beginning, the awakening, -*The Dance*. She wondered if the catabolism of the passion for life began in utero and was complete with brain death by age thirty-five or so, and only those anomalies such as their "Gathering" delayed the process. After all, even within the "Gathering", she was beginning to hear the rumblings of, "You should grow up!" They were only going to have their sixth reunion.

Thirty years since high-school and she felt more alive and vital than ever before in her life. She thought with a little amusement, *This is how you're supposed to feel just before you die, if you're a good person. Not now!* Not at age forty-seven, and by the average American's television induced standard she was too plump, too gray, and too old.

How many times was she told to, "Act your age!" As if someone else's idea of what matronly behavior *ought* to be should govern **her** life. For that matter, as if what anyone else's idea of what her behavior ought to be, in any area, should govern her life! She thought aggressively, *Don't you **should** on me!*

She conceded there were some things people in general could agree not to do out of convenience, like not stealing, not beating up others, etc. But, when it came to people agreeing on when would be the best time to stop being enthusiastic about living, or

4

quit on life, or accept another's idea of who 'self' is or must be in order to live up to someone else's idea of when life ended or began -- Bri refused. Others' opinions were not more important than hers, especially about herself.

Further, she did not concede or consent she must, at a certain age, step aside for youth nor that youth was better than who and what she was right this minute. She never did learn the script well enough to be in the same show as the rest. One of the problems, as she saw it, was: most people got the script down good, but kept doing dress rehearsal instead of the real performance. There's no coming back to the same scene in real life.

People talked about what they thought *real life* was, then waited for some time in some imaginary future to be real. As if letting the person next to you know who you really are could make you 'less than'. She remembered well those years she kept trying to fit into the concept: "Better to be thought a fool than open your mouth and remove all doubt."

Well! Fool or no, she was who and what she was. She would change what **she** saw fit to change. So what, if some (or all) thought her a fool. She had lived through enough hard times and good times to see who stood with her when the fun began.

She also learned: (Finally!) There are no free lunches. Her father tried to tell her when she was growing up. She watched him prostitute his values until he had to drink to numb the knowledge; he would never be what he really wanted to be. At a certain point in his life, he gave up all hope of ever trying. He became the American ideal and lost himself. She wondered, if he knew then, **that** is what is meant by the phrase "There are no free lunches."

Bri knew that we all pay in some way for the values we choose... and we all pay if we don't live by the values we choose. If the value is too different from the behavior-- one has to go, for sanity's sake. The value must change or the behavior must change, because if the payment for the difference is too great to be acceptable, you have to drink or drug or go nuts or have a heart attack or have a stroke or die.

Most people, she thought, *avoid knowing what their values are and attribute all those diseases to fatty foods, pollution, stress, or whatever is popular at the time. No matter. The results are the same. By whatever label you put on it:* **There are no free lunches.** *In some way, you pay every time you let yourself down or go against your own value system.*

Getting to know her own values was a trip, but living up to them certainly provided many a challenge and opportunity as well as joy and self-esteem. It took her a helluva long time, in the first place, to learn that's where self-esteem comes from. She used to think you got it from other people, or the job you had, or maybe from your husband. Maybe, you could just say you had such and such a value without having to live it. Perhaps you'd be able to live a certain way and not believe in it, and still have self-esteem: a 'fake it till you make it', laid back kind of attitude. *Here I go again-- thinking, thinking.*

Hazel would say, "There's a time for thinking and a time for doing." As she began to think about the coming "Gathering", her mind lighted on Hazel. Hazel is one of those incredibly loving people. They had been friends since the beginning of time. She often admonished Brighid, simply and lovingly, for being too critical of her humanness. Hazel was one of the few individuals she knew who could make humanness seem like the most Godly (or

Goddessly, as Bri preferred) of traits instead of the lowest common denominator.

Then, there was Mona. Mona, also, believed in doing, but with a minimum of effort and thinking and a maximum visible return. After all, if your outsides reflect your insides, it stands to reason: the more you have ('quality stuff' of course) for others to see, the more you have on the inside. Right!!? You don't have to flaunt it, but you do have to have it. It also stands to reason: if any kind of thinking or action won't *get* you immediate visible returns, it must be useless and a downright waste of valuable time, effort, and energy. One must always keep in mind the energy shortage.

Then, there was Kitten. She went to college in Texas and learned: control was power and power was control. She married a rich cattle and oil magnate and proceeded to *control* him through various feminine ways and when that was not possible, she maintained *power* by controlling herself. At least, **that** was not an illusion of power. The evidence of power spoke for itself. Of course, Brighid should get **herself** a little more disciplined and rigid if she wanted to be the master and not the victim. If one is to survive and not be anyone's victim: one must control one's universe and everyone in that universe.

Then there was Ollie. Ollie lived on the edge of poverty and emaciation, on more levels than the physical. She had her own experience of survival. The group had paid her way, several times, to the "Gathering". Despite all Ollie's efforts, and the group's efforts; the pattern of Ollie's life was looking like a sine wave on an oscilloscope. The area known as success was positioned just above the peak of the sine wave with a massive area of inertia, held down by gravity, in between.

Then there was... but there wasn't enough time to saunter through her memories right now. This was a time for doing! She needed to make plans for the "Gathering" in a few weeks. She would share at the "Gathering", with her friends, her peers, what she did in the last five years. She would share how she changed, what she kept in the last five years, and how she danced.

She also needed to get ready for the ritual tonight. The ritual tonight was a religious service, celebrating the monthly full moon with her Theamorphic group. Her religous group had planned a simple service tonight. They would set in motion healing energies to enable one of their group to get unstuck and progress further with his therapy.

All of a sudden, Bri had a gnawing ache somewhere in the back of her throat. It felt like trying to scream without the sound or mouth movements. It called to her awareness like the first realization of a bee sting. Something was wrong in the world as she knew it. She couldn't point to anything concrete, couldn't begin to explain the feeling in words, but "Something" was **very** wrong in the universe she lived in.

She tried to concentrate on *where* or, more specifically, *who* evoked these feelings and couldn't come up with an immediate answer. *Maybe, as the day goes by, something will manifest.* She got out of bed. Whatever state of blissful awareness she was in evaporated with that creeping sense of unrightness. She fingered her pentagram and acknowledged the Goddess within her.

She needed to prepare for that brake job and tranny work she had waiting for her at the shop. One of her ritual group had to talk with her before the ritual tonight and she suspected that time would have to be squeezed if she was going to be ready on time. She looked at the clock. *Oh! Great Goddess! I'm not going to be on time for work.* She shook her head, grabbed her energy back into her body and ran to the bathroom for her morning ablutions.

The day went quickly, with a minimum of gremlins in the moving parts. Brighid did, however, bang the bravery out of her hands. After cleaning them with the grease-removing solution, she fully intended to soak them and herself in those special bath salts she had made with the new pain-relieving essential oil formula she just developed.

Uummm! Bri could just feel the soft, warm water moving on her body, releasing the tension and pain as she breathed in the wonderful energizing fragrance. As she began the healing bath process, the ritual companion she expected arrived.

"Come on in, Fauwyn, we can talk while the elementals Earth, Air, and Water remind me how wonderful they are. Fire's been modified to warmth in the water, but I don't think it will mind, under the circumstances." Bri relaxed into the water.

"Bri, I'm really upset" Fauwyn began disconsolately. "How long have I been in the Pagan community? About four or five years, now, Bri?" Bri just nodded her head and let the woman vent, as she slid deeper into the tub. Fauwyn put the toilet top down, sat on it and continued.

"Am I stupid to believe in perfect trust and perfect love? Am I a sucker to trust in the Pagan community? It sure feels that way. Maybe they're just immature or inconsiderate and I shouldn't expect them to keep their word. I believe my word is my bond. Goddess knows, the first things we're taught are words can have power, to be careful what and how we say things. But even before that, I grew up with the idea my word was me. I don't understand! Are they liars? Are they immature? Do they just not care what they commit to? Are they unaware how a lie or breaking their word disintegrates trust? Or tell me, am I the one who's the fool for believing them in the first place? Is perfect trust and perfect love only given to *special* people and not to all? Maybe it's a big joke, an unbelievable old myth and I'm the infant for not recognizing what everybody else sees as a ruse? Tell me Bri, before I just give up believing in people entirely!" Fauwyn hung her head dismally.

Bri could empathize. Bri went through a period of similar awakening. Full of elation, Bri found The Lady and her true path. She was enraptured and inspired, enamored with the goodness in *"An it harm none"* Pagan peoples. Brighid overlooked her life experiences and everything she'd ever learned about people and put herself in a position to be taken advantage of. The acuteness of the pain she went through, as the effulgence of religious make-believe was replaced with spiritual acumen, was dampened but it remained a tender splinter in her ethereal skin.

"Did something in particular happen?" Brighid asked.

"Something?!" Fauwyn exclaimed, "A whole lot of *somethings*. I had made arrangements to go hiking with Brad. He not only didn't show up, he didn't call or anything. I made arrangements with Gerry to go to a lecture about 50 miles away. When I called him, he said he wasn't going to go or call me. He said he'd just come back from there and had to do his laundry. I asked Gail about it and she acted like I shouldn't have expected common courtesy. Like it was too mundane for highly evolved spiritual beings to keep their word. I told Karla something personal, risked being vulnerable; she and Rhiannon threw it in my face and rubbed my nose in it. *After* she was a witness and advocate for me in a legal matter, she tells me she won't appear in court." Fauwyn paused a moment.

"People will say they have such great experiences with this person or that one. My experience is so totally different and negative, I was beginning to wonder if my perceptions are off. Maybe I come across as such a rotten person, people just treat me like shit because they figure I deserve it. I know it can't be true when people treat me that way without even knowing me or interacting with me. I thought I was becoming paranoid until I realized; I was set up. They're making a mockery out of perfect trust and perfect love. The principles they talk about are just that-- talk. Bri, that's not testing to see if you really want to be in the community. That behavior is an excuse to hide fear, inferiority and smallness, not to mention just plain bad manners. They're trying to project an image of worldliness and holiness and specialness with nothing behind the image. Even illusion is made of something." Fauwyn sighed.

"I believe, I went through something real close to that when I first came to Paganism." Brighid got out of the tub and began to towel off. "I think I forgot all I had experienced, opened my heart, and blindly trusted people meant what they said and every word they spoke meant, to them, what it did to me. The edge is off the pain and I can tolerate socializing with most of them, but I still prefer not to be in circle with them, if I can avoid it. Remembering the different, little ways they appeared to consciously set out to obliterate my trust in them still smarts.

"I'm just as certain some of my perception is colored by previous pain, so a possibly innocuous event, here and there, appeared intentional, but my overall evaluation was accurate. More importantly, at that time, I was 'given', if you will, a practical demonstration that physical laws and spiritual laws are inseparable. The multiverse, being in constant change, always maintains balance. I got to see just how limited my vision is, in this form," Brighid said with a grin of chagrin. The poor woman looked like Brighid was talking another language.

"What exactly do you mean?" Fauwyn asked, "What did you do? Did you confront them and scream at them? Did you curse them, put it to them like they put it to you? What did you do?"

Brighid smiled gently at her, and replied, "First, cursing is out! There is **nothing** that will attach them to **you** like a curse will. You will put yourself in a position to **have** to interact with them and if they are unwilling to change their behavior... you're stuck in the same environment with them, still acting the way they do. If you think you feel bad now, when you can choose to leave their presence, imagine what it would be like to be unable to split. So I don't recommend cursing unless you want more of the same. Besides you can't use magic, effectively, to hide social inadequacies, or bully someone into leaving you alone or respecting you or not doing you harm for long." Bri began to put on her ceremonial robe. "Like any relationship-- two half-people don't make a whole person. Neither can a half-person and magic make one powerful, self-directed person. Attempting to take away a person's free will to make her/him treat you right will only draw that many more people who 'need fixing'. Magic is used only when other methods to focus **your** energies, not someone elses energies, have been eliminated." The young woman looked more distressed than when she walked in.

"Look," Brighid said, "There are better and easier ways to get noticed and feel powerful and accepted than to turn toward a religious path like Wicca. In fact, any spiritual path exacts its own fee for the learning you receive. There's always balance: for every force, there exists an equal and opposing force; energy is neither created nor destroyed; so as you learn, there is no void left in the place where the knowledge existed. You give something of yourself, of equal value, in return."

The young woman grimaced, "What about a spell put into motion, about being a Witch?" Fauwyn's voice trailed off looking at Brighid's face.

"What are the elements present in a spell?" Brighid asked. Bri could see this might have to continue after the ritual. In fact, this might be an all night session, from the looks of things. The woman replied cautiously,

"Well... There is intention, direction and power or energy behind it,"

"Right! So, what is the difference between a spell and a fervent prayer? Say, you have a mother whose child is on it's deathbed. The mother goes into the room, sits by the bed, begs, pleads, with all the feeling she can manifest. She speaks to the child; she speaks to the 'universe' or her deity, anyone or thing that will listen, to let her child live. You have intention; the life and well being of the child. You have direction; to deity, the universe and the child itself. Let's not forget the boundaries of free will and the responsibility we have to permit all creatures to learn or not learn as they choose, and to not make slaves out of them by doing it for them. You definitely have energy behind the mother's will for the child to live. Well?"

"What about being a Witch?" the young novice pleaded.

"Ah! Yes! About being a Witch. I thought we made the distinction clear enough in class that everyone understood. Obviously, something was missing... Let's start at the beginning. To be a Witch you don't necessarily have to work magic or cast spells, although that option is available, and the weight of responsibility lies a lot heavier being a Witch, because of the vows you take and the uncommon knowledge you focus on, receive, and use. Next, I can say I am the President of the United States but that won't make it so. I can claim anything I want and the proof is in the action and result." Bri looked for signs of comprehension.

"Witch is a sacred title granted to those who enhance life: granted by powers that make universes manifest, consciously." Bri continued, "It can be granted to those who've already proven themselves or to one who accepts the responsibility to enhance life whenever and wherever possible according to free will and for the good of all. It is not a position to be treated lightly or used to placate your own sense of unworthiness and fear by gaining power over others. To manipulate people, places, and things to buy 'safety' doesn't get lasting results, although we both know those that try to use it that way and they appear to get away with it." Bri looked to see if the student was following then continued.

"Remember. Nature abhors a vacuum and balance is always maintained. Energy is never lost. Pay now: Pay later. There are no free lunches. There are sorcerers, adepts, High Magicians who are not necessarily Witches. Although sorcerers, adepts and High Magicians can be Witches, also, if they enhance life with their craft. Energy doesn't care how you use it, but the rules that exist, exist for everyone. For people who do not choose to enhance life with their powers, as Thaddeus Golas says in the <u>Lazy Man's Guide to Enlightenment</u>, the Sea of Infinite Bliss wouldn't **feel** safe or right." Bri paused to let the woman mull over what had been said.

The young woman looked uneasy but less confused and Brighid continued, "Next, I did confront a few of them, those I thought might be reasonable, considering the way they talked. What an experience that was! They, not only, blatantly denied their behavior... they made me out to be some kind of degenerate, paranoid villain. They accused me of doing what I confronted them with. They didn't confront me, they accused me after I spoke up. That's nothing but a con-artist's double back to sidetrack a 'mark' from seeing what the con-artist is doing. Since it has been a spiritual axiom for me, if someone **really** bothers me, I have to look at: 'What is it I see in them, that I don't like in myself?' I had to do some evaluating of my own behavior. I recall part of a conversation with a woman named Donna, who claimed to be a Witch since she was very young. The gist was; if she said something, she had a perfect right and was always correct in doing so. If I said the very same thing, I was aggressive and antisocial. She was above censure and I was not. I basically gave up trying to communicate on an adult level with people who weren't."

"Well, what did you do?" Fauwyn asked troubled.

"I ended up doing what we're supposed to do in the first place." Brighid said.

"But what about them?" Fauwyn pushed on.

"I can't change them. Their actions will have the appropriate consequences and rewards. The very lie of 'evil' is that you can somehow evade or 'transmute' those consequences. Pay now, or later-- live in shadow or live in light. But don't forget by its very nature, light *creates* shadow. There's a lot of gray out there. We are all responsible for our own actions and reactions, victim and perpetrator alike," said Brighid. "The principles involved **require** I work on me, and as I do, I will attract those of like mind. I have to be honest here-- while I worked on myself, I often wondered if the people I attracted really reflected me-- **always**? My conclusion is: sometimes yes... sometimes no. You get to see where you want to go, where you came from and where you are now, all at the same time. And yes! Sometimes it's difficult to know which is which--

not as in healer, or life enhancer! pun! pun!" Brighid caught the novice off guard with the levity. Fauwyn began a tentative smile.

"It's important to observe perfect trust and perfect love in those around you, but it's far more important to be a person worthy of having the concept extended to you by others. You have just experienced the importance of honesty. Let's face it, even if you fool everyone in the universe by lying, how can you trust the person in the mirror when you know that person has just been untrustworthy? All you will see is a liar, an obliterator of trust. In the mirror, you see the only person who can dissolve your trust and self-esteem in an instant. You also see the only one who can restore it and keep it. Others can only point out what's already there. Others can't take away something that isn't there nor give you or add to something that doesn't exist. This initial principle has its roots in just about every other principle. It cannot be avoided nor evaded." Bri stopped a moment to get the cakes and juice out of the fridge.

"Principles don't start with someone else. I don't have the principles I do because someone else has them or thinks they're right. I have them because without them, I couldn't live with the self-loathing I would have to face every time I looked in the mirror. With them I can live my life to its fullest, trusting my own judgment." Brighid ended, hoping it wasn't too boring or abstract for the neophyte. She also hoped it wasn't too much lecturing rather than sharing. As they walked out the door to go to the ritual, the young woman was self-immersed in thought. *A good sign*, thought Bri.

They got to the park as the night air began to get a bit of a nip to it. The fire and friends were warm as they greeted one another, caught up on current events and went over what they hoped to accomplish with the ritual. The ritual had its intention specially focused tonight, but it was also a celebratory ritual, as all of their rituals celebrated the earth, its elements, and all that created, contained, reproduced, and maintained life. They gathered in a circle to begin their worship. A circle, where everyone can see everyone else, with no beginning and no ending.

They all joined hands, spoke aloud,

"This ritual and what we set in motion this night:

Harms none.
Is according to free will.
For the good of all.
In perfect trust
and perfect love
and perfect harmony."

They listened, as the Priestess spoke the:

Charge of the Goddess:

"Know that whenever you have need of anything,
OPEN TO ME

Set aside a time and space for me alone.

I am the wind and the breath of life within you.
I am the life of the sun, and the fire and heat in your body.
I am the oceans and the waters, and I course
in the fluids that ebb and flow in your being.
I am the earth and all matter,
I am the substance that houses and protects your spirit.

All acts of love and life are mine.
OPEN TO ME

In love I created you. I can never leave you.
And if you seek and cannot find me without,
turn and look within.

For there, I am ALWAYS till the end of form and time.*"*

The Priestess paused, "Lady, we honor your Immanence within us and in all things, let us feel your *PRESENCE.*"

Chapter 2

Judy was terribly shaken. She wasn't sure what she heard. It was loud. It could have been a scream. No one else, apparently, heard it. It left her with a sense something awful had just happened or was just about to happen and there was nothing she could do to stop **it** from happening.

She wondered if one of her patients had a crisis. She and her clients were bonded in a way that sometimes she knew one of them would be calling soon, but this didn't *feel* like one of her clients. As a psychotherapist, it would be inappropriate to call any of her patients, regardless of how urgent it felt. All she could do was wait it out.

She got up from her desk and walked to the window, staring out, not really looking at the street. The sun was bright. It was early morning. She was expecting Trish earlier than usual.

Maybe she just wasn't used to being in the office at this time of the morning-- that was probably it. She vaguely remembered what it was she was concerned about in the first place-- whatever it was, it was over now anyway. Trish should be here any minute, and she needed to be ready. Just about all of Judy's patients were sensitive to her moods and could personalize the effects of even a sour stomach, so she needed to ground and center before each one. Any carrying over of evaluating or residual emotion was immediately internalized by the person she had in front of her. In a way, it kept her on her toes.

By being so sensitive and vulnerable to Judy's "feel", each person demanded to be treated as an individual and be evaluated as such. They didn't do this overtly nor were they aware this was one of the consequences of their sensitivity.

Considering Judy's position, and how her clients viewed her importance to them, they would have been overwhelmed with fear that the very nature of *who* they were would be seen as a manipulative threat. Judy would then have to take an offensive/defensive position toward them, rather than a caring neutral position vital for progressive and healthy psychiatric growth.

They were, after all, survivors. Their senses were turned up to the max all the time. They were aware of their environment and the people in it, in a way ordinary people could never be. Each, in their own way, from their earliest memories had no one to depend on and turn to for protection, no realistic instruction for patterning, guidance and wisdom.

As survivors, most had no matching reference points with ordinary people and depended entirely upon themselves. With a traumatized child's perspective used as a basis for evaluating regular and everyday information, translation of ordinary events meant: their environment and the people in it behaved the way they did because of them. It was up to them, alone, to be sure "everything" was okay. Their survival depended upon it. It was like being in an excited state of fight-or-flight 24 hours a day. Their body functions were stretched to the limits, like a rubberband pulled to the max and kept there.

To compensate for the constant tension, their bio-systems reacted to even the smallest stimuli in a grossly exaggerated way to maintain some semblance of balance. Most of them had physical problems stemming from the unremitting, mobilized-for-crisis physiology in their bodies.

Judy was awed this condition lasted so long before the human body started to break down and show the inevitable, wearing effects of this type of physiology. She was also stressed that more doctors didn't recognize the symptoms. They treated each 'symptom' as though it was not connected to a whole.

*How could such 'smart' people ignore the obvious? What's happened to the 'scientific method', especially where medicine was concerned? Is medicine such an 'art' there can be no 'science' in it any more? Or was there ever any **science** in it in the first place? 'Caveat Emptor' even in medicine-- **especially** in medicine.*

Judy knew her professors would raise their eyebrows at what the psychotherapist experience had molded her into. One of the commitments she felt strongly about was her obligation to provide a safe environment for her patients to, appropriately, take over care of their own bodies and minds, so emotional maturity could begin.

She provided alternative ideas and options, ways to acquire new information on how and what to be 'responsible' for, in themselves and their interaction with people and their environment. They then had more 'options' from which to choose, instead of only the patterning learned in early childhood.

She defined the **Problem** as a traumatic survival response. The child developed exaggerated, sensitively heightened responses that appeared to control an uncontrollable and life-threatening environment and the dangerous people in it... to be able to survive. Once a problem was **Solved** and an answer found, that answer became 'Written In Stone', because of the trauma surrounding it.

Every issue was 'black or white' with no room for anything in between, and no room for new information or solutions that might

21

upset a very delicate life balance. Instead of answers leading to new questions, the very process of maturity, their process stopped when **The Solution** was found.

Like a robot, or one of Pavlov's dogs, they would return to the same set of ideas or behaviors that seemed to work the first time, when equivalent problems or situations presented themselves in the present. To control their world, *to survive*, there was no room for error or change-- both error and/or change could signify the interruption of survival. The threat of non-survival was so real and surrounded with so much trauma and terror, most continued survival behavior processing long after the "threat" ceased to exist.

Fortunately, we are not Pavlov's dogs. As humans, we have the capacity to change our earlier programming. It's possible to repattern and learn new skills. It's possible to become aware of and function in a life that is more than mere survival. It is **extremely** *difficult, because a person must know specifically how they learn. Sometimes, they must know how they learned a specific characteristic to reverse the process and develop a new process* **but it can be done.**

The **Solution**, obviously enough, is to develop living patterns that reflect and respond appropriately to present living situations, and create 'healthy' living patterns, instead of different 'survival' skills. Both her friends, Penny and Dee, communicated "Sanity in an insane world may well be the cosmic oxymoron.", but she had a Pollyanna spirit inside her that permitted her to think she contributed to the health and well-being of her clients.

In doing that, she was not setting her clients up for betrayal and ambush in a world that would take advantage of them, but providing them with skills to be whole and healthy individuals who deal with, maneuver around in, and have the ability to interact successfully in the world and with its people, as it is. Judy provided the safe place, encouragement, alternative ideas, new information and its sources but the people repatterned themselves.

That, essentially, was her goal as a therapist. She wasn't a savior, or a doctor-cure-all. She accepted there are and will be unresolved conflicts in everyone's life, but she adamantly refused to believe anyone had to be immobilized and stuck in the **Problem** forever. Her introspection would someday be published in the book she intended to write, but to bring the facts forth, as she saw them, without ruining her career, was, at best, a problem.

Trish walked into her office. Judy turned around with a welcoming smile only to erase it as she saw the dejected woman flop into the chair.

"Good morning," Judy said carefully. Trish looked at Judy with accusing eyes and a resentful expression... As if it were 'her fault' that Trish felt the way she did.

One of the first behavior patterns Judy insisted be stopped and relearned was fault-finding. Blaming and fault-finding did not lead to **Solutions**. They only succeeded in keeping the **Problem** alive in a perpetual cycle of finger-pointing, scapegoating, guilt, and crisis. In order to begin manifesting effective behavioral changes, thinking patterns had to be interrupted, examined, evaluated, and responsibility taken for new and appropriate responses. First, the **Problem** needed to be stated in as clear terms as possible. Then as many new and different **Solutions** as possible identified. The **Solutions** had to be implemented, making corrections and adjustments where necessary.

As Judy looked at Trish, she thought how she would express this concept in her book: *Emotion is appropriate as a response to behavior, not an irrational motivator of action. Cause or blame is only important to assure a person isn't doing the same things, expecting different results. More in line with the idea: a certain action or behavior will get a certain result or is the source of crisis (or option to change) when that result doesn't occur. Being victimized by change and/or the inability to suspend or control outside change personally could be considered a dilemma. Many of my clients were taught: 1.) New information or responses threaten survival and 2.) all comfort, nurturance and sustenance for survival is entirely dependent on that which is outside themselves.*

It creates quite a problem if you learned the only skills available to you between the ages of birth and five years old. Insanity may very well be doing the same thing and expecting different results but equally insane is expecting everyone to treat a person of thirty or forty as if they were twenty just because their learning had been suspended or they were unfamiliar with how to learn new responses. Life and expectation move on whether survivors do or not. Judy looked at Trish again. Trish's irate outburst brought Judy back to the present.

"That asshole! That idiot! Who the hell does he think he is!? Anyone who has control over somebody's life like that and can't stand to hear the truth should be strung up. Humiliated, the way he does others, then killed! Eliminated off the face of the earth!" Trish got out of the chair and began pacing back and forth like a caged tiger. "He's so puffed up with his own grandeur! Just because he can do good for ten people, the one he victimizes should be overlooked! Oh! Well! You can't win 'em all and the sacrifice of one for the good of the many just has to be, unless, of course, it's you who's being sacrificed!"

Trish stopped pacing, faced Judy and spoke, "How on earth can a person get well if the psychiatrist can't stand hearing the truth!!? The truth with the appropriate emotion behind it!! You're sick because you believed the lies in the first place... 'It didn't really happen that way', 'It's all in your head', 'Oh stop it! It wasn't **that** bad!'; then you're expected to get well by perpetuating another set of lies!!? You're sick because you're feelings can't be attached to behavior too painful to connect with and be able to survive. How can you **ever** connect appropriate feelings to behaviors if you can't express honestly what you feel about what was done to you? It doesn't make sense to me. I can see not being offensive, but when the very truth is offensive... should you lie?- Try to cover it up with inane and trite phrases? Try to make less of the truth so it won't be as offensive to **others**?!!"

Trish's voice rose with a whine, "Oh! Dear! I was tortured as a child and I was programmed to self-destruct if I told. I was programmed to be antisocial and display emotions inappropriate to the circumstances, so I would look nuts and no one would take me seriously. I was programmed not to be able to change these patterns in the most severe ways, but I won't go into the details because it didn't happen to **YOU**!" Trish mimicked sarcastically, "**YOU** shouldn't be bothered with how angry I am! **YOU** shouldn't be uncomfortable because I'm shattered! **YOU** shouldn't be affected because a wrong was perpetrated on ME-- **NOW SHOULD YOU**?" She paused a second, looking at something only she could see, and continued the tirade.

"What on earth could **YOU** do about it, anyway? It was my responsibility and my fault-- wasn't it?" Trish appeared to begin screaming to an imaginary person even though she was looking at Judy. "So what if I was an infant, a baby. Doesn't the bible say Lot gave his virgin daughters to the whole fucking crowd and isn't the bible our guide for moral behavior? Don't lay with another man you manly man but rape and pillage women and children **THEY** are GOWD'S designated sewage and hate receptacle!!

"Well," Trish spoke directly to Judy, "If I kidnapped that bunch that did all those slimy, painful, mind twisting things to me and shot off his dick, put her on a rack and stuck things up her, dislocated their joints, put their heads under water and sodomized them, over and over, so they wouldn't cry out, put their hands in cold water and put electricity through the dislocated joints-- a little mix up as to what cold and hot is... the better to tweek your mind with, my dear-- and shot off their hands and put a bullet through their mouths, thereby assuming the RESPONSIBILITY of justice IN MY LIFE!-- WELL!-- That would be another story entirely, **NOW WOULDN'T IT**!!!!" Trish was raging.

"**NO! NO! NO! YOU CAN'T** take matters into your own hands! Now, we have laws. **NO! NO!** It doesn't matter if **THEY** did that to **YOU**-- two wrongs don't make a right-- justice is a tricky word-- besides, who can understand-- we can't violate **THEIR** rights, even though we have evidence they violated your rights! Why! That would make US just as bad as **THEM**! Judy! **I WANT TO KILL THEM!** I want to torture them and make them feel every slimy thing they made **ME** feel! I don't want to violate their rights-- I want to violate their **bodies** and their **minds** the way they violated mine!!

"**JUUDDDDYYYYY!!!**"

The scream erupted from deep inside, reverberating through the air, rocking the foundation of detached feelings, shattering the aloofness that prevents synaptic connection. It echoed through Trish's convulsive sobs as she collapsed into the chair.

Judy let her scream and cry. Rage and hatred seemed an appropriate emotion for this situation even though many of her colleagues did not agree and were even frightened for their safety when their patients displayed "rage".

If these people can't display appropriate emotion in front of their therapist-- who can they display it to? If they can't display even inappropriate emotion in front of their therapist, who would explain why it was inappropriate and what was appropriate? Most people seek help when all their best efforts have failed. They seek new answers and ways.

If a therapist or psychiatrist can't stand to see REAL rage in a person, empathize, and provide new solutions, what are they doing in the position they're in but aggrandizing themselves, hoping like hell they never have to have the same emotions or never get caught with them. Being real doesn't have to occlude being effective, but if a choice has to be made...

"You saw the insurance company's psychiatrist?" Judy questioned.

"Yes. Yesterday." Trish sobbed.

"Do you want to talk about it?" Judy asked gently. Trish nodded her head up and down, trying to regain her composure.

"I told you I didn't want to go there." Trish sniffled, "He's an insurance whore! He didn't care one bit about me, only whether or not the insurance company was obligated to pay for your fees. I was telling him what an asshole the anesthetist was, about the stupid anesthesia not working, and he comes down on me and says, 'Don't speak about my colleagues that way.'-- It didn't matter that it was the truth-- I suppose he'd like me to think just because a person is a doctor, he couldn't possibly be an asshole or every doctor deserves respect no matter what he does.

"You know what he said to me!?" Trish looked perplexed, "'Just think, out of all the people a surgeon helps, if he makes one mistake out of a hundred and he lets that affect him.' Judy, does that mean it's okay to ignore that mistake? Should he never make any corrections of his mistakes because it might take his confidence away? Is confidence built on lies or overlooking the truth? Real confidence? Because he helps or saves thousands does it mean he's not accountable for one? What if he makes one mistake out of a thousand and *doesn't* let it affect him?"

"I can see you're upset, but what is the real issue?" asked Judy. Trish sat a minute and thought.

"I don't know if there's one real issue." she said. "I felt like I had to agree with every thing he said for him to give me a favorable-- no-- not favorable-- truthful, for even a truthful report, I had to lie. I had to betray me, to be able to act in my own best interest. I felt humiliated I just didn't state what my truth was and stick to my guns. In agreeing with him, I let-- even helped-- him to victimize me."

Judy thought a minute.

"Trish, did he ask you specifically about your opinion of those doctors? How did you get to where you offered him that opinion about what assholes they are?" Judy asked.

"Well..." Trish thought a long moment before continuing, "We were talking about my allergies to medication and then it got into the surgery and how I really didn't have any anesthesia and then about what the anesthetist said and what an asshole he was..."

Judy interrupted, "I can see how you got there, but tell me Trish, if you just hadn't said anything about the anesthetist being an asshole, just talked about the physical facts surrounding the surgery-- would that have betrayed yourself? Would you have felt victimized by not telling?"

Trish thought for a long while, then she said,

"Hmmm. I really don't know. I'll have to think about that. On the one hand, it certainly wasn't necessary to the physical account, but on the other, he seemed to discount my account of the physical facts as erroneous. He seemed to be asking about my emotional response to the physical happening. I'll think about that during the week."

"Don't forget, not next week, but the week after, we won't be having a session. I'll be out of town." Judy said.

"Where are you going?" Trish said, trying to hide the panic.

"I'm going to a special reunion," Judy said.

"Will you be gone all week?" Trish tried not to sound concerned.

"Yes, I'll be gone all week, but I've already spoken to a colleague of mine named Brad-- I'll give you the details and his number-- he's a really great guy and I'll fill him in on your progress and where we are now. Everything will be all right." Trish didn't look any more secure with that knowledge.

"You always seem to be gone when I need you the most," Trish said.

"It can't be helped, Trish. I've been planning this for a long time. Besides, have a little confidence in yourself and your protectors. You've all been in there a long time taking care of you. Now that you're all working together, I don't think anything can happen in a week that all of you, together, can't handle until I get back. What do you think?"

Trish asked with her eyes down, "You're not leaving because I spoke that way to the shrink? Are you?"

Judy smiled, "No, Trish. This was planned to happen years ago when I got out of high-school. It happens every five years."

Trish's face changed very slightly and she said, "I think we can handle it."

Trish's face changed very slightly again and she said, "I guess, I'm still not used to that. To feel my face change. It seems strange not to hear just noise in my head, and feel something besides me, inside me."

Trish seemed to be reflecting, "I think we'll be just fine now. We have an understanding; if one of us goes to jail-- all of us goes to jail or an institution and if one of us gets hurt, this physical body gets damaged and all of us will suffer eventually. We've had enough suffering-- time for good stuff." Judy wasn't sure if Trish was talking to her or not.

Trish finished and left. Judy had some time before the next client. Judy was going to do some of the mounds and mounds of paperwork, required by insurance companies and other agencies, but her thoughts kept going to the "Gathering". She was excited. She had lots to share, and she looked forward to the intimacy only this group provided. They were her link to her past. They reflected her hope for the future. They cried with her, laughed with her, encouraged her, hoorayed her accomplishments. She told them things she'd never tell her family. They preserved her continuity through time and space. She knew words and thoughts could not express her feelings. Time and space could not titrate nor precipitate them, either. She thought of each woman, and the conterminous place in her heart for each, but Hazel's place made her smile. She lingered in the memories of their friendship.

Hazel never ignored pain and sorrow of any kind, but somehow her very presence conveyed that pain and sorrow had no lasting claim on the human spirit. Joy, ecstasy, hope, abundance, health... these were innate to human spirit. Darkness needed fear, anger and chaos, the things that hide natural illumination, to feed off of to survive. If darkness is perceived as illumination that is taken away, hidden, overshadowed, blocked or interfered with, surely one wouldn't want to live with blindfolds on. It would be like trying to walk in the dark; you could hurt yourself simply by not seeing what's coming. Not even the misfortunes of childhood can take away your birthright of divinity and illumination. In Hazel's presence you not only knew it, every cell in your body knew it. It seemed like too many lifetimes ago since she was in Hazel's presence, and she desperately needed a good dose of Hazel to renew the *chispa* that everyday living appears determined to extinguish.

As a therapist, Judy certainly had her own support group to stay in balance while working with trauma victims. But Hazel provided more than balance, more than encouragement-- in Hazel's presence it was easy to remember connection to a life force so powerful, It created everything that exists. Everything! Though she was a small part of that life force, she was, nonetheless, connected to it, and felt it surging through her being. She basked in the warm memories until her next client arrived.

Judy's next appointment arrived, and the next, then lunch with her support group, then the next three clients and finally the people part of the work day was over. Now the monotonous, endless, duplicate and triplicate paperwork. The paperwork would always be tedious, because Judy was a people person. Her heart was into assisting people to recreate themselves as productive, communicative, interdependent, interrelating, and healthy people to whatever degree they were capable and willing. She assisted them to form boundaries of acceptance and love for whatever limitations appeared.

There was no joy comparable to watching someone make a connection and put into action a new skill for living more fully or destroying old limitations that kept them bound to sickness and misery. When the lights came on for them, her insides burgeoned with ecstasy and she was charged with power and energy and will to make it happen again and again.

Of course, there were bad times. There were frightening times, too. Like when Missy committed suicide right in her office-- she couldn't stop it. Missy had it too well planned. Missy had begun the process and was past the point of no return before she walked into the therapy session, although Judy didn't know it at the time.

Even though Missy needed to explain to Judy and say goodbye, she was determined to go, even to the end. The smile of peace Missy had on her face afterward was... well... Judy knew, then, that it was wrong to stop some people from attempting to move into the beyond. Life was truly unbearable for some.

The torture Missy went through on a daily basis, Judy had watched for a year. For whatever reason, Missy just couldn't heal the violation that wounded her. Judy suspected whatever had control of life and death, took mercy upon Missy and let her suffering end.

It was also a matter of respect for a person's sovereignty. Who was she to make the choices for another human being?

Choices. Each choice stands on its own. It simply depends where you want to learn from. Each choice is made now, not sometime in the past or sometime in the future. Each choice has its consequences-- good or bad or any of the endless possibilities in between. Each choice contributes to the possibilities of future choices.

Perspective can dampen the effects of our choices. Unfavorable or negative choices can sometimes be turned to advantage, especially when lesson learned. We all have infinite possibilities to choose from. Even where it looks like there are outside powers controlling events, like serendipity, we have made choices. Choices aligned to and in conjunction with other people in the past; all have contributed to our present circumstances.

Choices with consequences we were unaware of, possibly, but choices none the less. Perhaps the secret lies in making a choice, observing the consequence from the perspective of: Was this what I wanted? If not, what did I learn from this? How can I make this situation into the very best thing that could have happened to me? This is where the consequences of choice or chance or serendipity becomes creation. Like the saying, 'When life gives you lemons, why not make lemonade and sell it for a profit?!' This is where we have power. This is where we have control over our lives. This is where human and ALL are one.

Judy also knew most suicide attempts, even serious attempts to die, failed and left the people maimed and more helpless to stop victimization. *What a sad place to be. Not to be able to die and having to live with the fact you put yourself at the mercy of those who would take advantage of you. You were, then, powerless to stop anybody from doing anything they wanted to you.* She shook her head and shivered a little.

She also wondered about what they talked about in her support group today. They were comparing the ability to learn new or readjusted living skills after trauma. Comparing a person whose trauma was inflicted in childhood by family and/or 'community', with no opportunity to observe another way or learn the skills necessary to develop a "healthy" lifestyle, with: a person who had learned a "healthy" way of living at childhood through family of origin and/or 'community', or had a "healthy" family of origin and/or 'community' to go back to, after trauma was perpetrated on them, and relearn the skills for "healthy" living again.

Most of the group consensed that trauma victim's who had the previous "healthy" teachings or would be able to receive those teachings from a "healthy" support system, might have a hard time of it, depending on the individual circumstances of the trauma, but they had good chance of developing a successful, somewhat "healthy" lifestyle.

They agreed there would be minimal chance of repatterning for those who began life with trauma perpetrated by their family of origin and/or 'community', who had very little opportunity to compare their lifestyle with a "healthy" lifestyle.

For the latter, to develop a sense of social conscience was almost impossible, even ludicrous. Putting on a show of concern for others was easy, because it ultimately involved the survival of self. Real progress occurred when real guilt and shame over damaging behavior to others took place instead of fear that they were caught doing something wrong and survival would be interrupted. Real concern for the wants and needs of others, not attached to how their actions towards the needs of others will support their own survival, was a real breakthrough. The ultimate concern for one's survival was, of course, most appropriate for those growing up in a house of constant trauma. It would be more than insane to expect anything else from them, in the way of morality. Their only morality was survival. Even the desire to learn new skills had to come from something more traumatic than their childhoods, as inconceivable as that might be. Another possibility was a "safety zone" or an opening in their constant vigil for survival, like a parent dying.

Learning new social skills to be able to live above mere survival didn't, necessarily, give one the ability to feel or the ability to connect in an intimate or social sense. Nor did it bestow the courage to deal with those feelings and attach those feelings to the their initial behaviors once emerged. Judy chose to believe these survivors could make it.

Her group said there were those so well programmed that the interruption of the survival structure couldn't be done, even with a near death experience. These people were programmed with near death experiences, so how could they be retrained that way? They learned over and over and over again to be anti-social and how to survive. Not even as basic an instinct as socializing or the need for other human connection could be strong enough to break the chains of isolation that survival demanded. **"Don't talk. Don't trust. Don't feel."** The survivor's creed.

Those who wanted to change worked painfully hard to overcome these ineffective and limiting survival traits, often met with failure over and over again. If it is torment to watch their struggle, how did it feel inside them? As one of her clients put it: "At first, there's no feeling. When you're focusing on getting well: there's only accomplishment or no accomplishment. If you let yourself feel, you might have to stop, forever locked in despair, failure, endless emptiness and pain. If you can change the behavior response, and reprogram behavior: then you can check to see how that feels. Then, maybe, it's safe to investigate old memories and lethal feelings. But if you didn't have the possibility of comparing the regenerative feelings of the new, with the lethal old, the old would consume you and you'd be stuck in the terror indefinitely."

What kind of courage and concentration did it take to continue to try for something better, when you were aware the odds were against you? No matter how hard you tried, you might have to accept failure in this lifetime. You might never quite put enough of you together to make a whole person. There may not be enough pieces left. Judy wondered. *Paperwork, that's right.*

Paperwork would always annoy Judy. Paperwork felt diminishing compared to working with real people. *Damn those insurance companies! Someone should hold them accountable. When they agree to cover a person's medical bills, they agree to pay the fee charged, not half, not what they think it should be. Permitting a person to be treated is a nonverbal contract to pay the provider's schedule. You don't go to the grocery store and pay half-price or the price you think the commodity is worth. You don't go to a garment store and pay what you think it's worth... value for value.*

Hmmm... but look what pro-sport-players get paid compared to teacher's wages. Look how many people go to a football game and how many attend a concert or go to the library. Look how much money is spent on alcohol and drugs and how little is spent on learning or teaching healthy living and thinking habits. It's obvious where the quick profits lie.

When she and her husband were in Europe, she was impressed with the craftsmanship of the buildings. She was more impressed to learn that when a cathedral or institution was contracted for, it was contracted for several hundred years. The original contractor contracted for two or four hundred years and the evidence it was accomplished is still around today.

Couldn't you just imagine a contractor today, not only contracting for two hundred years for a building, but guaranteeing its finish, and being able to rely either on his family or his partner's family to honor the bargain? What kind of values did those people have and how did they teach them to their young? What kind of inner stuff made the kind of craftsmen who would be willing to labor most of their lives to create a piece of architecture, or any piece of work, they would not see finished in their lifetime. Something that would last thousands of years, through weather, earthquakes, war, and living.

Here you go! Got a deal for you! Would you like to spend grueling hours per day learning what character is, how to maintain it, and apply it to your life, waiting for unguaranteed results or would you like to go to the football game or watch TV. Someone, not real, is surely gonna' get killed, laid, and screwed royally. What's that you say?! Character loses?! But it's concerning someone real! It's about you!

Well, she had an idea it had something to do with the type of discipline she seemed unable to muster, right now, to do her paperwork.

In truth, she was still a little shaken with how the day began. No one called and no reported deaths. Not that it was entirely bad: no news is good news... most of the time. Still, she was curious about what it was. Judy picked up her things and made a solemn promise to set aside several hours tonight to do the paperwork. Mitch probably wouldn't be home yet.

She would treat him, this evening, to a special dinner. They had an equal opportunity kitchen and he was always superb with his "opportunity". Frankly, he was "superb" in everything he did, she thought warmly.

Once, she had the privilege of talking with a couple celebrating their sixty-third wedding anniversary. From another booth, she watched them cooing and delighting in each other's company, while the rest of their celebration party had gone to do something. She couldn't help it, she had to ask.

"How is it, after this many years, married to each other, you still are, obviously, very much in love with each other?"

They were a small couple, as many old people get with age, and the little old gentleman puffed up his chest a bit and replied, "Well, practice makes perfect!!"

The very prim and proper, dainty little old lady pats his hand very gently and lovingly said to him, "Oh! Dear! It's not perfection that counts--- it's the practice, practice, practice."

He obviously agreed as they turned back to continue delighting in each other. Judy had never forgotten and it looked like, since she told Mitch, he hadn't forgotten it either. *Hmmm! Practice! Practice! Practice!!... Practice first, paperwork second-- first the body then the mind- then the body/mind, then....*

Even though dinner was ready an hour ago, Mitch just had a chance to call. There was trouble on the site, he had secured it, eliminated the danger and would be home in about another hour.

Judy was a little disappointed even though she understood and equally deflated to think she could probably start her paperwork.

An hour and a half and much paperwork went by before Mitch finally got home. He walked in the door dragging, with that look that says "I just know I could have done more... or better... or something... if only..." *He's so hard on himself. He is such a perfectionist and that's probably what got, and kept him the job he has now.*

His company knew if something had to be done and done right, Mitch was the man. He was the best troubleshooter for any of half a dozen different manufacturing businesses. He spent years of long hours and sleepless nights learning from beginning to end, in detail, every aspect of every system. As he put his jacket away, she got up and walked to him and said,

"Well, if I'd have known the most wonderful, the sexiest, most masculine man would be walking through my door, why, I would have cooked him his favorite dish. Which, incidentally, is the best dish I make. I'd have his favorite bath salts, ready to go into a nice hot tub, and I'd be ready for absolutely anything he wanted." She brought out the bath salts she had been holding behind her back as she fit her body up to his in a warm hug with an '*I really think you're sexy*' kiss. He responded passionately.

"Anything?"

It was near impossible to move closer, but she managed a half-inch and nodded her head in enthusiastic consent.

"I'll bet there's spinach and Swiss quiche in the oven and now I have to make a choice between you, the bath, or the quiche first, don't I?" She nodded her agreement again, her body building delicious, intense desire. He kissed her passionately again,

"Hmmm! This is going to be a difficult choice and you're not going to help me, except by being the most desirable woman alive, are you?"

Affirmative.

"I think... I need to take a quick shower. I don't want these chemicals all over that beautiful body of yours, and then... There's absolutely no question... that I want," He gently and smoothly began running his hand down and up her side then slowly up her inner thigh.

"I absolutely need..." He gently fondled her breasts... "I absolutely must have... **You**... First."

He kissed her passionately, slowly and began succulently navigating his flicking, electric tongue down her neck. Her heart began to thunder, her breath to quicken. She knew the magic he could make with his enchanted tongue, with his gentle, sure hands and with his strong, hard-muscled body. Shower? He needed a quick what?

After all these years, he could still do this to her body/mind. As he headed for the bathroom, she vibrated in the lingering tingle of his touch, in the man scent of him, felt the wet of his tongue on her neck, the moist heat between her legs and the tense electricity a little higher up. She was unaware how she got back on the couch as her body/mind began to come back to the place and time of physical space she occupied. She wondered at how he could do this every time and how and why she was instantaneously responsive, receptive to him and participated in the whole of their love.

He was just as intense and focused at everything he did. She saw that over and over through the years. When he was with her, when he made love to her; he was completely, wholly, willingly with her. He had nothing else on his mind. He didn't want to be anywhere else or do anything else. There was no past. There was no future. There was only the present... loving... now. He focused his entire manhood on pleasing her, for as long as she wished, in what ever way she desired. His perfectionism would accept nothing less than her entire satisfaction and she could do no less than open to him and permit her body/mind to join their mutual ecstasy and rejoice. He, likewise, opened to her, withholding nothing. And she loved to pleasure him, she loved to watch him respond to her touch, to her body, to her womanness, to her love. The thought alone could make her heart beat fast, take her mind away, make her knees weak.

He came out of the shower with a towel wrapped around his lower half. She feasted her eyes on his broad, strong shoulders, the way his muscles rippled under his skin as he dried his hair, the way the soft, curly hair on his chest invited her to run her fingers through it, perhaps permitting her nails to gently explore the contours of his muscles underneath, the way his feet and toes made his calf muscles dance to a private syncopation.

He finished drying his hair and looked at her as if his thirsting eyes could never drink enough of her. As he moved toward her, his shoulders undulated and rounded the way they did when he embraced her. He grasped the towel as if she were in his tactile hands. His desire for her calling to her. Flaring nostrils breathing in her woman-scent. A parting, hungry mouth ready to taste her. Sensual arms and hands ready to touch her, arouse her secret places. His kinetic body, so male, so strong, so hard, yet so tender, held out a hand in invitation. Her hand went into his, as her body/mind vaporized all boundaries... and two separate flames burned as one sacred fire.

Chapter 3

Libby opened her eyes with a bit of a start... *What just happened?... Probably nothing.* She was just waking up... *What day is this?... What do I have on my calendar?... and... What?*

She moved her head to look around... *Yes, I'm in my own bed... No, this is not a dream.* She was, in fact, awake... *Wait a minute! Stop!*

She thought. She sat up and promised herself she would resume all this mental Ferris wheeling when she was fully awake, which was obviously not at this moment.

I hate it when I wake up like this! Usually, she woke up present and accounted for with the day's gameplan in her organized mind, ready to be implemented. All she needed was to start the action. That was before her accident. She heard Josie calling from downstairs.

She seldom needed stimulants like coffee to get her going, the way most of America seemed to. Part of what she identified as her aliveness stemmed from the fact that as a higher primate, her thinking abilities did not have any lapses in them. Her 'functioning' continued, no matter what else was going on. She trusted her body to do what it was supposed to do and her mind to function in an hierarchical way. Which left the most important things, exclusively, for her conscious consideration. She almost considered it lower primate functioning to have to be *aware* of every little detail of one's body and life. People who spend so much time and energy thinking about the minutest details of why did they have this pain... why did they say that... and why is my heart beating fast...

*Well, really... They exasperate me. Just do it! Some things require no real thought, just real action. If the right **things** aren't present, make them present, make it happen, move whatever needs moving, push it away, pull it to you, keep moving, get the job done, produce!*

She had learned these things almost on her teething ring, although she really didn't remember much about her childhood. *Not important. Emotion is superfluous to the task at hand.* As a woman in this society, she had to constantly be on guard that her decisions were logic-based and not emotion-based. That was the reason she was successful.

Successful in her own right; it was not her husband's success. It wasn't his efforts and hard work that made her business and life successful. As a matter of fact, she supposed, she would do nicely without Rafael after the divorce. He was a convenient ear while she was establishing herself, and yes, he provided the sex she needed to keep her body healthy.

He was definitely lots better than the gruesome bar scenes, the personals, or the dating agencies. He'd even cleaned house and cooked until they could afford a maid. Until recently, he hadn't pressured her for more than she could give, either. *We talked about our needs and agreed, before we were married. We knew what each of us wanted out of life and, I thought, from each other. When did all this change?* She tried to remember. *Was it after the accident? Oh well! I don't have time to think about it now. I have to get busy.*

Her business wouldn't wait while she meandered through her memories of the past. Besides she had an appointment with her therapist today. That was the time to go down memory lane. She had delegated one precious hour of her time, once a week, to straighten out whatever this was her doctor seemed to attribute to the growing numbness and bruises she had developed as of late. Her medical doctor could not find a physical reason for the symptoms, even after $5,000 worth of every test known to man.

When she started having dreams that woke her up, dreams she couldn't quite recall, leaving her with symptoms of terror, awful voices, terrible laughter, and that face with the eyes, he insisted she see a therapist. She was not especially pleased at devoting this much time to her doctor's fantasy, but to get him to find the real problem, she had to jump through the hoops... for the time being. *Just do it!* One of the problems seemed, the more she talked to this therapist, the more these 'symptoms' appeared to occur, so she tried to keep it light in therapy session. *If only Judy or Hazel lived closer. Judy is an excellent therapist and we've known each other since forever. I wouldn't have to explain every little stupid detail. Hazel would be great too, even though she's not a therapist. We used to talk about everything under the sun. There was nothing we didn't talk about. We solved the world's problems, but somehow overlooked our own.* She chuckled.

All throughout the long summer nights of high-school, late into the nights, for hours and hours, we'd re-create the wheel, tear it apart, and start all over again. I can hear her voice, now, echoing in my ears about some profound thing or other. Hazel always understood me and always accepted me for just who I am. I never had to justify every nook and cranny in my brain to her. She could hardly wait until the "Gathering".

In these last five years, she knew, Hazel definitely had her share of problems. She didn't know the details. It was funny how much Hazel was present in her thoughts along with what felt like some foreboding wind. She didn't know if the **wind** was pleasant or not, only of its presence. She would soon find out. *'Rocky Mountain*

Hiiigh, Colorado! Rocky Mountain Hiiiiigh, Colorado!' She didn't have time to be 'sick' now, at least not with anything that couldn't be cured right away with some pill or something.

Oh! Well, she'd spent much too much time on this annoyance already. There was time set aside for this in her schedule. Now was the time to get ready for the busy day ahead. *I have five appointments before my therapy appointment at lunch time.* She got up, did her twenty minute aerobic workout, took her shower, made her other morning ablutions within the fifteen minutes she'd allotted for such things and was putting on her girdle.

Her girdle was her special gift of comfort to herself. *No one wears these archaic things anymore,* she mused. But when she found out the sense of comfort and security this one object gave her, she was determined she would have one no matter what the cost... and it cost her plenty. This was the last company to make such a primitive undergarment. She was worth every bit of it. Even if she had to keep a permanent seamstress on her payroll for life, she would have the one comfort she allowed herself. *Besides, I can afford it!*

The phone rang. *Now, who could that be? I have fifteen minutes to eat and be out of here.* She answered the phone. It was Rafael. Her throat sank. *I have no time for this!*

"Hello, Libby?"

"Yes?" she answered perfunctorily.

"I need to speak with you about our municipal bonds and the futures we have on wheat. You heard about the flood, didn't you?" Rafael said.

"Yes, I heard about the flood, but I can't talk now, Rafael. Why don't you have your secretary call mine and book a time for us. Be sure to tell my secretary the agenda so I can have the necessary papers with me, and how much time you think it will take. If I remember correctly, we may have to put it off until next week sometime." she said.

"I'm afraid it can't be put off without a significant loss to us both, unless you are willing to assume the total losses?" Rafael cooed cheerfully.

"No! I'm not willing to assume the total losses. Tell my secretary the matter is urgent and I'll cue her this morning. Thanks, Rafael." She went to hang up.

"Wait a minute! Wait a minute!" he said, "I also called to see how your love life is and if I could be of some assistance...."

She slammed the phone down not knowing whether she was angry with him or with herself for letting herself get so horny. She heard that voice... that sneering, mocking voice... "You want it, doncha', baby? Be a good little girl, now." ... Laughter ... *GO AWAY!*

She had to admit, it was rather convenient having Rafael around, even if he was a little too kinky. She could ignore his dressing up in women's clothes. She didn't give a damn what a person wore or didn't wear, so long as they got the job done. She could ignore the handcuffs and even the riding crop (if he didn't hurt at the wrong time). She could also ignore any of the dozens of *different* things he not only liked, but began to require... but this last... this last... was the final straw.

He had hurt her. How he did it was hazy and she couldn't locate exactly where the pain was. It was almost like being in a dream where she could only see the top half. She could see something's going on in the bottom half but she couldn't identify exactly what. It gave her a vague sense of familiarity, somehow, but she couldn't quite remember and she couldn't remember why it should be repulsive and terrifying.

She didn't know the meaning behind the strange scenes that flashed across her mind so fast she couldn't quite comprehend what they were or what was happening in them or why she felt so dirty afterwards. She also didn't have time to spend wasting her thinking on this kind of dalliance. *I'll use my vibrator when I get home tonight, if I'm not too tired.*

One thing for sure, regular sex kept her body lubricated and fluid; irregular masturbating was beginning to tell in the dryness of her skin and the wrinkles beginning to appear and, worst of all, her body was increasingly more stiff when she got up and tried to exercise. *Damn that Rafael! Why'd he turn into a full blown pervert now? Especially right now!* She didn't have time to spend doing what was necessary to replace him. She ran down the stairs into the dining room. *Bless Josie! I must give her a raise this month. She's worth her weight in gold, but I'll never tell her that. I'm so glad she decided to stay with me when Rafael left.*

Ever since the accident, a year or so ago, Josie had become her right arm where the house was concerned. With Rafael leaving, she might even have to hire a second person to help Josie. Rafael had only been gone a couple of months and already the plants were dying, the mending was piling up and she ended up taking the dogs and cats to the groomer.

Maybe she'd sell the damn animals. *They never particularly responded to me anyway. Hmmm! Maybe, I'll give them to Rafael, since they're so fond of him... That would put a small crunch in his man-about-towning. At least he'd have to pay a fortune to kennels for those "pleasure weekends", wherever it was he was going now.* At that thought, she had to smirk malefically. *Damn him! Why'd he pick now to get weird?*

"Thanks, Josie!" she hollered into the kitchen, "I'll have juice and toast. I don't have time for anything else."

She took this morning's contracts out of her briefcase and began looking over the amendments Charles had made. *Lawyers may cost a fortune, but try running a business without one. You'd either spend all your time with your nose in law books or courtrooms.* Besides, that was one of the benefits Rafael brought to the marriage. Charles Ranley Manfred, III, was the best corporate lawyer on the whole East Coast and stopped taking new clients just about the time she and Rafael got married. Because he had taken care of Rafael's business for so long, he was coerced into helping Libby start her business. Then, like a proud father, just stayed on. With a significant retainer, of course!

She hoped that he wouldn't try to take sides in the pending divorce. She wouldn't know where to begin to try and find a lawyer of his competence, reputation, and experience. A good lawyer could make a business; an incompetent lawyer could insure litigation and bankruptcy court in a hurry. She had an appointment with Charles today at four o'clock. He was mysterious about the agenda.

Probably wants to talk about his retainer, now that Rafael and I are divorcing. That old scoundrel has collected two separate retainers for years. He knows perfectly well just what my business is doing and likely to do in the next five years or so. Bet he wants to up his retainer before all the messy divorce dividing and haggling starts. Well, I'll find out soon enough.

Then it happened... She heard the scream... It came from nowhere... ***What the hell is that!*** It was so loud and so intense, it never dawned on her it was in her head. She was the only one in the house to hear it... *But, there it is again...* ***What the hell is that?*** She spilled her juice on the table as her hand reflexively shook.

"Josie! Josie! What the hell was that!?" she shouted. Josie came out of the kitchen with a confused and startled expression on her face.

"What was what, Miss Libby?" she asked.

"That scream-- didn't you hear it? It was loud enough to wake up the dead." she choked out.

"No, Miss Libby. I din't hear anything 'cept you screamin' at me."

"I'm sorry Josie," she panted, still in shock, "I didn't mean to scream at you but it was so... so... terrible. I've never heard a scream like that before. I'm sorry, I'm still a little dazed", she said, shaken "What time is it?"

"Close to six a.m., Miss Libby. Time to go an' get the train. Will you want anything special for dinner tonight, Miss Libby." Josie looked at her worried, a little fearful.

"No, Josie what ever you want to fix is okay with me, but I'll probably be late, I'm meeting Charles at four and there's no telling how long that will take, or when the next train leaves. If you want, I can call you as I leave the city."

"That won't be necessary Miss Libby, I was thinkin' of fixin' stew and that won't dry out too fast, and I can pop the bread in the micro. But I won't time it to be done till after six, if that's okay?"

"Sure, Josie. Are you *sure* you didn't hear anything? Anything at all?"

"No, ma'am. Nuthin' at all." Josie looked at Libby cautiously, then went back into the kitchen.

It's a good thing therapy was today, at least she'd have something to say, or maybe she shouldn't say anything about this. If she didn't hurry, she'd miss her train, and she'd have to wait another hour to catch the next one into the city. *Damn... Other cities had half-hour service this time in the morning. Isn't it wonderful, the benefits of suburban life!*

As she got into her vintage Plymouth, Libby's mind drifted to the coming "Gathering". Just a few weeks away-- *God!* She hoped the divorce would be over by then. She didn't want to have anything take away from her participation in this year's sharing.

The "Gathering" was almost like inventorying every aspect of your soul, collecting every special piece, to present to your most loved, favorite relative... Or... No! Like presenting yourself to a host of seraphs specifically to receive the applause you and they agree you deserve. She got that unique excitement when she thought about her special group. There was Kitten and Mona, whom she could most relate with. Judy, Penny, Dee and Jo and the others. Then, there was Hazel. How did anyone describe Hazel? She was one of the most incredible people Libby had ever met. You could look into Hazel's eyes and see reflecting back at you, the best 'you' you could ever hope to be. Somehow, in Hazel's eyes, you became every bright, beautiful, intelligent, successful dream you ever had about yourself.

In Hazel's eyes, you knew you could do it. Whatever obstacles stood in the way of what you were and what you wanted to be, were to be tackled joyously, enthusiastically. Obstacles were nothing but ether barriers, that would blow over and out of the way, without much resistance. She could not fathom anyone disliking Hazel.

Hazel waited a long time to marry and have a family. She'd worked in the Peace Corps, all over the world. She'd acquired a foundation, in depth, in the magnificence of the human spirit. Then, she learned how to reflect that magnificence, through her eyes, back to the person she was looking at, and they could see their own divineness.

The feelings Hazel evoked were indescribable, like Hazel. For sure, Hazel was no beauty by magazine standards, until you looked into her eyes. Then, the short, overweight, graying woman transformed into nothing less than deity's representative here, on earth... Here, to inform you and make you aware of your own connection to all that exists.

Oh my! She was at the train station and didn't remember the drive. How, in the hell, did she avoid an accident? *Is this the kind of thing safe to talk about in therapy? God! I'll have to hurry, and I'll have to pick up the dog food when I get back from the city... Damn Rafael!*

The day had not gone exactly as she had planned. It was a good thing she was meeting Charles today. *That lousy Smith Brothers' contract negotiation turned into the worst free-for-all I've ever seen, complete with threats of a law suit. I have to ask Charles what the hell 'promissory estoppel' is.* The one semester of business law she had, in college, she had forgotten about, completely, since Charles was on the payroll.

The Logger's contract was 13 percent more than my highest guestimate and I'll have to review the figures again to determine whether the profit margin is enough to continue, then sign the contract. Memphis Security wouldn't accept the collateral I offered for the loan because of the pending divorce, regardless of the financial reports of the last five years and the projected growth rate.

No one was willing to estimate the liabilities of her pending divorce. The "tangibles" of her business were not in question. It was the "intangibles", so they said. The bottom line of this infuriated her beyond words. **They** considered her "unstable" because she was becoming unmarried. That made her too unpredictable a risk. *It's almost as if they thought Rafael was the brains of the business and with him leaving, the master mind of success was going with it.* She had defeated 'the good ol' boy' system before-- All by herself! (Well, with the help of Charles), and she'd do it again! But what a damn bother. The only contract that went right was the Sisters of the Moon contract and she really had gotten the better part of the deal.

Sisters' was an up-and-coming company run by three women with some great ideas. They were starting on a shoestring. It would take only one, out of the many possible mistakes, for the women to fall in on themselves. Well, she'd give it a try. The profits looked good to her, but it also looked as if too much depended on her for the successful blossoming of this venture.

She knew, even if the investment firm didn't, that she had made it this far without much help from anyone. She could afford to help these ambitious women. Though emotion was superfluous to the task at hand, she felt good being able to act like "Big Mama" or "Big Sister" to these upstart women, even though she would never have trusted another woman when she was starting out (or even now, for that matter). *The signed contract eliminates the need for* **trust**... *or insures it.*

Even her therapist got off on some wild track. Libby was talking, in general, about Rafael, her need for the physical relief of orgasm and how doing "it" herself wasn't filling the bill. She didn't even have enough time to hire someone to "do the job". All of a sudden, out of the blue, her therapist starts on this little monologue, like she's trying to teach Libby the facts of life. Her therapist starts out:

"Masturbation is basically good for two things-- first, to know what pleases you and be able to communicate that to another person and second, to take the edge off while you learn how to relate, sexually, to other humans."

Libby couldn't help but wonder. *Now, just what started this off?*

"If you don't learn these skills, adequately, in the time provided for them, just what in-the-hell are you going to do when masturbation stops working... and it will stop working! Sexually relating to another human is a helluva lot more than just orgasm. It's...",

Oh! Plleeeeeaze, Libby thought, as she refrained from rolling her eyes.

"...the touching, the looking, the talking, the 'small' stuff that communicates to yourself and the other human that you are both 'made in deity's image'. There is something more than elemental substance holding the 'dirt' together. There is a 'sameness' and a 'uniqueness' about you both, an independence. An interdependence, a quality of sharing the 'same' space while remaining completely whole and distinct. Sexuality is the sum of combining deity with mundane to create the dance that 'begins the original'."

Libby thought she was going to puke right then and there. Libby knew, without a shadow of a doubt, the sole purpose of sex was orgasm; the more the better. *Whatever gets that accomplished, between two consenting adults, is whatever is "holy".*

That wasn't the end of the day's frustrations, but from that point on, Libby had decided not to take the day so seriously. It was one of those days.

She got off the train at Grand Central and quickstepped to the lounge, where she was to meet Charles. She looked at her watch and wondered how long this would take. After seven, the trains no longer ran on the hour, but every two hours till eleven, then every four hours till the morning rush hour. She was also curious to know, what was so important they had to meet like this. Ordinarily, he would just send a fax or E-mail her if it required immediate attention.

She sat down, ordered a drink, got out the Smith contract and her business journal. Charles pulled out the chair and sat down.

"Well, hello, stranger." Charles grinned.

She looked up amiably as he sat down, breathed a sigh of relief, said, "I'm glad to see you Charles. I have a few questions to go over with you." She started to shove the contract under his hands.

"Wait a minute! Wait a minute! Let's get our drinks and relax a moment... and maybe... Let's move over there. To that corner.

There's more uninhabited space. Before the masses perceive unclaimed territory."

She really didn't want to take the time to do all the social protocols, just get to business. She needed to move on to the next items to deal with. But he called the meeting and any good business woman knows: *Let the rival call as many unimportant shots as possible and always wait; the loser talks first.* She looked at her watch. She'd never be able to catch the 5 o'clock, anyway. Maybe the 6. *If* they got to business. They were helped to the corner booth by the waitress, got settled in and Charles began to talk,

"Well, how's the animal farm? Are you ready to kennel the animals yet, or have you taken to long, leisurely walks in the great out-of-doors?"

She was confused for a minute. He had caught her off guard. She came prepared to talk about her business, not to listen to small talk. She was a bit annoyed but didn't dare show it. She was used to those kind of businessmen who always started a business deal around the barbecue pit in their mind. *Makes you wonder if they have to talk about football plays in order to have an erection.*

She knew how to deal with it.

"Well, actually, Charles, I've been so busy with the new proposals, the new line I'm incorporating, and the hold-up with Memphis Security, that I nearly forgot I had any animals. Were you interested in buying them or do you know someone who wants to purchase them? I hate letting them go. They were bought as an investment, a side venture for Rafael to dabble in. It seems his dabbling leads elsewhere lately and as you can see, I've neither time nor talent to profit from them. I'd be willing to let them go for a reasonable price."

Charles shifted in the booth a little, crossing his legs and extending his arm over the top and sliding down, just a little, to fit closer to her.

"Libby! Libby!" he said paternally, "You really must slow down some. Enjoy life, while you are still young and slim enough to move." He looked directly into her eyes and she looked away to hide the growing discomfort she felt. *What, exactly, is happening here? I've never seen Charles act in anything but a professional way, now he's "Mr. Let's Relax". I'm still in control. It's just more of the rest of this day.*

"Charles. Is there something wrong? You seem distracted. My business has blossomed recently, has the paper work exceeded your retainer? You are certainly familiar with the projections, and I'm prepared to offer you generous increases as these projections are accomplished." *The snake must be detented gently before it can be handled.*

"Have you heard anything from Rafael, lately?" he asked casually.

"We spoke this morning" she said patiently, "and we'll meet as soon as our secretaries set the appointment. Look, if it's the bond issue, there's really no need to worry. I have everything in proper order and if necessary, we can reissue with not too much loss." *I wish he'd get to the point.* She looked at her watch nervously.

"Are you on a tight schedule today?" he questioned "Do you have any other appointments today? Maybe a friend waiting at home?" He began to look around nonchalantly.

She was really getting edgy now... *What in the hell does that question have to do with anything?*

· "Charles, please forgive me for seeming a bit plebeian. It hasn't been one of my usually successful days and after we discuss why you called this meeting, I would like to talk to you about the Smith contract and ask you some questions concerning the community property laws in this state and Massachusetts. Then I have several hours work, some of which I can accomplish on the train. I'm sure you must know how concerned and curious I am when my lawyer and friend takes time from his busy schedule to mysteriously meet with me, rather than send me a fax." *There, now maybe he'll get to the point.* Charles shifted in the booth again. His arm came down.

"You know, I've always found you attractive. And from what Rafael's said about you, I believe we may have more in common than you know."

His hand went to her upper thigh and then directly to her crotch. She jumped, more from her own hormone response than from his surprise attack. She was genuinely shocked at his oddly unprofessional behavior.

"My retainer and whether or not I'll continue to work for you can be discussed later. I'd rather talk about us," he said.

Her face was burning, her body was responding to his touch like a hungry animal responds to the smell of food. She was disgusted at her body, shamed at her nature, angry at him for taking advantage of both, and ready to kill Rafael. She couldn't help seeing those eyes inside her mind, leering at her, waiting for her.

"What, exactly, did Rafael tell you?" she choked out, spitting on herself, "and what do you mean 'whether or not you'll continue to work for me'?"

He extended his arm on the table, so no one could see he was fondling her nipples as he continued to rub her crotch under the table. She felt powerless to stop him, overwhelmed by her own desire and disgust.

"Well," he said, "for years, now, Rafael has given us progress reports on your increasing libido, shall we say, and your willingness to participate in his 'games'. We're all interested. You only have to choose and you need never go without what you 'require'." His eyebrows raised as the hand under the table pushed in harder and her head began to swim.

She had no power to move his hands away and barely enough strength to grab the table with her hands so she would not fall. If she had taken the time to use the vibrator this morning, she would not have been this vulnerable. *If fishes were wishes... it's too late to do it now.* She was beginning to gasp and looked wildly around to be sure no one knew what was going on. *At least he had the courtesy to move to a dark, private spot. Damn Rafael!*

All of a sudden, he stopped. Just like that. She caught her breath. The ache in her abdomen began to be a pain, and her crotch throbbed. She knew she couldn't stand yet, or even move. She gasped a deep breath.

"I... a... um... I don't know what to say, Charles." she choked out.

"We'll talk about it some more, Libby, later." he said with a snigger to his voice.

"But... But... Charles... a... What was it you expected me to do now?" she squeaked, not believing he would leave her in this state.

"Well, Libby, maybe we'll talk about it tomorrow. Bring a change of clothes with you. For work. You won't need any night clothes. You and me and some of the boys will get together for some overnight, **intense** business dealings. If the negotiations work out tomorrow night, we'll talk about my 'retainer'. How does that sound?" He grabbed and rubbed her crotch again under the table.

She jolted like a bolt of electricity went through her. He moved closer to her. She could feel his maleness, as one of his hands twisted her nipple gently, and he pulled her hand down under the table to feel his semi-erection. Her head swam, and he crooned.

"Will we see you tomorrow?"

His fingers were moving fast and hard. She was gasping and almost ready. Then he stopped, again.

Something, a picture, flashed in her mind and was gone in an instant. She was left with a man's face and those eyes staring at her. There was something familiar-- something like this had happened before. Nausea was ramming its way up her sternum to her throat. She tried hard to bring back the information, but she couldn't quite remember. Then, the heat and pain almost made her double over. She was sweating and her hairline was sending droplets down her back.

"I... let... a... Ra... Charles," she couldn't speak.

"Well, you give me a call, later, with your answer. God, Libby! It isn't that hot in here. You're too young and active to be starting menopause, aren't you? You better get that checked. We don't want you *coming* down with anything."

He spoke smoothly and stroked her belly a few times, then got up and left her sitting there, in pain, in shame, in self-loathing. All that was left was her body, screaming for completion, and the voice of a dirty man... or was it a woman... laughing, speaking words she couldn't hear above the laughter.

She had several options, she thought madly. Then she knew, tonight, she would not take any of the options. She would never tell anyone what happened and she would seek no relief for the incredible pain. She would never admit to herself how her own body had betrayed her. Tears formed in her eyes. Grief and sadness too great to endure was beginning to lodge itself under her diaphragm. Yet the shame and guilt over her very nature, the nature that made her easy prey, and all those other words, would not permit the release of tears.

She probably deserved this for being who and what she was. She knew it, Rafael knew it, and God knows who else knew it, now. It looked like there was no way out of this alive. She tried to take a deep breath and could only manage short, incomplete gulps of air. She deserved that, too. Her very breath should, rightly, reflect her despicable nature. It was secret no more. What could she do? She didn't know.

One thing she did know; she couldn't leave the table until the pain subsided enough for her to walk. The waitress came over and put the check on the table and said, "The gentleman said to give the bill to you, that you would pay."

Something inside of her felt like it was going to break. Libby paid the bill and sat for a while longer. She looked at her watch, got up carefully, left the cafe to catch the next train.

It wasn't until she had gotten on the train and been riding for 15 minutes that she was able to get hold of her mind and go over the conversation. Even then, as she was recalling the words, her body shot electricity through her. She got that churning feeling in her stomach, and with all the discipline she could muster, she brought herself back to the words... *Just the words, damn it! Emotion is superfluous to the task at hand. Just the words.*

As she remembered what Charles said, the heat of anger began to stir. *Did he really say* **WE**? *Who the hell was* **WE**. *Surely, Rafael didn't say anything about our private life to any* **WE**. *Maybe he told Charles, as a* **close** *friend, and Charles went and blabbed it, like some ninny school jock. But, surely, not Rafael.* She thought of what Rafael had talked her into in the last year-and-a-half of their marriage. Her face turned heat-red. If she were Catholic, she wouldn't even tell a priest that. She felt her stomach moving up to the base of her throat, again, as if some giant phallus were being crammed into her mouth.

She recalled the last few times with Rafael. She was so disgusted with herself, she thought she would puke. Then her high-school friend Hazel's words washed into her mind from nowhere.

"Look, deary-- you can't do anything right this minute about what has gone on in the past. But... if you continue to be as disgusted with yourself as you now are, you'll end up with a heart attack, ulcers or cancer."

"What in the hell am I supposed to do?!!" Libby cried.

In that calm, loving way Hazel had, she simply said, "You must accept ALL of what you call your 'nature'. There is nothing wrong with your 'nature'. Now, your behavior may not suit your 'nature', or it may. One thing, for sure, the reason why you feel so bad is your behavior and your 'nature' are in conflict."

"Hazel, I can't stand being this filthy. My mind says this is wrong and my body won't let me stop. Hazel. I don't understand it! I am so strong in every other area of my life. I'm so disciplined, my secretary sometimes calls me iron-will. I didn't get to where I am by being Ms. Niceguy or by being a wimp!" Libby cried, "I hate myself so much, I feel like something is going to break!"

"Something will break. Either your body or your mind, if you don't change your value or your behavior." Hazel said.

"God! Hazel! You're talking in riddles!" Libby screamed.

"Look. If you don't love who and what you are, and you don't change into someone you can love, your body or your mind is going to break. If your body continues to give you clues your value system sucks, by breaking down, and you still don't change your value system-- keep pushing for your value system to be all right-- your body will get your attention or your mind will break. It's really as simple as that. Any of us can go on for years, living with minor differences and we get colds the flu, minor sprains and the like. Our body is saying, 'Hey! You! Listen up here! We got something we want you to look at!'" Hazel paused briefly to check if Libby was still with her.

"If you pay no attention," Hazel continued, "assert your *will* over the good direction of your body... depending upon your system, your health habits, and other physical factors-- you might get away with it for years before the first heart murmur or that first case of pneumonia, or that first big accident. Even then, most people like you, think there's nothing to worry about because you got away with it this time, you've got control of your universe. Nothing really serious happened and you get the idea you've just controlled the universe without having to pay a damn thing in return."

Then Hazel looked directly into Libby's eyes, "I tell you, right now, you never... **Hear me, NEVER**... get something for nothing. You never have to endure something without being able to get something from it-- but if you do not learn, and you continue to act like you are not enduring something; like there's nothing wrong or there's nothing that needs correcting, something... whether it is mental or physical in nature-- will stop you in your tracks to make you look.

"If all this process proceeds beyond whatever are your personal mental or physical limits, there is only one more option, and that is to start over again. The physical principles of physics are spiritual principles, and the spiritual principles will not 'override' the physical principles. There is only one way to transmute lead to gold, my dear. And, that principle has been known for eons. Lead is self-loathing and gold is self-love. The materials you have to work with are what you call your 'nature', your behavior and how they function together toward your highest good." Hazel said, "Do you understand?"

Libby had to admit she did not understand, but she remembered the love and life in Hazel's eyes as she said these things. Why she felt better after being in Hazel's presence, she hadn't a clue. She only knew life had more of a 'big picture' when Hazel talked than when she was alone in her own mind. Well, for sure, she didn't want to feel any worse than she did right now. Maybe, there was something to Hazel's thing about behavior and values and feeling sick. She wasn't sure, but she'd made a decision as she was reliving

Hazel's words: she would try to get another lawyer before she gave Charles her answer.

The sword in her gut began to burn less, though she still had the 'big dick' in her throat. She would call one of the women in her Business Women's Association and try to find a decent lawyer, maybe a woman. She had little confidence in professional women in traditional 'good ol' boy' positions. *How will they ever make a good showing if no one ever gives them a chance? That's what I'll do, then.* She'd give some woman a chance to be as good, but only if she came highly recommended and really knew her stuff. She'd have to have some kind of success record already, of course, but Libby would give it a try.

She felt vaguely uneasy at trusting a woman. In a flash, she saw the face and neck of her mother. She knew something was going on in the rest of the picture, but all she could feel was a vague pressure below her waist. *Can't remember it. Forget it.*

Libby wasn't used to moving in any direction that was not a sure thing. She hadn't gotten to where she was by 'trying'-- just 'doing'. Now that part was resolved, she would call up Rafael when she got home and ask him... just who in the hell is this **WE** Charles was talking about. The more she thought about it... the angrier she got. She wondered if she could find some thug to just shoot Rafael in the head. She wasn't a cruel person, she wouldn't want him to suffer. Just be gone.

*That way, the state wouldn't have to clothe, feed and shelter him. The **state** my ass. I've paid enough in taxes to support him in jail and maybe even one of his friends, all by myself.* She really was beginning to be pissed off now... *I would have to continue paying taxes, working like some whore for a pimp, while he was in jail, sitting doing nothing and I would get absolutely nothing from* *him! At least with a pimp, you get something, however little it is.* No... maybe it was best to kill him, even if she had to do it herself.

She would have to plan it really well, so she wouldn't end up cutting off her nose to spite her face, but she could do it. If worse comes to worst, she could always claim some type of mental thing. *I am, after all, seeing a therapist. Let's see...*

The conductor called off her stop and she realized the time had passed, again, without her knowing it. *Time flies when you're having fun,* she thought sarcastically.

When she finally got home, she called one of the women in the Association and got the name of a woman lawyer in the city. She left a message with the lawyer's answering service and the attorney called back within the hour. She was lucky to be able to get an appointment for tomorrow, after work. It would be another long day. Libby didn't like telling the woman lawyer as much about Charles and her business over the phone, as she had to do, but she knew the lawyer needed to have some background on her. She took it for granted, the woman lawyer would not go stirring things up with Charles until the contract for the retainer was signed. It simply was bad business to do that-- never mind unethical. *Who ever said lawyers were ethical,* she reminded herself, *as if there is some guardian of the universe protecting and enforcing the Doctrine of Fairness, so it's applied evenly like the windshield wiper fluid in my car. At least, I'm doing what I can,* she begged through the screaming of her body. Along with her girdle, she proved she was once more in control.

The next day was a long day, too. Libby looked forward to the new lawyer with about as much enthusiasm as she did getting the dog food, but both were necessary, now.

She hadn't realized the counselor's office was also where the woman lived. *Every tax write-off counts,* thought Libby.

The place was spacious, well decorated, orderly. The woman was well groomed, though a little too severely from Libby's point of view, even for New York, but who cared, so long as the woman knew her business.

When the woman got right to business, Libby was impressed. The attorney made a few references to Charles, admitting knowledge of and prior dealings with him. They talked about everything that needed talking about. It was late and Libby was exhausted. The woman offered her a drink before the long train ride home. Libby accepted the gesture of kindness.

As she sipped her drink, they talked about more personal things: her up and coming divorce, the animals...

Then, like some slinking dragon, crawling up from the black void behind her, the woman gently, lightly brushed her hand across the back of Libby's neck.

At first, Libby is confused... *do I have something on my collar that needs to be brushed off? She's looking at my neck as though there's something terrible that shouldn't be there.*

Libby shivers involuntarily.

The woman moved closer. Libby, thinking the woman was removing the terrible thing from her neck, moved her head to the side to give the woman working room. The woman brushed her lips over the skin of Libby's neck and moved to cup Libby's breast. Libby is stunned immobile. Libby faces the woman, shocked, speechless, questioning.

The woman passionately, tenderly kissed Libby full on the mouth, her tongue moving softly over Libby's lips and in and out of her mouth. Her hands caressed Libby's curves, squeezing, massaging, moving the muscles, gently. Even through the shock, Libby is aware her body is responding.

How strange, I never thought my body would respond to the touch of a woman.

Then, a flash in her mind, again. Some other woman, then her mother's face, a pain in her abdomen wiping away all sensation of pleasure, then blur.

The woman was still doing what she was doing and Libby's body was still responding, but Libby was now concerned about the scene that just thunderbolted across her mind, leaving in its wake a terrible pain under her diaphragm and lower abdomen.

She felt filthy and afraid. *Afraid of what? Why does my body respond that way?* She felt fingers all over her body and inside her body. *Whose hands are invading me?* Intense terror was building. *I have to get out of here!*

She pushed the woman away, grabbed her briefcase and ran out of the flat. *'You have to get to the train station before you hurt yourself.'*

She shook her head. *Who is speaking inside my head? What did they mean by "before you hurt yourself."? How would I hurt myself?*

'Regardless of what goes on in your head', the roaring was ferocious, *'You will... Do you hear me?... You will act normal!*

*For appearance's sake: You **will** slow down'*,... and Libby slowed down.

*'You **will** change the expression on your face'*,... and the expression on her face changed. Her face appeared calm but alert-- she was still in New York. *'That's better.'*

Who are you and what are you doing in my head? she asked. No answer. *I'm not nuts. I've learned how to survive, too well, that's all... that's all!*, she reasoned.

Her moment of panic passed and she put the whole thing aside, for later. She had things to do which required her attention. *Emotion is superfluous to the task at hand.* She heard sleazy laughter somewhere. *Yes, that's it! Emotion is superfluous to the task at hand.*

She didn't remember getting home or the next few days very well, but, apparently, they passed as they were supposed to. She wasn't in jail, or an institution, or with someone she didn't know. She was right here, at her desk and... *What day is this?* She looked at the calendar-- *Friday? Is it Friday, already? How wonderful!* She could enjoy a restful, solitary, peaceful weekend at home. She needed to clean out her car and do some stuff in the yard. Most of all, she needed the rest, since the awful headache that never let her sleep was finally going away. *What headache? Oh! Well!* It was nearly gone and she felt a little achy, but she looked forward to the weekend. She would leave on Wednesday for the "Gathering", according to the calendar. She was so excited. She wasn't about to let anything spoil it for her.

* * * *

They were meeting in Hazel's city, Colorado Springs-- *'Rocky Mountain Hiiiiigh, Colorado, doo, do-doo'. What a fine Saturday this is turning out to be.* She had packed for the "Gathering" this morning and now she was cleaning out the car. It was an Indian summer day, much too warm to be fall, really.

She permitted herself a rarity, today. So rare, in fact, she had a hard time finding them, and when she did, they were sizes too big. The last time she wore shorts, she must have weighed at least forty pounds heavier. Maybe more.

To add to her sense of wild abandon and rare freedom (and to celebrate her elation of the coming "Gathering"), she also decided to not wear any underwear. No girdle, no bra. Well, she was wearing panties, *but that's as good as no underwear.* She was going to spend the next week with only women, *for God's sakes.* Of course, you couldn't tell much, with the bagginess and dark colors of her outfit. It's not like she was even going to the store like this. She was just flopping around the house. HER house, in fact. But the wildness and freedom she felt sent new stirrings through her, along with some voice in her head saying something about being a 'lady'. *'Ladies don't...'*

Of course, nobody's gonna notice. Nobody can even see me! Nobody is looking at me. Why should they? I'm not the center of anyone's universe at present. Those feelings, that everyone **knows** she's naked underneath and bad were just in her mind. *And who cares anyway? You can't really see the street from the garage. The open garage looks out into a big beautiful field in the back.* As she stepped back out of the car and straightened up, she had two handfuls of papers and trash. She turned around and jumped back, startled.

"Charles! What are you doing here? Why didn't you call first?" she felt nakedly vulnerable, all of a sudden. He started to answer and took a step forward. "No! Charles, please don't." She tried to move back, to be less vulnerable, but she was caught between the open door and the seat of the car.

I'm not getting in the car. Her heart started to pound. Her breathing became shallow and quicker. She felt like something was stuck in her throat and covering her mouth.

"You never called us, Libby. Shame on you, for not even responding to our offer with a refusal or even a different proposal. After all I've done for you and your business." He was so close, now, she couldn't move to get in the car even if she wanted to, and she wanted to be anywhere else but here. Trapped. Helpless to prevent him from doing whatever he wanted to do. She was going to scream when he reminded her.

"Now, Libby, don't be a bad girl and drop that trash and make a big mess all over the garage floor."

She had forgotten about her hands. Her fingers paralyzed around the trash in her hands, her mind gripped in fear. Her confusion was leading her in circles. What was the right thing to do here? *Am I dreaming this? If this is real... Why? What have I missed? Should I have seen this coming?* She turned to look at her hands and he had her blouse up and was gently sucking on her breast. Her head swam. She tried to pull away. He not only pulled her closer but tickled his fingers up the back of her leg to her buttocks, around her hip, over her thigh, up her inner leg, rippling his fingers in the hair of her crotch, opening the slit, gently rubbing her clitoris. He lifted his head from her breast and said,

"Don't drop that nasty trash on the floor, now. Be a good girl!" and bent his head to pull her nipple in his teeth, rubbing her vulva more vigorously and sliding his finger into her opening.

71

She vaguely remembered looking at her hands and seeing two other men standing there, grinning at her, before she came the first time. *It's been too long!*, she pleaded with her mind, *too long!* Her eyes were closed, her body vibrating waves of pleasure, and still the eyes grinned at her. The roaring laughter was getting louder. *'No! No! Make them stop! Make them stop! It's gonna hurt! It's gonna hurt!'* someone screamed inside her mind. *Who's in there?* She tried to pay attention to what Charles was doing and a vague someone else with him. She tried to distinguish the voices in her head and which one was her own. She couldn't focus in on any one thing.

"There, now" Charles said, "That's some of what you wanted, isn't it, now? Tell me, you want it. Tell me you don't want me to stop." He was still rubbing her clitoris, gently then vigorously.

She was barely aware they had put her on the trunk of the car. There was a voice in her head saying she should not be letting them do this to her. She should be fighting them, or trying to stop them in some way. They were violating her! Another voice was saying, she really wanted this all along and as long as it feels this good, don't stop. It was almost as if someone was whispering, closely, in her ear. She knew she was just getting started. She knew she could have, at least, fifteen orgasms. Rafael had counted up to fifteen, then stopped counting... *Rafael, that bastard, this is his fault, but...* everything stopped, the world went night, her body peaked, spasmed and she climaxed again. What were they doing to her? Her whole body was alive... electricity shooting pain and pleasure in alternating waves. Now her mind was coming back.

"Look. We've all got to make her pop so she can't claim it was rape." some strange man was saying.

"We'll give her the stuff, and she'll beg us not to stop." said another strange voice above her.

"No, we can't, till she's come without it then we can have some fun. Until then, she could always claim one of us raped her-- you know how the law is, Jock Face. You *are* Chief of Police."

She tried to move her head to see him but there was one in her, one at her head and one at each arm, and the world was going night again, and she popped. She loathed her body for betraying her. She couldn't scream, even though there was nothing visibly covering her mouth. She couldn't fight. There was more holding her down than four big men. She couldn't make her body not respond. Tears of helpless, hopeless abnegation rolled down her cheeks.

"Who are you? Charles, who are these men?" she sputtered out between alternating waves of nausea, repugnance, and ecstasy.

"Oh! I'm sorry. I didn't mean to be so rude, my dear. Let me introduce you formally." The man who was at her head was now inside her, Charles was holding down her right arm, the man who had just been inside her was over to the side bending over something that looked like a black bag, and the man who had not yet been inside her was holding down her left arm, pinching her nipples hard.

"You, of course, know me, and the man inside you, doing such a poor job of making you come-- it helps to manipulate the clitoris, genius. Shit, no wonder you have such a hard time of it." He grabbed the battery powered vibrator, opened the labia and put the vibrator right on her clitoris and continued to pump away. She tried to resist. The pain of his roughness echoed through her body. All those previous gentle manipulations were gone.

"This is Jock-Face. He is Chief of Police. I can't tell you where, right now, but all you really need to know is: he would be more than a credible witness. The man on your left is Balls. You'll know why in a minute. He is a prominent judge. I'm surprised you don't recognize him. He is virtually unimpeachable. And, last, but not least, to see to it you are not really hurt *too* badly is our illustrious M.D., who, alas, happens to be on the board of advising professors for one of our most prestigious schools of psychiatry. May I introduce Stick."

The world was going night again. Her body bunched up, and bang, she came.

"Well, well Libby dear. We are so glad you're enjoying yourself so much. Now, aren't you glad we invited ourselves here? You seem to have needed all that we have provided you. We had no idea... have no fear, there's more to **come.** We never expected such a warm welcome. We would have **come** sooner, if we had known how much you really needed us. Rafael told us just what you like and just how you like it." She was terrified now. Rafael hurt her badly, really badly. As Jock Face moved to her left, Balls took Jock Face's place inside her. She tried to struggle free, even though it was ridiculous.

"Oh! Yeah! You really want it don'cha, baby?" Thundering laughter inside her head. Four big men certainly had power over her and there was little she could do about that now.

"Why?" she asked, tears still in her eyes, "You don't know me. You can't hate me?" she asked Balls, but he was busy. Charles bent over her and started sucking and biting her breast again. This time he was hurting her.

"Why! We're doing you a big favor. And we know much more about you than you can possibly imagine. We're not exactly strangers, Libby," someone was saying, as he sniggered.

A warm breeze blew over her body and the world went night, she came... but, this time, as she came back, Stick had a tourniquet on her arm and was injecting something into her. Balls had her legs up and Charles was smearing Vaseline around her asshole.

She panicked. Before her eyes, she flashed on a scene and this time her mind broke open. The laughter was getting so loud she wasn't able to hear anything else clearly. The arm she saw was a little girl's and someone was putting something in that arm, also. Something was hurting inside her body. She tried to scream and a hand came out of nowhere to stop the screaming. Her body was moving up and down with the pain... then the bugs of electricity crawling all over her, making her body jerk. Flash... *'Don't let them hurt me, Daddy! They're hurting me!!* **No, Daddy! That hurts***!'...* Flash... *'Nooooooo!!... Mommy, don't do that!! You're hurting me!!'*, she heard the child scream. Libby couldn't tell anymore, if it was pain or something else, and she knew she'd be a bad little girl if she told anyone-- then... she went away.

* * * *

She woke up Monday morning to Josie calling up the stairs, "You'll be late for the train, Miss Libby, if you don't get up, right now!"

Good God, is it that late?

She would work Monday and Tuesday and be off to the "Gathering" Wednesday. She must be catching cold-- her body hurt all over, so badly... a couple of aspirins would get it.

She wasn't about to let anything spoil it for her.

Chapter 4

"Look, Ollie!! He's just a nerd. A real jerk! What has he done for you, lately or ever? Isn't there a rock song, or something about that?" Lea railed.

"Well, he's just had some hard luck lately." Ollie winced.

Lea just doesn't know how long it took to find Michael and just how long those days and nights were without him, thought Ollie. *She's always had a man of her own, even when she and John broke up for a while, a few years back.*

As a matter of fact, she had men crawling out of the woodwork, just to get a date with her. It was like she was a virgin again or a Special Edition Whitman's Sampler or something. It was sickening how they begged and pleaded with her to pay attention to them. In the end, she went back to John. She just doesn't know what it's like to be lonely and desperate for someone to just touch you, and to do without. The more Ollie thought, the more resentful she was beginning to get.

She's not only always had someone there but someone else has always provided for her. She's always got her dinner paid for, and the door opened for her. I bet they accept it and count themselves lucky to be out with her when she says 'Not tonight' or just 'No'. I bet nobody ever forced her and made her do it when she didn't want to. John's always right there kissin' her toes if she wants, when she wants it. Easy for her to say I can do without and I don't need anybody. How the hell would she know?

Ollie was working herself up into a migraine. Her disability check wasn't coming for a few more weeks. She wouldn't have any money for medication until then; always short half-way through the month.

Mona was supposed to join them shortly and Ollie found she wasn't looking forward to it as much as she did when she sat down. They were going to carpool to Colorado Springs. This luncheon (as Mona liked to call it) at Wendy's was supposed to be a planning session, because the "Gathering" was only a few weeks away.

Ollie would have to borrow the money, but everybody knew she'd pay it back as soon as her check came in. Ollie kept her reputation for being "good for it" clean as an ammonia-washed window. It seemed she spent about the same amount of money each month... *That's stupid. I only make $600 a month. How can I spend any more?...* but it seemed to run out toward the middle of the month.

Ollie wished she could manage her money a little better, or maybe the right word was different; manage her money different. She couldn't seem to get out of the rut. Ollie's best efforts always led her back to the same place... poverty. Every time she was close to getting on her feet, something would happen. The car, the household appliances, the plumbing, her favorite shirt or pants would rip and couldn't be mended again. She'd need underwear, or shoes, or the utilities bill was higher this time by more than she could pay and on and on and on ad nauseam.

Now Michael was in her life. She spent more on gas; he used the car. She spent more on food; he ate at her house most of the time and he ate a lot. He needed cigarettes and shaving cream and razor blades... but she could use those too. At least up until yesterday, when he said he didn't want her touching his stuff. He was getting a bit moody lately. He'd lost his dishwashing job at one of the local restaurants and lost some of his pride with it. He really didn't mean to take it out on her, he was just nervous about being dependent on her. They hadn't known each other very long and he was probably embarrassed to be down on his luck so soon after they met.

Ollie knew how he liked to impress people. Like the time a few weeks ago, when he needed a new suit to look for a job. He was applying for a vacuum cleaner salesman's job. He said, "To be a success, you gotta look like a success. Nobody's goin' to buy a vacuum cleaner from a guy in jeans or a busboy's uniform. I won't be able t' get in the door. If I can just get in the door, I c'n make up to $500 a week in k'mish'ns."

The manager showed him all the people who made more than $500 a week after being with the company for only a couple of months and he looked just as good as any of them. "'Course, none of them's 'round here. They's all in much bigger cities, so's it might take me a little longer... but not by much, you see... cause I'm supposed to get these leads from the sec'tary and I'll only have to make a few 'cold calls' a week."

So, Ollie spent most of the utilities money to get him a new suit. It wasn't one of the good brands. Actually, they went to Goodwill and got one real reasonable. *What's in a label, anyway, and if it fits and it's clean, who cares who's worn it before?* He wanted to go to one of the local department stores to buy one off the rack. He fits into rack clothes, and he said she was lucky he did because it was a lot more expensive to get tailor-made. In the end, they still had to go to Goodwill. He got angry at her and wouldn't touch her for a whole week. She begged him to understand she couldn't afford it. Finally he understood, but he still avoided touching her and tried to stay on his side of the bed.

"Hey!! Come back, Ollie," Lea said. "Here comes Mona. Where'd you go? You looked all far away." Ollie just shrugged and looked up to see Mona coming into the place. Mona always looked as though every time she walked into a fast food restaurant, touching the door handle made her hands greasy-- any fast food restaurant.

It was all Ollie could afford. They always had to accommodate Ollie's purse or buy her lunch. One time, Mona said something about the lowest common denominator, but Ollie didn't understand it and was afraid to ask. Ollie was afraid Mona would laugh at her and say something else she didn't understand and then she'd really feel stupid. Michael called her stupid but in a nice way. She knew he really didn't mean it.

"Gooch, dears!" Mona greeted them.

"Hi, Mona!" they responded with varied enthusiasm.

"Your hairdresser is doing much better these days, Lea. Is it the same one or did you finally get rid of the little twit?" Mona eyed Lea's hair looking for defective contours in her coiffure. Mona didn't expect an answer. Mona looked Ollie up and down a couple of times. Ollie thought Mona was going to say something to her. Mona must have changed her mind and just sat down.

"Well dears, have we worked out the details, yet, of the trip to Colorado Springs? Has anyone found out if there's skiing there this time of year? How many miles is it and how many hotels with golf courses along the way?" Mona eyed them, as if expecting them to produce their theses and stand ready for orals.

Lea thought, *No matter how beautiful Mona is, there's something about Mona that reminds me of a black widow spider-- after feeding.*

* * * *

Ollie was cooking dinner, thinking about the plans they had made that afternoon. She'd have to tell the landlady Michael would be here by himself so the woman wouldn't think a strange man was entering her apartment while she was away. After they figured up the traveling expenses and how much the week's stay would cost, Ollie figured out it would probably take close to five months to pay the money back if she lived real light. *If Michael does good on the sales job, maybe he could help out. At least, pay for his own gas and if he intends to stay here, half the rent and utilities. That would sure help.*

She didn't like his moodiness and he stayed away from her more often now than when they first started going together. Oh, he still touched her occasionally and made love to her when she could talk him into it. She really didn't beg him, but it boosted his male ego a little when she played the part of the wanton wench.

She wasn't really interested in those kinds of games, master and slave, French maid, all of those things, but he seemed more aroused than when they had straight sex. She chuckled a little to think she could really suspect he didn't care for sex at all. *Look at what a sex maniac he was when we first got together. The first week or so he just couldn't get enough of me.* She thought about it; maybe she'd get out that French maid outfit he seemed to like so well. Maybe she could entice him tonight, if he wasn't too tired. *But if I ask him to help with the finances, he might feel "pressured" and lose all interest. That's the way he is. He's kinda' late now.* She was deciding whether or not to ask him for help or try the French maid outfit, when he walked in the door.

"Whew!! I'm tired!" he said as he slopped down in the dining room chair.

I'm not sure even the French maid outfit would work tonight, anyway. His eyes glistened a bit but he didn't smell of alcohol. He seemed to develop a slight case of the sniffles lately, and was a bit edgy. She hoped he wasn't coming down with a cold, being out in the weather.

"How was your day? Did you make any sales, today?" she asked cheerfully.

"Look, Ollie! Don't pressure me, I'm doin' the best I can. I'll get you some money as soon as I can. I have expenses too, ya' know."

"Michael, I was just making conversation. Asking you about your day."

"Well, just drop it, will ya'. Ya' make me feel like some kind of mooch, spongin' off ya' everytime ya' ask." he growled back.

"Michael, I don't know what to say to you anymore." She was nearly in tears.

"And don't start ya' goddamn cryin' again. I'm so sick of everytime I open my mouth you're cryin'-- one of these days I'm gonna give ya' somethin' t' cry about. Do ya' hear me!" He was screaming and raised the back of his hand to her as she flinched to get out of his way. He went into the living room, turned on the TV moderately loud and threw himself on the couch. "How long before dinner's ready?" he snarled into the kitchen.

"Not long, Michael. Michael?" she asked quickly. "Do you know where the blender is, I can't seem to find it? I wanted to make a cake for my birthday next week before I go on my trip."

"Yeah" he said. He got up off the couch and walked into the kitchen with an indefinable look on his face.

"Yeah. I hocked the blender. I don't want no big deal made outta a little, cheap kitchen appliance. I needed a pack of cigarettes... and whatta ya' mean you're goin' on a trip? A trip to where? And how long ya' gonna be gone and what am I supposed to do while you're gone and where am I gonna stay while you're gone?" He was nearly in her face. She smelled a strange smell on him. When he became aware she noticed the smell he immediately backed off. She was flustered by his behavior.

"It's a five-year-thing I go to with some old classmates," she stuttered out. "Of course, you can stay here, while I'm gone-- if you want to. I'll be gone about a week. What was that about the blender?" she asked.

"Look, don't change the subject," he was looking a little angry. "Just where are you goin' and who with?" He grabbed her by the arms. He was hurting her.

"Some old classmates of mine... just some women. We get together every five years. Michael you're hurting me!" *Was he jealous? Did he care that much?*

"*Where?* You still haven't answered me yet. **Where?**"

"Colorado Springs, Colorado, Michael. Please!" She was afraid he was going to break her arms. All of a sudden, he released her as the expression on his face changed and her body vibrated like a rubber band.

"Whole week ya' say?" He had a strange grin on his face.

"Yes, Michael. Michael, what are you grinning at?" she tried to ask as carefully as she could. He seemed preoccupied for a moment.

"Oh! Nuthin'!" he said, "When's dinner gonna be ready, baby? I'm starvin'-- how d' ya' expect a man to have the strength to give ya' a good tumblin' if ya' don't restore his energy after a hard day's work, my winsome wench!" He clenched and squeezed her breast and crotch for a few seconds, then went into the living room to wait for dinner.

Ollie was stunned. She didn't know what to say or think. *Is he relieved to know I'm going to be with women classmates... for only a week? Will he really 'give me a tumble' tonight?* He could change his mood quicker than static electricity could pop. He had done this before. When it came time to go to bed, he was too tired, or had a headache, or some TV program put him in a bad mood so all he really wanted to do was argue and maybe rough her up a bit.

Worse was the time he was finished and just left her all worked up. He said he was too tired to finish the job and just don't pressure him, and sneered at her when she began to finish it. He said something about being able to control herself and being a pussy. She stopped what she was doing and lay awake, hurting all night, afraid to start crying. It would wake him up and he'd get pissed off at her for interrupting his sleep. He had to work the next day and be up early.

Will he really 'give me a tumble' tonight?

She was forty-eight years old. She still believed love was supposed to grow. Not like the song that says the first time is the best and everything after was less or something like that. As she thought, she realized love had never grown for her. It was more or less the way the song said. With all the men she'd been with, after the first time there seemed to be something missing. She couldn't exactly put her finger on it. Maybe she really ought to give up on the idea that "love" grows or gets deeper. *I mean after all, I'm forty-eight and nothing like that's even got close to me, in my whole life. Maybe that kind of thinking is childish dreams.*

Her mother used to tell her, "Dreams aren't goin' to feed you. You'd better get your head outta' the clouds and your feet back down on earth. Life is too tough to keep any illusion like love or justice or honor... or mercy, for that matter. Those are things for people with enough food and money and leisure time to ponder such things, not for workin' people."

She just couldn't help but remember when he couldn't get enough of her. She tried hard to hold onto the feeling--- she'd give anything to get that Michael back again.

* * * *

Lea was getting ready for dinner and the show after. John had gotten two tickets to that marvelous new dinner theatre with the long running Broadway hit.

She had to ask him for everything, the man had no creativity, no imagination. All he ever did was work and wait for her to suggest something for them to do. The last time he suggested anything, he wanted to go to the stupid football game and out dancing, like they were back in college or something.

*Really! No imagination. Well, I can't exactly say he had **no** imagination,* she smirked. *He did want to go to that topless place a couple of times- he thought it would fire me up a little, but how can I get fired up when I know all I have to come home to is John.* At least he didn't say anything if every now and then she entertained herself with a young stud or two. It relieved the boredom. She wasn't really interested in the sex part: the fantasy playing was like being on stage. Too bad there wasn't any applause. She always did a fine job of acting and never an ovation. *Maybe someday.*

"Are you just about ready, honey?" he shouted from the other room. She was sitting in front of the mirror, adjusting the last wayward strand of hair as he walked into the room and came up behind her and started to kiss her neck. She pulled away.

"Please, John. I've worked for an hour trying to look decent for the theatre and in one minute your clumsiness is going to destroy all my work. You know how I like to look when we go out. You never know who we're going to see. Would you want them to think you have a slut for a wife?" *He looks a bit injured, but so what,* she thought annoyed. *He still hasn't learned, after all these years to keep his hands off. Just because we're married, it doesn't mean he can paw at me like some animal in heat.*

"It's just that... I... a.... thought you might... a... with the dinner and the theatre and all..." he stumbled over his words.

She turned to him with her eyebrows raised, scowling in contempt. "You thought what, John? Say it! You thought what?" He bowed his head in shame, turned around to walk through the door, murmuring.

"I just wanted to touch you, even if you'd never touch me back."

She couldn't hear what he mumbled and was just as glad. Because if she heard it, she would have to respond and that would be annoying just before dinner and what promised to be a lovely evening out.

She supposed he would want to paw at her when they got home, but she could take care of that. Even if he had to do **it**, disgusting as it was, it would only take a few minutes and he'd be done. Of course, she'd be messy and sticky and have to wash the nastiness off and out of her, but everything washes. *"It all comes out in the wash!"*

She especially hated it, if he wanted to spend time putting his hands on her first or wanted to linger on her after he was through. She thought she had taken care of that sufficiently the last time he tried it... he hadn't done it since. She may need to remind him tonight. *He'll be drinking,* she thought with distaste. *He might forget and try to maul me before he gets in and does his business.*

As she thought, her mind wandered back to the first time ever. It was with him and it had hurt a bit, but it was her mother she remembered most. Lea didn't know how her mother found out, but she did. Her mother was waiting for them when they got home. Her mother was always cold, *but this night absolute zero had nothing on Mother. Mother simply told John quietly to leave and he did.* Lea was there all alone with her. The very air was electric with tension. Lea didn't remember everything her mother said. *But I'll never forget how Mother wrinkled up her face in loathing and disgust and looked at me as if I were some slimy, inhuman, creature up from the depths of the oozing, filthy mud. Gritty with shame and guilt.*

Lea did remember something about being ruined and used merchandise and her value being like that of any other whore. Her mother wasn't even concerned she was hurting a bit-- in fact, a lot. Her mother did not tell her it would hurt like that. Her mother told her nothing at all, except you had to let your husband do it after you were married, if you couldn't talk him out of it. She had told her it would be sticky and nasty and you needed to be very careful to wash it all off and all out of you so you didn't smell like putrefying meat or dead fish. Lea hadn't a clue what her mother meant until the first time. *But Mother never told me it would hurt...* Lea sat there, lost in memories for a while.

Well, she thought, coming back to the present, *it doesn't hurt now; it's simply unpleasant and nasty. I'm glad I can talk John out of it most of the time.*

The time they broke up, all those men-- wanting to put their hands on her, she couldn't stand it. Some of them weren't going to take 'No' for an answer and she was terrified. Although nothing much happened, it could have if she hadn't decided to go back to John.

He wasn't much, and he was terribly dull but he provided for her and when she said "No" he respected her wishes. They both knew she controlled the way their relationship would be. She supposed he had a whore or two over the years, but he was married to her. *He was the first. He's the one who took away my purity. He owes it to me to stay with me... Provide for me since he was the one who **ruined** me for anyone else.*

Her thoughts then went back to the afternoons planning for the "Gathering". This time, she would not have much to share. The last five years of her life hadn't brought much. To tell the truth, the last five years of her life were somewhat boring.

She thought of volunteering for something, like the hospital or some community service project but she couldn't stand blood and gore. It was a wonder she could take care of herself during the time of her woman's curse; so the hospital was out.

Most of the community service projects worked with indigents. They made her uncomfortable. She always had the feeling they

87

knew something about her she didn't know. Something dirty. And they weren't going to tell her what 'It' was. They always looked at her as if something was missing, or like her inseam was torn, like she was deformed, used. She'd wear her best casual clothes and have her hair done the day before and they always made her feel that somehow she just wasn't good enough to volunteer to help them. *Well, I don't have to put up with that. I don't need them, they need me. The hell with them!*

Her volunteer work idea had been short lived.

She thought of starting her own business; a boutique. She dreamed of catering to women like Mona, and Julie and Kitten. Catering to women only. Where she didn't have to put up with any disgusting men. The only problem was: most of the successful lending institutions, realty and merchandising businesses were populated with men. So, there was no way out of it, she'd have to deal with *them*. That brought her back to the last "Gathering".

Hazel suggested maybe it wasn't *men* she was uncomfortable with but her *feelings* about men and poverty and all the other things that made her uncomfortable. Hazel was a nice person and all, but Lea hadn't a clue what Hazel meant sometimes. Even though Hazel's words could make Lea feel uncomfortable, the woman, herself, seemed to have a calming effect on Lea. She thought about it a couple of times and gave it up when she felt her mind going around in circles.

Lea perceived Mona absolutely detested Hazel's 'goodness and light' attitude and trying to play everybody's guru. Mona thought Brighid was a kook, Ollie a K-Mart special, Chris and Penny lowlifes because they weren't about to make anything of themselves. Judy was just as nuts as her yo-yo patients, and though Dee did something constructive, she was always hung up on 'being in the light', whatever that was. To Lea, out of the whole group, the only ones Mona seemed to like were big businesswomen like Libby, Kitten and Julie. As for Jo-- Lea doubted seriously Mona even considered her human and breathing. Mona severely limited those she thought deserved credit for thinking: Jo was not one of them.

Lea considered for a moment what Mona might think of her and gave it up quickly. Lea knew Mona had a certain kind of respect for her because she went back to John and had control of their relationship, but that was as far as she would delve. Something in Mona's mannerisms reminded Lea of her mother when she disapproved of her. She wasn't ready to defy Mona's favor.

As for the group, Lea, herself, really had no opinions one way or another. They were what they were and she was who she was. They really didn't contribute to her life nor take away from it. They were a connection to her youth. The dazzling, adventurous time of her high school days. She was the senior prom queen, the president of the junior class, voted most popular and most likely to succeed-- two years in a row-- and had tons of friends sign her year book. *Where did I put my class ring? And the letter sweater the whole football team made especially for me? Where are they now? Why was life so exciting then and so dull now?*

In high school, she dreamed of being a princess, like Grace Kelly. She'd jet all over the world, have subjects bow to her and a dashing prince to kiss her finger tips. Then, in college, she met John, and though he wasn't a dashing prince, he had a promising future. He came from a decent family who had property and investments. Their courting was okay, so long as she managed to keep him in the front seat and his hands to himself... but he was no worse than all the other boys. She had lots of dates and lots of friends and lots of interesting things to do.

Maybe, when I get back from this "Gathering" I'll try to look up some of the old crowd. Try to start some kind of a club or something, where we can talk and do interesting things. Like we used to do. Yes! Now, that will be my new project, when I get back.

"Honey, if you don't hurry, we'll be late for the hors d'oeuvres and the cash bar," he shouted from the next room.

He's going to try it again tonight. I just know it. Well, I'll nip that in the bud! She grabbed her evening purse and started out the door to enjoy a lovely evening.

* * * *

Mona was exasperated with her travel agent. She wanted to go to the West Indies after the "Gathering". The agent couldn't get a booking on the day Mona wanted to leave. *I'll have to find another agency. After their initial wooing, the discount they give just isn't enough to keep my business. They've had trouble, lately, getting the exact arrangements I want. As a matter of fact,* she thought peevishly, *it's the only reason why I have to car-pool with those two whippets. I would be just as happy to leave both of them behind.*

She was considering speaking to a few 'chosen' at the "Gathering" this year and start their own "Gathering" without the impoverished collective. Most of the collective group was a waste of time, money and effort. The few that made the "Gathering" worthwhile for her, well... it would be to her advantage to cultivate those relationships on more fertile soil, so to speak.

There were many who thought they understood Mona but few who could match her ability to reason. That alone, never mind her life experiences, put her in a solitary position most of the time.

90

She worked all her life using the philosophy of minimum input/ maximum gain successfully. This group of virtual losers' net profit to her was waning so quickly they were about to become a black hole. She never liked wasting time and resources, especially on self defeating, no-return, nonprofit activities. That's one of the reasons she never married-- talk about self defeating, no return and non profit. She could use her talents, the talents she chose to use, as she saw fit with no accountability to anyone at anytime. She saw absolutely no sense answering to the whims of a half-wit, arguing or making concessions to an inflated bag of testosterone.

The only thing she would ever plead or beg for would be a chance to get ahead or even before she died. She wasn't sure who or what, if anything, she'd have to bargain with to do it, but negotiating was her forte. She had learned her lessons well. She came from a poor background and vowed, by the time she was thirteen, she would never stay poor. She would not spend a lifetime doing without. And she damn sure wasn't going to put out all the effort she saw her mother and father put out to receive so little in return. Day after day and night after night, watching the loan-sharks, the government, the church taking preemptive rights over their meager earnings. They left only the most meager scraps for them to survive on. She loved her parents, if that was the right word, for providing for her and keeping her alive till she could get out on her own. They would never understand her, but she just couldn't pretend to not know what she did know.

She saw what government of the people, by the people, and for the people was in the riots of Selma and Watts. She saw it on the Berkeley campus. She saw it on the faces of her neighbors after the I.R.S. confiscated everything they had. She saw it in the McCarthy trials. *Oh! Yeah! Freedom in America. Let's talk about a little love... Love Canal that is.* Let's not forget justice-- like what was done at the rape trial to her best friend who was gang raped. Her friend ended up committing suicide when they were all set free after a plea-bargaining session. Mona still couldn't figure out how the attorney of the accused convinced the jury her best friend, a virgin before the rape, was a whore-who-asked-for-it.

She'd been to old folks homes and orphanages and knew, beyond a shadow of a doubt, the only one who was going to take care of her was herself, and she'd better get busy. She wasn't a sociopath nor was she totally amoral. She made conclusions from the evidence of her surroundings. She decided, if she met the Buddha on the road, she'd shake his hand, wish him well and see if he'd buy dinner... And if Jesus really did let all that happen to himself, she was out of there in a hurry. Modern psychiatry had names for people like that.

She wasn't one of them and didn't want to hang around them. Something might rub off or someone might think she was like that by association and try something funny with her. She designed her future much too carefully, and worked toward those ends much too hard to grant anyone any kind of *gratis* to what was hers-- **anyone**.

When she first started making money, she tried to repay her parents for what they had given her. When she saw them report the money as income and all the "agencies" finished taking their share, she said forget it. That was the first and last time the I.R.S. bothered her. She cut her business teeth on that one, and never had to learn a lesson twice. By the time she was thirty, she was well on her way to being the richest woman in the United States, paying the least taxes. By the time she was thirty-five she retired on the interest accumulated yearly on her investments and could still afford to play futures and commodities when she wanted to. She had nests all over the world sheltering her assets that could be converted to gold at the drop of a hat.

Every time someone told her some money making longshot was impossible, she'd study, she'd spend grueling hours teaching herself... disciplining herself, bending her mind, body and will to learn the business and how to conquer it, and compel it to turn a profit for her. Success could not evade will, knowledge, hard work, wise judgment and most of all, tenacious persistence, for long.

She'd been asked many times to teach and thought often enough about it but there would be only three things she would write on any board as principles to success. She would be willing to share the three guiding principles that she had developed early on, only because she had observed these qualities were lacking in most people's training and especially in women's training over and over again. She could envision herself writing on a blackboard:

Principles to Success:

1) **Focus** *on the solution/s and* **apply** *it/them to the proper problem.*

2) **Take responsibility**-- *blame is superfluous to the task at hand-- all failures and mistakes, everyone's, exist for you to learn by- so, do it- take responsibility and fix 'it'- learning occurs in the doing. It will be you who learns or someone else who gets the opportunity:* **Commit! Choose! Make the decision!**

3) **See the big picture**-- *there are no free lunches and there's no such thing as a self made anything since the big bang- everything that exists interrelates to everything else.*

She had no doubt money made her desirable and what money didn't fix, in that area, she wouldn't spend a nanosecond of thought on. When she wasn't busy making money or enjoying a good learning challenge or the creativity of the world's best artists, her thoughts, occasionally, turned to sexuality. She had been a virgin for a long time and wondered, when she was young, if she were abnormal in that realm. She really didn't have too much desire for sex or physical sensuality or emotionality.

Real excitement, for her, came with accomplishing an especially challenging learning project, with mastering the impossible and herself along with it. When she started making real money she finally found time enough to try sex and could afford the best. She paid to learn and experience everything one could offer in the sexual realm and would still prefer mastering something that would challenge her actuarial acumen. Let the longshot copper futures she bought in a bear market, the one everyone said was on a critical path, suddenly, overnight (as she calculated it would) increase its p-e ratio by 200. She'd skim a little more and then out with a nice windfall promptly converted to non-taxable securities, and--- and, let this happen within a few hours... *Welllllll, that's much better than sex any day, no matter what the position or who the artist is.*

Just thinking about some of the deals she made recently could make her heart beat fast, her breathing heavy, and her forehead sweat. Who the hell cared if she was abnormal. She was healthy, wealthy, and wise. There were very few who would dare to tell her otherwise, to her face, and they were ignorant at the very least.

Her mind wandered back to the plans for the "Gathering". She wasn't at all happy with the present arrangements. She would have to travel at the rate, pace, and level of Lea and Ollie She didn't mind spending money and could afford to pay their way to travel, so they all could travel to her standards. It wasn't even a matter of profit or return. It was a matter of self defeating, however. Not to her especially, but to both of them.

Through the years, she had occasion to lend or give money to many people and learned, along the way, a concept expressed by the Chinese and the Jews concerning giving, responsibility and self esteem. Basically put, it said: if one is not willing to be responsible for a person for the rest of their life and not willing to be the key igniting their self-respect; don't give them anything they can earn. Even though the concept of responsibility and self-respect earning is a two way street, the person seeking self-respect can't throw the responsibility of it on someone else. Due to the very nature of those who have and those who have-not, more responsibility lies on those who have, because in having, they realize the nature of getting and its rewards. Those who have-not are yet to realize the connection between cause and effect, action and reaction, responsibility and self-respect. It seemed nearly everyone wanted a hero. Which meant someone to do it for them. Someone who will make the changes for them, wave a magic wand over them, pave the way. All they should have to do is step on the moving walkway and collect their due (which, of course, should be the same as the heroes).

It's nice to think those who are more gifted will share the fruits of their efforts with those less fortunate, but it is, by no means, an **obligation***. It's nice to think someone's there to bail you out if the water's too deep, (parents, friends, lovers, children, monarchs, presidents, congress, big business, etc.), but again, there's no* **obligation***, implied or contracted. If a people take responsibility for their own self-esteem, they may consciously decline 'help' rather than turn over to others the criterion by which their value is measured. The new concept of either permitting or not permitting others to have a personal* **affect** *is ridiculous. It's equivalent to someone holding her breath and not letting it* **affect** *her. Why on earth would any persons want or choose to be or stay anywhere where they were unaffected by those they were in the company of?*

For that matter, why would anyone want to be unaffected by the place, or circumstances or anything she was involved in? Alcoholics and drug addicts do their thing to be unaffected, the average person has TV. The consequences are the same. When a person gives up the choices she has to someone or something else, she chooses to live unconsciously, every time. Every time anyone closes her eyes, turns her head, goes along with the crowd without investigation, or lets somebody smarter, prettier, more powerful, more experienced, etc. make her decisions, she gives over, maybe not consciously but willingly, her self-esteem. She turns the responsibility of 'self' over to 'them'.

The principles she learned came back to her easily now although the learning was not so easily won. Her mind began to stroll down this corridor for a while. *No wonder most of society feels victimized. Society has given over to 'others' the power to do anything they want. The average persons trust these 'others' will do the right things in a life they themselves want no responsibility for. Then cry 'victim' when the wrong decision is made.*

*The problem, after it becomes multigenerational and self-perpetuating, is not making conscious decisions, it's becoming conscious in the first place. The problem is not to beware of things easily gained, but **which** things are hard earned in the first place. The problem becomes not just having values but in knowing **what** to value; not in earning self-esteem but in knowing **what** earns self-esteem and keeps it. Perhaps the advantage in beginning with nothing is I had a better opportunity to see what is valuable or really... I was able to see that I am valuable, without all those 'things' getting in the way. I only had myself as a*

resource, and an insatiable desire to extend to my fullest capacity.
The seeds for accomplishment fell on healthy soil and the vista for
self actualization grew abundantly.

From that perspective, all gained is added to what is already, not
trying to make up for what never was. Born into a generation of
relative abundance, compared to centuries before, how can anyone
believe themselves impoverished? Mona surmised that no one
dares to say, for abundance to translate into self-worth, individual
action accompanied by social conscience and consciousness must
be valued. *Giving Ollie what I've earned wouldn't give Ollie her*
own achievement. Effectively, it would take away Ollie's need to
create change. Giving to Lea wouldn't make her conscious.

Most of the group attending the "Gathering" started out, relatively
speaking, with the same hypothesis, but the process and
conclusions were universes apart. Their processes were not wrong,
simply ineffectual, for Mona's values. From Mona's perspective,
she wondered if their methods were insufficient for their own
values also, but it was, truly, none of her concern. She could only
decide for herself, act, evaluate the results, make corrections,
where necessary, and not perfect her mistakes. She had no
intention of permitting indigents to hang onto her as a lifeline, nor
letting ineffectuals leech on her.

That's where she and Hazel disagreed. Hazel believed if people
knew any better, really knew, they would do better: good is
inherent. Mona believed, not only, people knew what the choices
were, but no amount of education would make the bad choose
good, if those were the appropriate nouns. Mona couldn't fathom
Hazel's process. From all appearances Hazel was intelligent. Hazel
had traveled, had real life experiences from which to base her
evaluations on. Hazel was not deficient or defective. Hazel made
some quantum leap in thinking which Mona didn't understand.

To Mona, the equivalent of Hazel's thinking would be something like: Here is an apple tree. You water it. You feed it. You give it lots of sunshine and clean air. You watch the apple blossoms bloom and you just know you're gonna get the most wonderful watermelons from that tree. Hazel made no sense to Mona; therefore no point wasting time on Hazel. Well, enough!

Mona had heard something strange a few days ago, the morning they had planned the trip. She knew who it was and would wait to get the details when she got to the "Gathering". She had some financial fun to accomplish before then... first things first.

Chapter 5

Penny was a round, soft, fairy woman. Even in maturity, she had the gentleness and beauty of the ethereal about her. The best of the Irish was in her blood, which also meant to those who mistakenly thought gentleness was wimpy, the rock hard toughness and strength of the indomitable Irish could come out in dragon-sword fire when her ire was awakened. That ire could most easily be brought from its sleep when she perceived cruelty or injustice to the small and powerless. Her mouth could make baby food out of the biggest brute, and grown men would cower from a bolt of lightning flashing in the electrically charged words she could invect at them.

Yet, that same mouth, with the kindness and power of a healer, could make life bearable for one more day to a young woman so violated by life and love that she was convinced, before talking to Penny, that this unendurable pain would follow to the realms beyond death.

Penny's perspective of humanity was tempered with the most inhumane experiences of ghetto life, violent parents and being on the wrong end... the poor end... of the American system. She forged nights filled with terror, loneliness, and darkness into a heart that beat with the spirit of a high priestess and messenger of the Goddess. More than once, she had not only enhanced life, but, in fact, saved it, unbeknownst to her, just by being who and what she was; herself. She understood the value of truth given in love and knew it could change lives for the better. The gift she was currently bringing to the world was of a small business owner, artist, learner and teacher of the human spirit.

Penny wore her past gracefully, like a loose fitting garment. It was neither shield or barrier nor was it a banner; it simply... was real.

She approached the events in her life, to the present, as an artistic, finely crafted mosaic; a delicate lacework weaving the essence that was her; and the masterpiece wasn't finished yet... The last note of the symphony hadn't been written. Considering everything, she wasn't going to rush it. The coming "Gathering" would be another learning and growing experience for Penny.

Jo smiled as she thought how Penny's friendship helped to heal the mind break she was blissfully unaware of in herself. When Jo had joined Alcoholics Anonymous many years ago, she was totally unable to see what others saw, that her mind was shattered and fragmented. Penny was one of the rare and few in A.A. who befriended her and told her the truth gently, without being cruel. Most people were just afraid of Jo and stayed away.

Through the steps of Alcoholics Anonymous, an atheist group in the program, a remarkable sponsor, and Penny, Jo was able to find enough pieces, or make new ones, to put what was left of herself into a somewhat functional whole. Many people talked about how the "fellowship" made it possible for them to recover. Well, for all Jo saw or felt of that, she could get more "fellowship" from an angry rhinoceros.

Jo recognized that, although she managed to be functional, the likelihood she would ever know a consistent feeling of fellowship and ease around familiar people was small to nonexistent. She'd never been able to comprehend or grasp what other people seemed to evaluate, do so casually, and take for granted as friendship. Sometimes the pain of this difference was overwhelming.

In her early sobriety, it was more than enough to worry about just learning to survive sober and be functional. Now, she had time to spend on more than mere survival, the skills necessary to learn this thing called friendship continually flung darts of ignorance, inadequacy, and ineptness... tortured and eluded her like a mirage out of reach. With the continual encouragement of the few like Penny and her sponsor, she could focus on the direction she was heading, the goal, and give herself permission to look back to evaluate only the successes, and those only with a newly developed sense of humor and gentleness.

No... Jo wouldn't give up... she'd already done the impossible in her life; the miracles would take a little longer.

Jo considered how lucky she was to have any brains left, at all. She could barely remember what she had done drinking or the drugs she took, sometimes at the same time. She was informed in early sobriety how many of the people who did what she had done, died or would "never come back" because they were wet brains. Perspective might not be everything, but it could sure take away the value in real accomplishment or it could turn the most impossible problem into a challenge and opportunity. It could turn indifference into *chispa*.

One big "for instance"; when Jo was learning how to be functional... It looked like, from where she was sitting, "crazy people" got taken care of and didn't seem to have it too bad. They certainly didn't have to struggle like she did, against unattainable odds, for so little in return. Jo mentioned it to her sponsor in the form of a whining complaint. Her sponsor didn't say too much, but shortly after, they had an opportunity to bring a meeting to one of the psychiatric units.

Jo looked carefully at the inmates. Profound understanding took place as she looked into eyes that couldn't hide their horror of awareness. Those eyes imprisoned the last shadows of human beings... lost in torment... stalked by their own excruciating and demented nightmares... without hope of release... Jo shuddered, and had a perspective gestalt she never forgot. She feared even toying around with the idea of insanity as an option to an easier softer way.

Jo, also, was grateful to her sponsor for showing her in the only way she was capable of learning at the time. The smile returned to her mouth, remembering Penny and her sponsor. She sent a silent prayer for their blessings and well being to whomever was responsible for distributing such commodities.

Jo walked into the coffee shop to meet Penny and Dee to discuss the details of traveling to the "Gathering". Jo knew she would do most of the driving because it wasn't one of her depletion activities as it was for both Penny and Dee, each for different reasons.

Jo didn't mind at all. What Dee and Penny contributed was more than enough to compensate for not driving. In fact, their combined talents meshed into a magnanimous working unit measuring more than the sum of its parts. Jo often wondered why they didn't start some kind of business together. They complemented each other so well. She was sure anything they got into would surely be a success. Together, their assets were enhanced and exponentiated. Their liabilities were diminished and deflected.

Most recently they had discussed the dynamics of relationships, in general. Dee and Penny were married. Penny was finding her "family by nature" and developing a relationship with them. Dee was unbonding with her "family of origin" and forming new bonds by choice. Jo was unmarried for over twenty years and without any significant others including "family" for close to fifteen of those years. Although to Jo, her sponsor in A.A., Penny, and Dee were more than "family" could ever be. Her "family of origin" gave her "life", her "chosen" taught her it was possible to live it. Jo was currently adding her therapist to her "chosen family".

Jo had found out she was multiple personality, a condition caused by the physical torture and mind twisting done to her in early childhood by her parents and "other people" she could not identify. She had begun to remember her childhood when injuries from a car accident triggered memories of the torture. The injuries of the accident and the traumatic body memories were in the same spots. After seventeen years of sobriety and reforming her life, she had to begin to redevelop her "values" all over again.

The car accident triggered the onset of the memories and the body memories retraumatized body places used by her torturers to program fear, shame, guilt, and silence, in the same manner that Neuro-Linguistic Programming patterns and sets triggers. This made her body/mind feel like being newly sober without the pain numbing fog of anesthetic chemicals still left in the brain. Some of the "memories" were like a "virtual reality" experience. The reaction they produced in her body, however, were as far from the unreality of "virtual reality" as the real pain of a broken bone before medication.

Guesswork replaced certainty of perception, just as it had done seventeen years prior. Her body bruised, swelled, bled, opened in lesions, broke out in rashes; muscles would cramp and pull together in spasm as if the trauma were happening right now, every time she spoke out loud the truth of what she remembered happening to her. Memories caused her heart to batter her rib cage and she hyperventilated as weird scenes crossed in front of her vision path. She could only see what a small child would see in those circumstances so that visions were half complete, or seen through the water her face was held down in, or drug-fogged because of the chemicals her torturers gave her as a child to intensify and intentionally distort her perception. The only advantage that came from doing drugs in her active alcoholism was that Jo could identify drug distorted memories. She did, after all, have experience as an adult in these matters, in depth. Tsk, tsk.

Memories were definitely not the same as the experience. They lacked the endorphins. It would be hard to get hooked on memories. Memories are not nearly as friendly as the experience. In the actual experience even terror and pain had compensating chemicals to go along with them. Not so with memories. The pain and terror were there without the compensation. Being seventeen years sober also meant the kindness, extended to the mental disabilities of "newcomers" in A.A., was not extended to Jo. At seventeen years of sobriety she was expected to have someone else's idea of "quality" sobriety, whatever that was. She was supposed to display the type of functionality "society" and A.A. could be pleased with, so A.A. could say it "works when you work it". The only thing keeping her out of the funny farms was, in fact, working the A.A. twelve steps, as she'd been shown by her sponsor and a few alcoholic women she grew to trust, as she understood them.

As for the men in A.A., it appeared to Jo, the "principles" didn't apply to their dealings with the women in A.A. The current wave of misogyny and disrespect perpetrated by recovering alcoholic males on recovering alcoholic women was becoming tantamount to murder. It seemed to Jo more recently, alcoholic males had some preposterous notion that women, especially alcoholic women, fell into two categories. They were either virgin/wife or whore. Some alcoholic males, even males with "time" who were still active, untreated sex offenders, seemed to feel capable and qualified to judge the sober behavior of recovering alcoholic females and deign which woman deserved "respect". New comers were giving these males "authority status" without question or investigation, to the harm and detriment of the females involved..

For this type of alcoholic male to respect, bless, and grant valid "quality sobriety" status to an alcoholic woman, she needed to fit into the virgin\wife half of the persona. Even women who managed to stay within the ridiculous virgin\wife half of the whore/virgin\wife persona were subject to harassment and devaluation when they didn't agree with these pompous males at meetings. Experience, strength and hope took second place as credibility and sway was given to the nebulous, untenable **'opinions'** of swaggering males.

After traveling, Jo knew that all over the world alcoholic women are stigmatized as 'bad', undisciplined, sexual deviants needing to get good instead of sick people needing to get well. Recovering alcoholic women are sensitive to these attitudes and often try to live up to hideous standards not imposed on alcoholic males. Headway to correct the erroneous, moralistic attitude toward female alcoholics was making progress... until recently. A.A. was a money maker and more potent than religion in keeping the uncontrollable in-line for certain unscrupulous people and groups... a new source of power to munch on.

When Jo came in, seventeen years prior to stay sober and clean, "tough love" did not mean exclusion if you did not conform to someone else's set of values. It meant telling your own experience, strength, and hope. It was an aide and guide, not a rule laid down to follow. People who had little sobriety were listened to and respect was given to those who had stayed sober and clean continuously.

It's a sad statement about Alcoholics Anonymous today that most women who come in as 'sick' as I was, will be turned over to the euphemistically referred to "mental health" system. Jo shook her head somberly. Although Trauma and Recovery, by Judith Lewis Herman, M.D., Professor of Psychiatry at Harvard Medical School has done a lot recently to aid health care professionals in treating alcoholic women more appropriately, few have read the book.

Alcoholic women, instead of being offered the same opportunity to recover as Jo, end up on medication. Drugging them was a way of silencing and controlling them, dooming them to the ever-lost, without anyone batting an eye. It seemed Alcoholics Anonymous would rather a woman be labeled "crazy" mistakenly than an alcoholic with other problems... solvable problems... such as mental disorder due to trauma. The uncomfortable and unmentionable are preferred controlled rather than recovered.

Out of the women Jo had been privileged to share her experience, strength, and hope with, not one, not one was untraumatized and unvictimized by the society she lived in. Even AA members began doing what society had done for generations. When these women started getting well and telling their true stories; they quickly became aware it wasn't nice to tell the truth if it was nasty and didn't have a typical happy ending. Unresolved nastiness, after some "time" in the program, resulted in pariah status. Ostracizing an alcoholic who adopted AA meant they would be fated to a living death -- drinking.

Instead of being free from alcohol and drugs as a parameter of respect, the way it was when Jo came in, regardless of a person's ideology, now there were current societal, television standards as parameters of respect. *How did Alcoholics Anonymous lose its connection to the "Well of Compassion" and its primary purpose? Did it begin the day Alcoholics Anonymous gave over the privilege of working with wet alcoholics to the detox centers and the treatment facilities? Why had so many people "forgotten" the value in getting sober and staying sober for its own sake, the way the "Big Book" expressed it? Hell! People are arbitrarily* *changing **that** without permission. When did only certain brands of religiosity become acceptable in Alcoholics Anonymous?*

Soon, any resemblance of A.A., as it was, when it started out, would be wiped out entirely. Staying sober wasn't the only thing, for sure, but without it... Something of value is lost for Alcoholics Anonymous.

In her early sobriety, it was inconceivable to Jo to think in terms of a "therapist" as being more important than her society of A.A. In truth, the therapist she had was quite unique as therapists go. Jo sponsored "therapists" in A.A. who became "therapists" before they got sober, and... *Frankly, if that's recovery in the 'mental health' system, way too many people can only hope for slavery to the system through drugs, rather than recovery.*

She had been sober long enough to appreciate recovery and its process. She had been through too much to surrender recovery and substitute being controlled through drugs. She would not keep quiet. **"<u>Victim No More: Silent No More!!</u>"** was the battle cry of the recovering survivor, alcoholic or not.

Her therapist's insistence on "cleanness" as well as sobriety and gradual recovery, lent respect to all her personalities. The process to recover from her trauma required it. Her therapist's willingness to go through the memories and aid in the process of recovery, which was frightening even to the strong of heart, made the woman so special. Her therapist dealt with the more terrifying aspects of this type of recovery, in a way assisting Jo's recovery and change. Since frightening feelings that were merely controlled could resurface at the most inconvenient times to sabotage progress, vitriolic feelings dealt with right away had their controlling power removed right away. So, just as her sponsor, Penny and Dee became "family by choice" through doing what families are supposed to do, her therapist became "family by choice". Her discoveries and recoveries in therapy added to the richness of her discussions with Penny and Dee.

If it hadn't been for therapy, they wouldn't have been discussing "relationships" in the way they did over the last several months. Dee's voice would echo in her mind and rock it with a distant vision of recovery. "Afterthought: I realized the idea 'end' is an illusion because it's all a spiral, but I see us getting to that space of wide-armed, open hearted connection that breathes with power, through every inhalation and gives it forth with every exhalation. No effort, no barriers."

Dee also spoke several times about moving into that space that is love, sitting and grounding yourself in love, and initiating all your decisions and actions from that space, operating from a space of love. What that meant to Jo was: when you want a change in your life... say, you want to be more loving to yourself and others: you make up your mind to love-- you **create** thoughts, and actions and feelings reflecting and supporting what it is to be loving so everything-- absolutely everything-- you do and say and think expresses your new direction. Every cell of your body and mind becomes aware of your decision to love and contributes to your efforts to make this change come about. Even the most simple and mundane ideas and decisions revolve around *'What does it mean to be loving?', 'What do I do when I'm most loving?', 'What does it feel like and look like and how do others react to me when I'm accomplishing my goal to love?'*

Like a feedback loop where the original output goes out and becomes input, corrections are made over and over until a leap is made- a connection to change is made, the final output desired **manifests**... a vision to look forward to indeed.

Dee also said "When the language of your vision holds a solution, your words will have power." Jo reflected on the dynamic changes, quantum leaps in her direction of associative thinking, where the very process kept some of her in the wide eyed wonder of entering a secret garden.

Diane Mariechild said in her book <u>Mother Wit: A Feminist Guide to Psychic Development</u>, "..., we have all perpetrated the use of violence either by actively harming others or by ignoring our own needs, thereby allowing ourselves to be harmed." On the same page of the same book Ms. Mariechild says, "You can act out of a space of love and abundance or you can act out of a space of fear and limitation. You cannot act from both spaces simultaneously."

Yes, through therapy a vision of "love and abundance" isn't a misty distortion of heat, unreachable and unbelievable. *Ecstatic joy of communion with the ALL is surely the glitch that produces the moment when I'm able to simultaneously see the before and the satori, and step over to the new-- firm and committed, looking back without loss, looking forward with anticipation.* Real progress is when there is a knowing, a gestalt coupled with a behavioral change that manifests: All time is now and there is no separation between all that exists and the **ALL**, <u>ever</u>. Hope is having the experience at least once.

Jo found a small smile on her face and a heart-pounding flush of life as she continued to walk, nearly bringing tears of intense gratitude and joy to her eyes. Maybe, just maybe, she would not end up like those she saw in the institution, trapped in their own, everlasting, nightmare.

Yes... Jo had <u>evidence</u> of hope... "*evidence*".

The small smile on Jo's face turned into a wide, broad happy-face of a smile as she caught sight of Penny and Dee sitting at a table, engrossed in what was obviously an intense discussion of something. People at other tables looked up and smiled at her, which she acknowledged by looking directly at them and smiling back. *What a vision*, Jo thought, as she joined her family. Penny and Dee looked up to smile and acknowledge her presence and continue their discussion... *Evidence of hope, not shatter-proof but no longer fragile.*

Something like calm began to settle in her stomach, without the emptiness that an unagitated state used to produce in her, or the hard rock of the temporary ceasing of turmoil. This was full and warm and satisfying like a nourishing, clean wet energy, everflowing, undulating, embraced by the thin membrane of human skin.

She mused: she had never, in her wildest dreams, ever, thought she would feel a sense of goodness about being feminine. That she could center in it and be comfortable in it was like attaching a perfectly fitting, formerly lost, part of her natural self back in place. She sat down and waited for a pause in the conversation.

"Hey, there!" Jo grinned. The other two looked at her and grinned back.

"How in the hell are ya'?" crowed Penny.

"Well, you finally got here! We were talking about being alone and time alone and independence and interdependence and we want your input." challenged Dee good naturedly, in the way of old friends.

"Can I get some coffee first?" Jo saluted.

"I don't know," Penny looked at Dee half seriously with one eyebrow cocked up. "You know her and chemicals... Are we ready for that?" she nodded at Jo. They all chuckled.

"Will she transform to a guru or something weird?" Dee gibed at Jo fondly.

Jo put a seriously intense look on her face and in a near whisper, croaked, "I will turn into a web of blithering mush, veerrrry soon! I can feel it coming on and the only cure for this condition has been proven to be a rare combination of chemicals to be found in the coffee in this shop alone. Quickly... Before... Blither... Blither... It's happening... Blither... Blither," Jo began to twitch.

They all roared in laughter.

They finished their plans to get to the "Gathering" and settled back into the original conversation.

"Well, you know, there's no such thing as independence but I'd never tell that to someone deeply attached to the illusion. Hell, you could get yourself killed today by one of those well-meaning, self-sufficient, do-it-your-selfers." Penny said as if to test the air, looking over her granny glasses.

"I think I know what you mean," Dee spoke out loud, as she thought, "but what's so illusory about earning your own money, picking your own home, going to the store and picking out your own clothes or deciding to be in relationship or not?

"I don't have to be married to Bob, you know, or anyone else, for that matter," Dee continued. "I've made the choice to raise my children and what values I chose to emphasize in their training. It's just sometimes being alone seems like a sublime nirvana somewhere in the future. Then I'll be able to concentrate and focus on what I consider to be the reason I'm here-- my work, so to speak. Surely you can't think being alone is not independent?

"Just look at Jo and how far she's come-- she's not only alone but she's happily independent." Dee illustrated. "She comes and goes as she pleases, she doesn't have to ask for anyone else's time schedule. When she's hungry, she eats; when she needs to shit, she doesn't have to wait in line; she cleans up only when she wants to and only after herself. Do you know how much time I'd have, not to mention how neat my house would stay, if there was only me there? And I might be able to keep a thought long enough to write it down without being interrupted."

Penny slid in for a slam-dunk, "You can do that now if you changed your priorities, but that's not the issue. How many people raise their own seeds, or food, harvest or hunt to weave their own cloth and make their own clothing, mine the raw materials, process them and craft their own tools and make their own machines, never mind make their own transportation, beginning with acquiring the raw materials and fuel, manufacturing each part, putting together each piece including the nuts and bolts, find and process fuel from scratch? Hell, when was the last time you or I or anyone made anything from scratch?"

Dee looked a bit confused.

"We are talking about independence, aren't we?" Penny questioned. Dee nodded yes and Penny continued, "While we're on the subject, who's engineering our biochemistry by controlling what food is available to eat and what properties that food will have? By the year 2000 we won't even be able to find a seed **'they'** haven't produced with all this hybridization. The clothes on our bodies are chemically processed to someone else's orders. Our bodies will be so dependent upon what some controlling son-of-a-bitch wishes to feed us, clothe us in and chemically control us with; if we try to wildcraft a stinkin' tomato or kill a deer and wear its hide, we'll get the symptoms of poisoning. What we eat, what we wear, what we breath, what stimulates our olfactory, auditory and visual senses affect our body chemistry enough to change the very nature of who we are and how we will behave. Where do you think you got the idea of what independence is? Where do you think you get the chemistry to have any feelings about independence or any other emotion at all?"

Dee shook her head in confusion, "Wait a minute you lost me! First you're talking about biochemistry, then you're talking about food, then you're talking about emotions. Are you making some kind of connection I'm not getting?"

"You bet I am! Do you think any of those are separate? Do you think they don't interact with each other to produce the final result that is you?" Penny paused a moment, "We're not only what we eat. We're what we think and how we act. What we eat isn't under our own control and what we think and how we act is subjected to things like TV, radio, subliminals, colors, noise, air pollution, the chemicals we know about and those we don't know about. We are programmed by some one or some thing outside our control. So I ask you... How about some programmed depression so you can't protest what somebody else does to you but you can still have the mind to know they're doing it and the energy to produce?! Some forms of depression don't involve not being able to move. You move just fine, it's feeling good, or enthusiastic, or motivated to change you can't quite get up to! So much for independence!" Penny sat back and folded her arms as she arched her triumphant back and cocked her head.

They both looked at Jo for some input. "Well...?" They both raised one eyebrow at the same time with a head down, horns up position as they shot a somewhat heated "Speak Up!" glance at Jo.

Jo looked a little uncomfortable as she looked from one to the other. She was obviously thinking and not sure how to verbalize the essence of truth that was hers. "Hmmmm..." Jo started out. "I don't know where to begin, exactly." She paused. "For all intents and purposes, I haven't been married in over twenty years. We all know the intensity of certain perceptions change when you're in intimate relationships, or even with having a TV, which I haven't had in fifteen years, or with having enough money to placate the illusion of independence. Which, I do, by the way, agree with Penny, is an illusion for some of the same reasons. I also believe we have illusions concerning choice because the choices we are permitted to make are few and keep us within controllable boundaries. One example would be food, as Penny pointed out. With all that is available, most of us have given up the right to have a say in our own lives for the convenience of not having to grow, manufacture, process, create, et cetera the things we consume or use to stay alive in. Giving up choice in some areas gives some of us time to do other things besides merely subsistence survival."

Jo bit at her lip as she thought of the words to continue. "I also believe that what choice we have involves being able to choose our direction, but not necessarily the circumstances surrounding that direction. Some people have 'Principles' of convenience. As soon as it becomes a little tough or they 'feel' out of control, they make the necessary changes to stay in some imagined comfort zone. Being able to have direction and choose your surrounding circumstances, equivalent to staying in some comfort zone, is real mastery and is much easier the fewer people or requirements of your choice there are. A person can have very little they value and very few people they relate to and appear to have total control over their lives. What's the saying?... If you don't mind: It don't matter." Jo paused briefly to gather momentum.

"Choosing a direction, a value or principle because you believe in it, because it's right for you, it's the only alternative that makes any sense to you or it's the least of all the evils and then sticking with that choice, no matter what, can be more difficult and cause so much more pain. Often it looks to some as unnecessary pain; more than most people are willing to imagine. The reality of interdependence requires a person to modify their direction to consider others or be doomed to extermination by isolation. The way our current survival requirements are set up, exactly how little can one person survive in the elements with, alone, or want to continue living like that indefinitely... who knows? But... I'm fascinated with your perspective or what appears to be your perspective of my aloneness as some kind of nirvana."

Jo took a deep breath and continued, "When I have 'others' in my life to have intimate contact with-- my daughter, a man, a roommate, someone living with me or the like-- 'outside' relationships are not as intense and not as important and do not consume as much of my thinking and active time. In this, I don't think I'm all that different than other people. But I am very different than most people, in that I don't go around manufacturing 'intimate relationships' to take away the intensity and reality of my 'aloneness', such as it is. Although 'intimacy' differs in activities and intensity, et cetera most at least provide some kind of body contact and background noise and the knowledge, at some point and time, another human being will walk through the same door you walk through."

Jo shifted in her chair, her face solemn, speaking slowly, the silence screaming for an explanation. "I am very familiar with the sounds of air moving in and out of my lungs, with the feel of blood as it moves through my heart, with the atmosphere of my skin. I am familiar with the sounds of the fridge, the fan, the electric heater, the creaking of the houses breathing their silent watchfulness, the midnight sounds and smells and movements I can't quite identify. I am familiar with that twist of perception that puts a body into survival mode so all the senses are heightened to a sharpness bordering on pain. Each noise is magnified and there are voices in every nasal breath. I am familiar with the phone that doesn't ring for days, or weeks or months and I wonder if I have affected life and people so little that my existence will go unnoticed, I will pass away with no one to cry for me. I am familiar with the great ideas no one will hear about or laugh at because I will forget them by morning and what would it matter anyway? I am familiar with the nightmares that leave my whole body pounding out the fear in my heart and the wet dreams wasted and left to die alone in the night and not a soul to confirm or deny: *'Was this real?', 'Is this real?', 'Am I real?'*

"That little trek of homelessness in '92, where I was up in the mountains camping out gave me new perspective and familiarity with the sounds in my head, and the weather of fear on and in my body. It gave me new perspective on hunger-- hunger for food-- hunger for evidence of human life-- hunger for evidence of something greater than-- hunger for reason to be alive, more than just the inability to die before it's my time. These perspectives were added to what I had already." Jo stopped and listened and waited a moment. Penny and Dee's breathless silence encouraged her to go on.

"Most people, at some time or other, desire and maybe even require being 'alone'. The amount of time differs with each person... but see if you can imagine being 'alone' *indefinitely*-- I, of course, mean without intimate contact. There are no sounds other than what you make. There is no talk, no touching, no movement, no smells other than yours-- *indefinitely*. All sensory input of other humans is 'outside' your sphere. You hear your own heartbeat in your own ears, *indefinitely*. You hear, see, feel your own breath-- you know when you're lying to yourself. You know when you're ill by the telltale of your body reactions and this will go on *indefinitely*. If you're sick, you are the only one to cook for you, get a cup of tea for you. You must move, even if you can't, you must be strong, *indefinitely*. If you have a sudden injury or accident, **you** must call the doctor because no one's coming home in a couple of hours or a couple of days or a couple of years to help or comfort. You will have to do this *indefinitely*. When your body and mind ache with desire and longing for another's touch, you sit there unsatisfied, *indefinitely*. You made the 'choice' long ago, after suffering the consequences of too many of the 'same' kinds of men doing the 'same' kinds of things, leaving you not only alone, but empty afterwards.

"Oh! Occasionally you try it again, just to be sure-- a one night stand- the singles clubs- the church socials. But you can't pretend to not know what you do know. Innocence has long gone and the minute he opens his mouth with the same old shit, you just can't pretend, this time it will be different. If you didn't know or you could wash away the years of 'Where are you from?' and 'What do you do?' If you could erase the fear and contempt when 'they' find out you really are stronger-- you don't have the same illusions-- you prefer to be aware, alive, and responsible... But you can't pretend to not know what you've experienced." Jo looked down. She just couldn't look into their eyes and go on.

She gasped for breath and exhaled shallowly but continued. "One of the definitions of insanity is doing the same things over again and expecting different results, so you try a lot of 'different' things, expecting 'different' results. Penny, you said once that being sane--

ie. aware, alive, responsible-- in an insane world is the real insanity. I have a tendency to agree with you.

"Inevitably, somewhere in all that trying 'different' things, you meet a special person here and there. At first, you hang on for dear life because the intelligence, the life, the visions you share in your brief moments of friendship are the only thing that point to any hope of 'something more'. But the other person begins to feel smothered.

"You don't know why your needs are so great... You don't know why there aren't more people in your life to share this with. You've certainly tried... You don't know why there's such a difference in your needs and your friends because you share so much in common. You see your friend has many more people to share with... Try as you might, you haven't been able to negotiate that same talent. You watch your friend-- the closest thing to intimacy you're gonna get-- slip away or run away.

"Through the years," Jo continued, "you learn not to hang on. You learn to choose your friends carefully, not giving your precious gifts to those who would take advantage of your loneliness and you have to trust that if you don't have a death grip on the relationship, it won't die.

"And through the years you learn to take, with love, just what they are able to give... It doesn't matter what your needs are. It's better to have what is offered than to go back to nothingness-- *indefinitely.* And you treasure those communications as life-giving manna." She stopped a moment and tried to collect herself but the tears wouldn't stop, so she just kept on talking.

"You know, it's not hard to imagine going through life's rough spots alone. Most of us have to do it some time or other. It builds character... But can you imagine having to go through life not being able to share, **with anyone who cares**, your joys, your victories, your accomplishments, your abundance-- when you finally have some-- or the beauty you feel coursing through your very existence... *indefinitely*?" She looked up and saw their stunned, silent faces.

She wished, with everything in her, she hadn't said too much and their relationship hadn't changed...

But she couldn't pretend to not know what she did know.

Chapter 6

Chris didn't like the vague uneasiness she was still feeling while making her breakfast. It had started right about the time she was making rounds and didn't get any better while giving report. Hazel flashed into her mind briefly.

That was strange. Hazel's face flashed in her mind. Not a memory of something they did together or a photograph of Hazel, just Hazel's face, no body, no give-away expression, no emotion, no animation, just Hazel's face.

She and Hazel were best friends forever. Time and distance couldn't alter what love in friendship wove together. That's what made the vision so strange. The vision looked like a weird still life painting breaking through an opening in big puffy clouds. Though Hazel's mouth never moved in the vision, she heard Hazel's voice in her mind trying to tell her something she couldn't quite make out.

It was almost time for the "Gathering". She intended to go; having made arrangements for time off, plane tickets, hotel reservations... the whole thing already. She had even been excited before this morning. Now, she had unaccountable reservations whether or not to go, except to see Hazel. She would find out then, probably, if there was anything to it.

This is stupid! There's been nothing identifiable to make any change in anything. So just quit the shit! Right now! Let the damn thing go! Whatever it is! She was tired. She was hungry. She was emotionally drained.

On her floor, she had two expirations, one mother- one child. Neither of them could have been prevented. The mother was diabetic and went into convulsions unexpectedly for no apparent reason. It happened so suddenly. There was no warning. It was over before the machines were in the room. The baby was toxic and deformed, screamed his first breath and never screamed another. There would be an autopsy, of course, and she most definitely was not looking forward to the endless reports, paperwork, and hearings.

Finally in a safe and undemanding place, she pushed her eggs away and gave in to the overpowering sadness and grief for the lost humans. With tears she retched away the sorrow of the powerlessness and inadequacy of medical art in the face of death's call. She knew she'd be okay after some sleep, food and maybe some life-affirming warmth from family.

I know this kind of thing goes along with the territory. I'm grateful it doesn't happen too often- but you'd think after all these years it just wouldn't be as devastating.

Her body was quickly reaching the point of exhaustion where it would refuse to move. She'd better do something like motivate towards the bed or she'd awaken to her face in the eggs. *Eggs are good for the complexion, aren't they?* As the thought dashed across the space of her mind, her head was on the table. Her body relaxed and it was the last she was aware of till the early afternoon.

She was aware of a distinct pain in her neck and back. An urgent pressure let her know she needed to urinate. *I think I need a chiropractor*, her dazed brain said as her body took inventory of the pain still left after the bladder was relieved.

"Do I have to participate in this?" She heard herself ask her brain. The brain did a spot-check of the body parts, especially those resisting movement, gave her an affirmative to which she just

groaned. Her body at full speed wouldn't register a mark even on the finest caliber speedometer, so she ordered her brain to quit nagging her. She spoke kindly to her body, asking it to maneuver towards the bed with a promised reward of being put on something soft, gentle and kind to it. She went to bed and back to sleep.

She came to in the evening with a start, not remembering how she got in the bed. *What time is it? Did I miss a night of work? Is it morning or night?* She quickly looked for a clock and was relieved to know she still had some time before she'd have to get ready for work.

I hate it when I'm so tired I sleep away the time I need to accomplish other things. I doubly hate it when I don't wake up ready to function. Uhhh! Who's been pounding on my body while I was away? She tried to move... *and what was that strange dream? Hazel was trying to hurry us up. To do? What? What was she saying? What were we supposed to be doing?* She had a feeling of incompleteness. *Something's left undone and it's important to do it... as a matter of fact, there was some urgency. To what?* She searched the paths of awareness in her brain, all the files, all the numerics, all the abstracts, dates, times. She went everywhere in her brain she could go and still found nothing sensible to give meaning to the insistent feelings demanding attention.

She could give Hazel a call, right now. She checked the clock again. No. She had just enough time to eat... *Oh! That's right! Eggs on the table.* Groan! *Food, shower, get ready for work, go to the all night grocery store and then to work. The store can't wait, the call can.*

She was being silly about the urgency but not about how good it would be to talk with Hazel. She'd call tomorrow when she got off work. In the mean time... *'Up and at 'em'*, the dictator inside her cried. *How is the family group doing? When is the last time I saw them? Must be too long because my body is strongly indicating desertion if I don't get some physical and emotional contact soon-real soon.*

She was so glad she joined the polyfi'ed group marriage. She needed the love and intimacy of a family and to give love to a family. Being bisexual and healthy along with her other circumstances presented a situation perfectly resolved by being part of a seven-adult, six-child polyfidelitous marriage.

Her needs, even in the group marriage, were special enough to warrant a small place of her own. A place where she could fall asleep in her eggs with no one to be bothered or bother her. When she got off work she didn't need children running around trying to get her attention or dancing on her while she had her face in the eggs.

Chris' place was a little efficiency off the garage. When she was able, she was always welcome at the dinner table, in the family games and outings, in the planning sessions, and of course, always in someone's bed.

She contributed her part of the expenses, nurturing, counseling, offering her wisdom and love with enthusiasm. Her contributions were well received. They had all been together, now, for fifteen years.

She remembered when they all birthed Ronnie. She chuckled remembering how everyone wanted to help Jessica feel loved and cared for while she was in labor. The confusion when everyone realized there was only room for so many people around one birthing woman.

The way everyone tried to be thoughtful of everyone else's wants and needs permitted her and Jessica to deliver baby Veronica.

All noise, all movement, all calling out directives to get this and do that stopped instantly with the baby's first loud cry of life. The awe of the moment when a small unmoving, unbreathing creature, just coming out of its mother's womb, becomes a real live, moving, breathing, wailing, miniature human being is worthy of the silent, reverent attention accorded it by all present.

Life -- how miraculous!

Hazel's hand had helped her find a suitable way to live. Chris had been dying day by day in a quiet, desperate world, giving her life force daily, never replenished. The constant draining of her body's life with nothing and no one to nourish and revitalize her was all Chris had to look forward to. It was Hazel who suggested she write to this advertisement in a magazine about several families pooling their resources together to try and meet each others' needs. She liked the advertisement. All she'd had to lose by checking it out was a couple of dollars in calls and paperwork. Not a bad trade if it worked out.

As they met, talked, and got to know each other, hope had begun to renew her. Life might just have more to it than giving and giving and giving till you dried up and died because you had no more to give. After much talk, working out things like finances, the kids, the sleeping arrangements, the shopping arrangements, the property arrangements, they agreed to try it for a year.

That first year was tough. If you think trusting, sharing, and relating to one spouse and any number of children is difficult, try doing the same with six adults and any number of children. She thought a moment and decided: *In some things it's easier, and in others it's magnifyingly difficult.* There were arguments, and tears, and sleepless nights not compensated by lovemaking. There were personal boundaries and territories to establish and semantics to clarify. There were all sorts of situations, feelings, surprises, disappointments and limitations never taken into account because none of the people involved had ever done this before. One by one problems were dealt with, resolved, worked on until agreement was reached by all.

Many a morning she would come home tired, dragging, to find a house full of people waiting for her input. She would give the last ounce of energy in her, knowing sometime soon one or more of the family would rain their love on her.

She would feed her soul, nourish her spirit, fill up to overflowing the golden, ambient, supple liquid of life replenishing her empty reservoir. Surely, this was the secret to eternal youth: the constant giving forth and filling up, because life is a constantly rhythmic capacitive - inductive flux.

She and Hazel often talked about the nature of relationships, sovereignty, spirit, and perspective. The limits we put on ourselves and the limits others put on us, or try to, often have nothing to do with the third-dimensional reality we are currently living in. All too often limits have a lot to do with the way we perceive what third-dimensional reality ought to be to fit our own belief system. Who knows how many times we act out our own karmic dramas with people closest to us. Our loves have nothing to do with the reality we are currently attached to. We are dealing with our mothers or our ex-boyfriends, someone from our karmic past.

In love, these people, sometimes knowingly, sometimes completely unaware, will act out a drama of ours, one totally foreign to them and their stuff, transforming themselves into people they are not, so we can finally resolve something we need to deal with. Like the time Natalie started screaming at Chris,

"Look! I'm tired of you expecting me to do all your dirty laundry. Just because I don't have a job right now, it doesn't mean I'm going to be your slave or anybody else's!" Natalie started to storm out the laundry room door and Chris called her back and shook her head in wonder.

"Natalie? What is this all about?" Chris asked.

"You know!! You know very well!! You left your dirty laundry right here!" Natalie pounded on the counter. "You expected me do your stuff. You knew I was doing my laundry today. I always do my laundry on Tuesday. You didn't even ask me- if you'da asked me I might not've minded," Natalie pursed her lips and folded her arms tightly. "But you just left your dirty things there, like I was the maid or something and I was just supposed to do it because you left it there."

"Wait. Wait, Natalie." Chris was shaking her head, "I forgot today was Tuesday. I've lost track of what day it is. That's all. I didn't mean anything by it. I'm just tired."

What came out later, after much talk was that Natalie grew up in a family who figured children should be used as servants. To be valued one must be an adult, must 'have a job' and 'bring in money'. If one didn't fit into the criterion of adult: i.e. working, bringing in money... they must be worthless and no better than a slave. Natalie needed to pay for taking up space, air, food, and resources in some menial way to match her menial value. So she cleaned up after the valuable, moneymaking adults.

Natalie's sole function was to make the valuable, moneymaking, jobholding adults comfortable. Of course that was impossible, because their life was soooo much harder than hers could ever be if she wasn't 'working'. Self-worth was granted by the adults around her, rather than from something within. It could be attacked, diminished and even withdrawn-- taken away by those adults who didn't have any self-worth, for they surely deserved some. Which meant it was necessary to protect, fight for, and hold on to hers, to keep the enemy from getting it.

What a challenge for the whole family. First to help Natalie with the concept that self-worth is something inside herself. It's acquired by what she does and who she is to herself. Secondly, Natalie needed to gestalt: there are no enemies, at least in the household. The give-and-take of the rhythmic flux had its trial by fire on that one. Natalie still had her moments of doubt and fear, but the changes possible in an atmosphere of love are nothing less than amazing-- possibly Amazing Grace.

Chris remembered the last conversation she had with Hazel about this very subject. Hazel had been talking very strangely, not quite depressed or fatalistic but almost like she was channelling information. She looked as if she could be a Hazel in a lifetime ten lives in the future. They were talking about loving, sharing, being rid of karmic stuff, finally awakening to being Divinity and all it entailed.

Hazel was saying, "You know being Divinity could easily have its drawbacks."

Chris looked at Hazel as if she had gone mad. "What are you talking about?"

"Well, imagine you managed to 'get' how to create eternal abundance, eternal bliss, and eternal love. You are aware and can shift from this plane straight to the Prime Source. There you'd be; just a patch of energy within a greater patch of energy being blissful, and loving. With the powers to manifest anything- absolutely anything- in any state you are in, you wouldn't need anything. You'd be aware you had no boundaries; you actually shared everything because everything is you."

Chris thought a minute, "Sounds good to me!!"

Hazel grinned. "As a sovereign, complete entity, you would never give anything to anyone or need anything from anyone because you are everything and everyone. Not only would it be sad, it would be boring."

Chris went 'glitch', "You've lost me."

"Okay. Here we are on a three dimensional plane, somewhat limited or appearing to be limited in the amount of abundance, love, bliss, and so on we can obtain here. Say everyone was aware they were able to manifest all the abundance they wanted, contain all the love possible within themselves, have all the energy they need available to them, and so on-- who would you share it with?

"If you didn't give it away, what would you do with it? If you knew that no matter who stole it, took it, destroyed it, used it-- you are able to manifest more. Even if you were the only one who could and no one else believed they could or everyone else believed they could and did, what would be the point?"

"Earth to Hazel. Isn't it time you came back now?" Chris asked cautiously.

"No! No!" Hazel pursued, "Think about it. If you realized you were Divine and truly everyone else was Divine and there were simply some people who didn't want to be aware of their Divinity for whatever reason... but there you were - able to manifest absolutely anything with no desire to be what is called negative in this world - no desire to manipulate or rule over anything. You don't even have a need for an ego to protect what you are not, because you are all.

"If you didn't have others to share your abundance with, others to be joyous or jealous or something with all your abundance-- what's the point? You can eat only so many steaks before you get tired of steak. You can have only so many diamonds, so many planets, so many answers to all the questions possible, so many games and variations. You name it and there's only so much any being could want, need, do, or be before it gets boring... then sad, especially if we are eternal beings. Even if you choose negativity or evil, there's only so much to do before it wears itself thin. If you flopped back and forth between good and evil, switching to a different one each lifetime, there's only so much before it becomes the same game, same tune, same plane, same possibilities, same station. So what's the point?"

"First thing, whatever is your 'Prime Creator' probably has an answer for you 'cause I don't. What exactly brought you to this point?" Chris asked, feeling a little strange like maybe planes shifted or maybe they moved into another dimension when she wasn't looking.

"Really!" Hazel continued, "Think about it. So you work your way up to being a 'Prime Creator', having experienced and created all there is to experience and create. Then you raise up and become a part of a unit of 'Prime Creators' until you rise up far enough to the original 'Prime Creator' and the thing starts all over again or raises to another level of 'Prime Creators'. Somewhere in there, whoever's at the current top could sure be bored or sad being in this eternal state of bliss."

Chris paused a minute, raised her eyebrows and said, "Did you hear what you just said?"

"Sure I did!" Hazel was excited- she was on fire.

Chris pursed her lips and gestalted a decision. "Maybe it would be better to just focus on the next few months rather than the next few eternities. At least you'd have people to share this great abundance with and nobody would have to deal with the mess that's left behind when you transcend... Your third dimensional, elemental form and all. You know."

Hazel's head jerked around. "What do you mean?"

"You know. The body is made up of so much calcium, phosphorus, magnesium and that kind of stuff. I've noticed when souls leave the physical form, somebody's got to clean up what's left or it begins to smell. Small things like that... Very necessary on this dimension- goes along with those of us who choose to ignore our Divinity and remain in third dimensional reality - all that." Chris was beginning to be seriously concerned for Hazel. "Besides, I heard a nasty rumor somewhere; you gotta love it here, just the way it is, before you can leave it," Chris commented

Hazel cocked her head, smiled. "Loving doesn't mean you can't attach emotions, nor do you have to approve, simply accept or surrender, if you will."

Chris shook her head and replied. "I still don't see how you equate bliss with sadness, even with a time factor of eternity. Valium used to be the cure for that, or a good bottle of ninety proof something, or even multiple orgasms. Have you tried any of those lately?" They looked at each other and guffawed till tears ran down their faces and they had to hold their sides to keep from hurting.

Chris would need to start packing for the "Gathering" soon. *Why am I thinking so much about Hazel?* Chris wondered, put it to the back of her mind and smiled inside thinking how good it would be to be in Hazel's presence again.

She checked in briefly with the family, got hugs, kisses and complaints of too little attention. Chris gave solemn promises to remedy the delinquent situations as soon as possible, oohed and ahhed report cards, drawings, math tests, new nail polish, and other achievements.

She took care of necessary things and went to work with Hazel still on her mind.

Chapter 7

Kitten tapped her long fingernails on the mahogany bar. Her soft blond hair haloed a face that looked 30, not 48, and crowned a slender, lithe, supple body. Wherever she went eyes followed. All eyes; the eyes of admiration, the eyes of curiosity, the eyes of the lurking, the eyes of the profane. No one, at least in this little Texas town would ever approach her without her permission, or more correctly, without the Duke's permission.

When she'd married the richest and most powerful oil and cattle man in Texas, she had no idea how impoverished and trapped she would be. Oh sure, she had everything she could possibly want to buy- but she owned nothing. She had as many people to surround her and do for her as any human could possibly handle at any one time- but not one person she could talk to or be real with. She could educate her mind and body in any discipline she desired- but she would never use that education for any other purpose than to add to her husband's image. She could have all the contrary opinions, beliefs, and values she wanted to have. The last time she expressed those contrary opinions to the wrong group of people, when it got back to the Duke, he beat her until she bled and swelled up. Then he fucked her and went on to his regularly scheduled business meeting.

She tried to press charges but not one person would listen. It was like she became invisible. She was treated by the old doc, cleaned up by her maids, healed up by the natural forces in her body. All to the tune the Duke whistled... And if she didn't stay in her place, like a proper woman and wife should, she'd have no place and be replaced. As she knuckled under to the rhythms of the Duke and learned how to be a Good Ol' Texas Gurl, people began to see her again, but nobody said a word about what the Duke did.

He was the life force in that part of Texas and anything he wanted to do was 'jest fine'. He signed the paychecks of more than a million people and owned enough banks to hold the profits of his oil fields, his cattle, his investment companies, his land holdings, his inheritance, his... on and on.

Kitten couldn't help wonder why he married her until she found out her background and bloodline matched what the Duke needed to produce the sons he wanted. A breeding mare... that's all he wanted from her. As long as she popped out one of those round, fat testicled creatures every two years, for as long as the Duke said, and stayed in her place, she could have almost anything in the world she wanted that money could buy.

She remembered when she carried a girl child in her womb. She remembered only too well how she begged him to let her have the baby. She went by ambulance to the hospital, received the finest care money could buy, including tranquilizers to ease the pain of the "miscarriage induced for the necessary health of the mother". She tapped her nails on the airport's private, by membership only, mahogany bar and got up to meet the plane.

Julie was a short, dark haired, tropical looking woman with an I.Q. much bigger than a body her size should hold. This was unusual, considering the average family she came from, but many unusual things about Julie lent a helping hand to those who wanted to take advantage of a ripe and juicy, shy, often overlooked, and somewhat exotic gamine.

Although Julie's I.Q. was extraordinarily high, she didn't seem to be able to learn certain skills having to do with socializing in the same time frame as her peers. On the other hand, her body development seemed to want to stay on a par with her I.Q. Her budding breasts, at nine years old, had turned into 38D's by the time she was twelve and the waist and hips of a child were replaced with those of a woman's by the time she was thirteen. Her inherent shyness made speaking and being noticed more excruciating than keeping silent about those nasty little boys and the dirty little things they did to her and made her do.

Somewhere around the age of seventeen, in her first year of college, it dawned on her she no longer had to put up with males and their demands. She also realized she had a brain, which was far more important than what she had between her legs or on her chest. That one item alone, if trained and used properly, could put her in a position to never have to put up with the kind of harassment she had to put up with as a minority female ever again. She quit nursing school and started for a law degree. Soon she was on the dean's list. Soon enough she graduated magna cum laude, and she was very quickly employed by an all-women firm in the metropolitan New York area.

Her career grew by leaps and bounds. She forgot the average little town she came from, the average little boys, the average little family she was raised by. She forgot their average little values, hopes and dreams that she was raised very carefully to have and she became Julie, Esq., the most successful corporate attorney in the metropolitan area.

She landed the Duke account through a recommendation from her classmate, Kitten. Of course, the Duke thoroughly investigated Julie and ran her through the novice hoops, but she passed all the tests and signed a retainer agreement. The Duke never needed to pause where her professional services were rendered. She became an expert through hard work and an ambition to succeed as great as her I.Q. Julie headed the team concerned primarily with the Duke's banking interests and all litigations the Duke might require on the personal legal front. Some of those fronts involved cash transactions to low income parents of willing and sometimes not so willing girls when he was younger. More recently, these legal fronts involved similar transactions and negotiations solicited by his sons. The Duke sure did know how to raise good ol' boys proper. Most recently, the youngest was being held on assault and rape charges, not to mention drunk and disorderly-- sowin' wild oats, yeh know! Everyone will be glad when the boys get over this lil' ole' phase and settle down and start a family, an' all. All boys do it, ya' know! Julie had a sour taste in her mouth but would continue to take the paychecks the Duke signed to the tune of five figures each month. Males!

Kitten met Julie as she got off the plane. "How was the flight?" asked Kitten as she picked up Julie's grip.

"Oh thanks! I suppose I'll never get used to you doing that." Julie nodded in the direction of the grip. "I caught up on some paper work during the flight, so unless the weather was really turbulent, I had no idea if there was a sun until I got off the plane. How's Duke and the boys?"

"Texas hospitality!" Kitten nodded at the grip. "Everyone's jest fine. Well, 'cept for the little mess Junior's into, you know. And a few little things I think the Duke wants to see you about. Won't take up too much time before the "Gathering". I thought for the teensiest moment the Duke wasn't goin' to let me go this year until I reminded him I was goin' with you an' he thought it over an' said I could go."

"What did you do?... Threaten to hide his cattle prod?" Julie side spoke to Kitten. Kitten half smiled and spoke in a quiet tone.

"I would never lower myself to be a whinin' woman twistin' off at the mouth, but I have my ways." Kitten side glanced at Julie with a

135

half-grin/half-smirk as the chauffeur opened the Rolls. "Does Andre' need to go around and get your other bags?" .

"No, I sent the others on to Colorado Springs. The airline will store them until we get there." Julie replied. On the drive to the ranch, they caught up on business and gossip.

"Is the Duke in residence at this time?" Julie asked casually.

The driver took a quick look in the mirror to see if Julie's remark had been sarcastic. Julie's face remained very neutral and Kitten replied, with a broad smile.

"Why, no. He's not. He's taken a little trip down to Dallas to see about a land purchase and said he would talk with you in detail when we get back from the Gathering."

Julie's face broke out in a grin and she kept her eyes looking out the window. "How long do you think it will take us to get there?"

Kitten thought a moment, "I suppose we could make it in a little more than twelve hours, dependin' on how many stops we make and how many speed towns we get caught in, but I was thinkin' we could leave a couple days early an maybe we girls could go shoppin' along the way. There's some fine booteries up to Amarilla', an some outlets along th' way for just about everthin' a girl could wish for. What do you say?" Kitten begged Julie excitedly.

"You're doing the driving.... You **are** doing the driving, aren't you?" Julie nodded toward the chauffeur.

"Oh! For sure! The Duke wanted us to take the Leer. You know how protective he is about what's his, an' all. Wellll, I started woman whaaillin' 'bout not bein' able t' shop an' all, an' I thought right then an' there he was gonna backhand me, so I ran out th' room, slammin' th' door t' give 'em time t' think 'bout it." Kitten defended herself excitedly, batting her eyes. The driver shot a transparent glance in the rear view mirror.

"Wellll, I guess he thought it over, an' installed a mobile phone, an' while we're on th' road we're s'posed t' call regular to let him know we're okay. He says since you're gonna' be with me, at least there'll be one good head if we git in any li'l trouble." Kitten nodded her head affirmative as Julie tried not to let her face show the distaste in her mouth for the Duke's implication of Kitten's thinking ability and simply turned toward the window again, expressionless.

The chauffeur opened the door at the front entrance, the women walked to the door as maids and butler approached in greeting and to take the bag. "It goes to the Bluebonnet room adjoinin' mine, Maria."

"Yes, Miss Kitten."

"I'll show you there so you can refresh yourself, an' we kin catch up on the gossip. It's just been toooo long since we actually had time t' just sit an' talk girl-talk, what with you clawin' out a name for yourself in that man's world way up to New York City. Why, I bet you're just dyin' t' do some woman things." Kitten flapped her hand down and put an arm around Julie's waist, leading her up stairs, entourage following.

When they were in the suite, Kitten took Julie on a grand tour of the "tiny li'l extension of her 'room' saved for 'special' guests", while the servants unpacked Julie's bag and put her things neatly in drawers and closets. As Kitten was finishing the tour, the last of the maids was waiting for instructions.

"Will Miss want me to draw a bath for Miss Julie?"

Kitten looked at Julie. Julie signaled "No". Kitten replied, "No, thank you, Sancha. We'll be jest fine. You can leave now an', please see to it nobody disturbs Miss Julie till she's ready to come out of her room. She'll ring if she needs anythin'" Kitten looked at Julie and Julie nodded affirmatively. The maid left.

They both stood there for indeterminable minutes, until they were sure all the servants were busy doing something. Then Kitten leaped into Julie's arms, passionately kissing Julie's face, cupping Julie's warm round body. Julie's hungry mouth found Kitten's neck, as her hands found Kitten's full pointed breast, stroked her waist, her hips, her bottom, then found hot nectar as Kitten's legs opened to Julie.

"It feels like it keeps getting longer and longer between times, and harder and harder to keep up the charade." Kitten breathlessly sobbed.

"Shh...Shh." Julie comforted, "Just love me now. All we have is now."

First they shared each other to make the desperate longing go away. Then they shared each other to fill each other up, then, again, for the joy. As dusk was settling in, they lay woven in each other's arms. Julie stroked Kitten's hair and asked, "When will the royal ass be coming back?"

Kitten only moved a breath's distance, to look at Julie's beautiful face. "He said he would probably be back in the morning, or real late tonight, so not to wait up for him."

Julie pulled Kitten possessively to her. "He's not still trying to stick it to you is he?" Julie looked into Kitten's glowing face, cherishing every line, running her finger softly down Kitten's cheek.

"Oh! No! Although, I *am* his lawful wedded wife and the mother of his children. He has the right to **take** me whenever he wants, you know. And since I maintain the proper Christian attitude of disgust at his sexuality and gratitude for the fact he's got some sweet young thing in town and rides a couple of the maids ever' now an' ag'in, he leaves me alone for the most part. You'd think as old as he is, he'd give up *some* of his foolishness, but ever' now an' a'gin I see where he's payin' some strange doctor bill or sets aside an education trust for some new baby boy. He knows I know, an' I'd never ask what he does with what's his. I just care about him leavin' me alone...."

Kitten looked as if she'd smelled something putrid. "I think he thinks I'm all dried up or somethin', an' since I don't take to no other man, he don't care what I do, or who with. So long as I don't come up pregnant an' nobody knows, he can act the part of the respectful Christian husband to his appropriately sex-hating, good Christian wife in public."

Kitten almost looked as serious as the preacher who counseled her to the truth and light espoused in the Bible. Kitten straightened her shoulders, put her head up and began her recitation. "You know it's **my** job, as the wife, to set Christian limits on an otherwise **rampant** animal nature. Because it was **WOMAN** who first introduced man to the sin of **LUST**. Why! From that time on, just like a ballistic missile, ever hoverin' to strike and penetrate its target, man's animal body needs woman's **Christian** guidance to clamp **that** *'thang'* down. How else he can be the direct intercedent to God and the spiritual umbrella he's s'posed to be for woman and her children? How would we have any salvation at all?! Uh-hm, ever'one must play their part no matter how wicked or disgustin'." Julie chuckled a little, then more seriously tried to sit up to look directly at Kitten but they were too tangled up in each other. Julie still spoke a little concerned as they untangled.

"He doesn't suspect us, does he? Hazel would never betray us, would she? She's the only other living being who knows about us, isn't she?"

"Who knows?" Kitten shrugged, "What would it matter? So long as we're discreet and I'm available, so he can show ever'body his dominance over what's *his*." Kitten was beginning to crinkle up her nose as if unsavory slime were slithering its way off her body.

Julie protectively, gently rolled over onto Kitten, chest to chest, belly to belly, up on her elbows so she could feast her eyes on her beloved. "Come away with me," Julie whispered, "Come away with me. I have enough put away and invested. We'll never have to worry. Let me love you for the rest of our lives. Leave that raging maniac so he can't ever hurt you again. I'll take care of you. I'll love you. I'll never hurt you." Julie breathed passionately as she looked down, drinking in Kitten's smiling face. Before Kitten had time to change expression, Julie was kissing her ardently, moving to life's rhythm pulsing inside her, stirring Kitten's desire once again. Julie began frantically but lightly to explore Kitten's body once again as if she'd never touched such a treasure before. Kitten couldn't help but giggle, gently trying to keep hold of Julie's playful hands so she could speak.

"You know he'd follow us anywhere in the world. No one gits away with takin' one of the Duke's possessions. He'd have us killed in bed together an' nobody-- **nobody**, would ever know or find out." Kitten tried to convey the seriousness of what she was saying in her voice. Julie stopped being playful and just held Kitten as tightly as she could, burying her face in Kitten's breast, trying to ignore the reality of Kitten's words. Kitten cradled Julie, stroking her wet, disheveled hair, grieving their mutual sorrow, silently.

Before long, they untangled again, looked lovingly but sadly at one another, each going to her own bathroom to shower and dress for dinner. They had what they had. Some people would live an entire lifetime and not find what Julie and Kitten found in each other. Whatever else they could never have, they at least had that.

After dinner, Kitten and Julie went into the parlor for after-dinner drinks and conversation. "I don't think I'm nearly as excited about going to the "Gathering" this time as I have been at other times." said Kitten reflectively.

"I'm not so sure, after this year, I'll be able to fit it in, very frankly." Julie said as she looked at Kitten longingly.

"Oh! Why is that?" Kitten returned the look, as she tried to make small talk while the servants moved about to perform their services.

"Two of the team members contracted to your husband are retiring this year, and naturally, I, too, am thinking of retiring," Kitten looked panicked as Julie continued.

"I'll have to groom not only my successor, but also hire and train two aspirees, so to speak. Not only will it take time, but a lot of time, and my work load isn't shared among the other team members. Only my successor incumbent is privy to my actual assignments. The corporate procedure, in this case, will be different than most because of the contracts we signed with your husband. He made sure no one individual could bring down the whole structure if they left. Each person is accountable for a clearly defined and recognizable area."

When Julie talked about business, Kitten became aware why her husband hired the more than competent attorney. Julie's posture, mannerisms, and even her face changed and gave out an aura of power. It suggested something along the lines of a steamroller approaching at light speed. It insured cooperation in any and all business matters concerning the Duke. It was obvious, only business dealings favorable to the Duke kept one from being "steamed" or "rolled", so to speak.

"Besides," said Julie, "I had some interesting precognitions about future 'Gatherings'. It's been thirty years, and it seems almost redundant to the original axiom to take the time to 'gather'. Those who have used this time to set up patterns of mastery have achieved. Those who haven't, aren't likely to suddenly develop an interest in procedures designed to govern the body and control the mind to affect achievement. More to the point: those who want to continue growing synergistically have developed disciplines, incorporating them as part of their lifestyle," Julie said matter-of-factly.

Kitten ruminated mentally and commented, "We do have late bloomers in our group and I don't mean undergarment!" Kitten felt an annoyed vagueness, bordering on free-floating something or other. She knew her so called "accomplishments" were really her husband's and not her own, but she claimed them anyway. Without the advantage of her husband, or rather, what he was able to provide, she couldn't have done the things she had done. Her life would have been... well, much different.

She had been doing a lot of looking back lately. Intruding thoughts warned that if she were to do anything of her own, the last chance was approaching. As the wheel of time rotated and the hand of accomplishment shined the last spotlight in her direction, she reviewed her past and there was nothing she could identify as Kitten. There was no creation (not even the 'boys'), accomplishment, legacy of her own. To Kitten, she was always an extension of someone else, a *small* part of somebody else. She didn't even have the identity of being a filler-in in someone else's life. The more she thought, the more fear and grief wrapped around her. She had no identity at all which meant she couldn't prove she even existed. She was so minute a part of everything and nothing, her very presence or lack of, wouldn't even be noticed. She counted for nothing and took up breathing space besides. The ropes of guilt and shame pulled tighter around her throat and stomach, her bowels stopped as if to affirm the audacity of her desire for recognition.

I'll have to get out the Ex-Lax again... maybe even throw up... Yes! You can't have too much money and you can't be too thin. As waves of nausea passed through her, she remembered why she didn't like these "Gatherings" too well. *All that emphasis on achievement and talk about stagnancy. What nonsense! If they'd all just do what they're supposed to do... Get a man who would provide for them and treat him right, they wouldn't have to worry about all that other stuff. Everyone knows that's what women are supposed to do. It's a woman's place to be submissive and accepting. It's the natural thing to do.* Her stomach really started heaving now. She rushed into the bathroom and closed the door.

The early morning sunlight was bright for an autumn day, as Kitten reached drowsily behind her for Julie. She jumped up, awake, to remember Julie went to the other room before morning so the Duke wouldn't find them weaved into each other's bodies. *Everything was ready to be loaded into the Volvo last night... Or was it the Subaru?*

Kitten tried to guess the time by the angle of the sun. *Most of the things have probably been loaded by now and all we really have to do is shower, dress, eat and take off.* She was looking forward to waking up in Julie's arms tomorrow morning. Through closed eyelids Kitten was imagining the feeling of Julie's touch on her skin when she heard a knock on the door. It brought her back to the present with the same sensation a loud crack of lightning would bring. "Enter," she pulled the cover to her neck and tried to look alert and pleasant.

The Duke was a tall, big, Aryan looking man, a Teutonic God in the flesh. As he walked to her bed, his eyes scanned the room, her bed, and Kitten, herself, in one incorporate information flash. She felt his *Presence* nearly assault her as it preceded him before he was within five feet of the bed. As he approached, what felt like a blow flattened her to the bed. She thought he would take her right then. He looked as if he contemplated it and thought otherwise as he looked, or more accurately, critically examined her. *What is he evaluating?* She couldn't speak. She could barely breathe.

Finally, as a vise is loosened, his *Presence* backed off and returned to him; she was able to sit up and breathe again. "The Volvo is packed and loaded. When you and Julie are ready, meet me downstairs and I'll introduce you to the men monitoring your trip."

The Duke had spoken.

"Monitor?"

"By radio. To be sure ya'll are safe all the way. Besides the weather turnin' at any time, there's no tellin' who's on the road nowadays or what can happen to any vehicle."

"Oh." she murmured.

Taking one last leer around the room, he headed out the door again. *Well, I've received my orders just like the rest of the hired han's. Guess that's the way, when you're bought and paid for.* She thought she might puke again, but she tried to concentrate on the trip, and Julie. She went to shower and do morning.

Julie and the Duke were talking in the breakfast room when Kitten came in. Julie looked up, gave a nod, a brief smile, then went back to the conversation. As soon as breakfast was brought in, the Duke excused himself.

"I think he's going to find the white, dominant males who will be 'monitoring' our trip, to introduce us to them." Julie whispered. Kitten only nodded her head in acknowledgment as she slowly ate what was put before her, not at all sure it would stay down.

Well, if I kept down all I had to eat, I'd be as big as a house! a prim voice inside Kitten chided. *We'll be leaving soon and maybe my stomach will settle down. Being within reaching distance of him is becoming an ordeal.* She wasn't sure there was any way out. She began sweating. She was finding it impossible to chew. She put down the fork and her eyes surveyed the contents of her plate. There went her stomach as she ran to the bathroom trying not to make a mess.

Julie was receiving instructions from the Duke and one of the 'guardians' of the trip when Kitten arrived outside. "So you got it straight? Every couple of hours or so. We'll work it out along the way. The big guy wants us to keep real good tabs on ya'll, so nothin' bad has a chance to move in while he's not there to protect ya'll. Haw! Haw! Haw!" The goon guffawed.

Kitten was introduced to them all, but it was the one with the strange eyes that gave her the creeps. She and Julie very briefly talked about the strange-eyed man after they got into the car and were a'ways from the ranch. They didn't really want to spoil what looked like a wonderful trip.

"You've met them, talked to them and you know what to do now? Don't you?" Duke asked the strange-eyed one, as the men dispersed. The man gave Duke the high sign. "....the other one? Is it taken care of?" Duke asked.

The strange-eyed man nodded his head, "Taken care of a couple of weeks ago," and left.

The Duke had business to attend to.

Chapter 8

What could be said about the sixth "Gathering"? They were all close to living half a century and a little more than half their life expectancy. Up to this point, had they truly kept the "catabolic brain" away? Were they each still growing and excited about life? Were there new horizons to meet and conquer? What would this "Gathering" bring?

Bri was anticipating the warmth of old friendship, the wonder of creative accomplishment and the new ideas that would light in her. As she was unpacking her suitcase, she could almost feel the glowing approval she would bask in when she told of her last five years. She could hardly wait for the others to arrive.

It was strange there was no answer at Hazel's house. Hazel knew about the "Gathering", it was in *her* city. Hazel'd never forget "The Gathering", but she wasn't at the hotel and there was no answer at her house.

Maybe something came up... or she's on the way... or at the store. Since Hazel's divorce about three and a half-four years ago, Hazel's changed everything about herself. Oh! She's still Hazel, of course, but it seems the stuffings got temporarily knocked out of her. No amount of encouragement brings forth that special zest for life Hazel exudes. Hazel never complains or bad-mouths Jack, her ex. Hazel, actually, never dwells on the subject of marriage or divorce much. But when she speaks about it, it's like communicating with someone who's just found out something really important didn't exist or wasn't what they thought it was. Yeah! Sure! They'll recover, but it's just gonna take some time for 'em to catch their breath. Out of all the people in the world, Hazel is the very best at making lemonade out of life's lemons. Goddess knows, she's had enough practice. The phone rang. *That must be Hazel now.*

"Oh, hi, Ollie... No, I just thought you were Hazel. There was no answer when I tried to call her. How was the trip? Boy! You don't sound too enthusiastic... Well, you can call home later this evening and be sure what's his name? Yeah, Michael, and tell him you arrived safely. So, how's everybody?... How was the trip?... Oh! Yeah!... I already asked that... Um... Have you heard from anyone else?... Yeah, I think we scheduled the first meeting at two, after lunch. Okay, I'll see you then."

What's churning in the pit of my stomach? Hazel must be looking to the sightseeing, that's it. There's so much to see, and it must be the strange water making my stomach do flip-flops. I always have a case of the trots when I drink strange water.

They all began arriving. As is the way of old friends, they shared good times remembered, news of families and friends: 'Aunt Bessie passed away... Marguerite had her third last spring... Oh!No! your sister's gonna be a GREAT grandmother! That's impossible- How old were you when she had... You're going to retire?... You may finally get that business you've always wanted started this year?... Married how long?... Divorced how long?...'

Time passed so quickly, no one could believe it was two o'clock already. Let's see... everyone's here? They were all looking around a little nervously. Where's Hazel? This is her place and where is she? She must have gotten' caught in traffic, or something where she couldn't call.

The buzz of comraderie silenced as the awareness of a missing *presence* became louder and louder. The room became sanctuary quiet, each looking uncomfortably to the other for explanation of

148

this unusual predicament. After what seemed like a light year of silence, Mona quipped out, "Did anyone call?"

Three women answered "Yes!" simultaneously. Silence, again.

Suddenly, someone noticed a man and young woman standing at the door, looking uncomfortable and solemn. Chris recognized them first. "Come in Anya, Jack!" She moved toward the door. "Where's your mother?" Chris spoke to the younger version of Hazel standing before her.

The young woman looked at the man, at Chris, at the group of women and walked in, slowly dragging her feet with much effort. Chris put her arm around the girl, "What's wrong, Anya?" The young woman looked up at Chris with tears in her eyes. She turned to look at the intense group of women and put her head down, unable to speak directly to the group. She took a deep breath.

"My mother," Anya choked, "was found in her car, in the mountains, frozen dead..." She began convulsively crying, unable to go on. The man approached and folded Anya into his arms.

"I'm Jack, Hazel's ex-husband," he said as tears threatened. "Hazel was found about two weeks ago, in her car. They thought she was dead... until they put the machines on her. The coroner can't determine *if* she's dead, nor the cause of deaa... what ever she is. No one knows why she was where she was or what happened. There's no evidence of m... m... mur... someone else or... or... suicide..."

"Hazel would never commit suicide!!" screamed one angry woman.

The room broke out of its stunned silence to a roar of confusion, anger and disbelief.

"NO! NO! She can't be dead..."
"Surely anyone but Hazel!..."
"What do you mean they don't know the cause of whatever it is she is? She had to get there from something!..."
"This is a joke, right?..."
"Where in the mountains?..."

They all spoke at once as the young woman buried her face into her father's chest, her shoulders shaking her startlement, confusion, and grief.

"Wait a minute! Wait a minute!" someone shouted. "Let's all sit down and let them explain. Here... why don't both of you sit down. None of this makes sense."

The room quieted into soundless shock. All sat down before weak knees gave way, the young woman sitting on her father's lap with her head still buried in his chest. Jack looked bewildered.

"There were no marks, no residue of poison, no virus or bacteria, no evidence of stroke or other body malfunction, no struggle... One minute she was alive, the next she wasn't... or at least it doesn't look like she is. The brain machine registers something, I forget what they call it. The heart machine registers something and blood tests say there is some chemical saying she's not dead. They don't know what she is but after this long they say she couldn't be any more than a vegetable. If she doesn't make some kind of change in two or three weeks they'll consider taking the life support systems off..." his voice began to break. "I want them to keep them on as long as... as long as..." Finally, Jack began to break. Tears streaming down his face threatened to become incoherent sobbing as he put his hand to his face and his body shook with wet emotion. Several women had tears running down their faces, as disbelief turned into stomach churning, gut wrenching realization.

"No! No! Hazel would never permit life support systems to keep her alive. You must take her off! You must take her off!" Chris screamed.

Dee and Penny grabbed Chris and quieted her as eons passed in the small room. Father and daughter stood, supporting each other, grief and confusion twisting wet faces.

"I think we need to go now," he said. Father and daughter leaned on each other as they left, leaving a wake of shock, sorrow, and uncertainty behind them.

"Maybe we should just go home this year and decide what to do next year. That will give us a year to think about it." Mona broke the silence.

"No!" Chris erupted, "Hazel would never've wanted that!"

"Hazel isn't here." Mona said matter of factly.

"And she's not dead yet, either!" Chris snarled through clenched teeth as Dee and Penny kept her from lunging at Mona.

"Why don't we just go back to our rooms and meet in the morning to decide what to do?" said Bri.

Most of the women who could move at all nodded their heads to the suggestion. They needed some time to assimilate this turn of fate. They were all too young to die, most of all Hazel... or what ever it is she was... and Hazel alive, vibrant! Yes!... but a vegetable? Never. **Never** a vegetable!

This couldn't be... but it was. What did it mean universally? What did it mean individually? As they gathered their things, they looked at one another, trying to affirm, questioning. "Yes... We are ALL too young to be dead. And if Hazel wasn't dead... What was she? If she wasn't dead now, she would pull through soon, wouldn't she?" No one in the group would permit Hazel to be a vegetable- **NO ONE.**

If any of it was true, then WHY?... and of all people, why Hazel?... How? They went to their rooms: encompassed by their own puzzlement, shrouded in their own disbelief, doubting their own futures. The death, even virtual death, of someone you know always mirrors your own questions of mortality. It's mirrored back to you in a way you can't ignore or put aside till later, when it's your turn.

When they arrived, they paired off in rooms the way they always did. The thirteenth, the hostess, always had the good fortune of spending a night in each room, sharing more and getting a little closer to each of the others... That would not happen this time.

Bri and Ollie leaned on each other's shoulders back to their room, each in their own silent turmoil. Jo and Chris held each other's hands, tears streaming down their faces, dazed in uncertainty.

Mona led the way, snapping a quick pace, expecting Lea to follow, which she did, looking to Mona for direction. Penny and Dee held each other, openly crying, daring anyone to deny them the right to grief.

Julie and Kitten moved slowly to their room, maintaining distance and a balanced pose for the outer world, silently wondering what this meant, not daring to look at each other. Libby gibbered to Judy in confusion, afraid silence would bring on the voices only Libby could hear. Libby would not speak out loud of the strange scenes superimposing themselves on her vision like ghosts playing on the tapestry of present reality.

* * * *

"Well, this is not how I would have planned it but it is the opportunity I wanted." said Mona to no one in particular.

Lea said nothing, just waited for Mona's direction as she hung up Mona's jacket. Mona regretted Hazel's demise but life was for the living and this was the opportunity she'd waited for. She was sure a few others felt the same way. Lea finally spoke.

"Did he say no one knows why Hazel... is the way she is? That's not possible, is it? You have to either be alive or die from something, don't you? Hazel would NEVER have committed... done it... um... you know..." Mona came out of her self-absorbed critical assessment a little annoyed to find Lea there, apparently asking her something she hadn't heard.

"What were you saying?" Mona whipped.

"Oh, nothing... I was just wondering what made Hazel... if she... um... a... Why she was in the m... Why was she by herself...?" Lea sputtered and trailed off.

"Who knows?-- Who cares? She did her thing and now she's gone. I never understood what her thing was, but whatever it was, she had a good time doing it. Maybe she got bored and just decided to leave. Who knows? Unless she decides to come back and tell us, what we do know is: she's gone and we have to decide if we want to continue doing this... thing... or not. She left us with an opportunity to make some necessary changes. I think we can all be grateful, if that's the word. All of us need to move on."

Lea looked at Mona, as she began to comprehend what Mona was saying. Lea felt a tightening around her throat as the vision of giving up the last remnants of the past looked like a dandelion seed flower just found by a gust of wind. Lea did not see seeds blowing in the wind to their new growing destination, she saw a pitiful, ravaged, dying flower, whose delicate beauty had been chewed by a cruel wind and left to wither.

She sank into the chair as if the wind had stopped blowing abruptly. If Mona was right, she couldn't be a cheerleader anymore, even if it was every five years. She wouldn't be the girl most likely to succeed anymore and what good would it be if she found the letter sweater the football team gave her? It probably had holes in it and wouldn't even keep her warm in the winter. Then it hit her. All she really had was John.

There was an ice mountain beginning to grow up the back of her spine, up Lea's neck. John was the only one who understood her. He was the only one who had ever treated her like a princess, in his own way. She thought of the day after day dullness. He would come home after working, await an audience with her, pay homage to her. All these years, he was the only one to bow and bend knee to her. He was the only one who ever cared about pleasing her, not just himself. *But he's so dull. He's so unimaginative. He's so... so... ordinary.*

Not even every five years... there would be no more leading the cheers... there would be no connection to high-school days... there would be no reason to look forward to getting excited... she would never feel that... way... that young... that alive... again.

As she crossed her arms and slunk down in the chair, she felt age moving across her body like a desiccating wind, sucking the life juices from her very bones. She was afraid to look in the mirror. She noticed, for the first time, the dry reptile-like lines on her hands, the jellylike sagging of the once firm breasts she had her arms crossed under. Her slightly dry skin began to loosen and droop around soft muscles. When did this happen? Why hadn't she noticed this before? A wave of panic brought a tentative solution of joining the health club.

Movement! That's what I need! Movement!. If you don't stop moving it, can't catch you. That must be the secret. Don't ever stop! Don't ever look back! Don't ever let IT know you're thinking about IT!

The panic swept away and silent resignation quieted all through her. Someone pulled the plugs on the bottom of her feet that held in all her life energy and it was draining into the floor. Her body felt like lead, immovable. She knew she was still here and she was still alive. She could hear her heart and her breath and her thoughts. She just couldn't move. She tried to think what it meant. What possible significance could this have in her everyday life? But all Lea could manage was...

*Hazel's daughter is so young and beautiful... so moist and fluid... so **young**.*

* * * *

Julie unlocked the door and opened it as Kitten walked through. Julie entered, closed the door, locked it and turned a stunned face to the water-streaked face sitting at the table. Hazel was the only one in the whole world they had shared the joy of their secret with.

Hazel, always approving of love in any form. Hazel: non-judgemental, safe, trustworthy. How could the world not have Hazel anymore? There were a lot of people, places and things the world could do without or never miss once gone... but not Hazel. Hazel didn't need the world, it was the other way around... the world needed Hazel. How could she leave? How could she just up and leave-- no good-byes, no forwarding address, no reason for leaving? Hazel had work to do here, she just couldn't leave like that. No! She *wouldn't* leave like that: Hazel would never permit it to happen.

"Something's not right," Julie shook her head as she sat down and nestled Kitten in her arms. "Something's very wrong. She'd never leave that way. She'd just never leave that way."

Kitten sobbed in Julie's arms. Kitten couldn't say anything. She felt equal only in Hazel's presence, smart even, maybe like she could mean something in the world. Now Hazel was gone. Julie loved her whether she contributed to the world or not. In Hazel's presence she knew she had something to contribute and desired to contribute it. The desire to do something grand would surge up from the pit of Kitten's stomach and surround her with electric energy demanding life, demanding accomplishment. Would she ever have that feeling again without Hazel's presence?

Julie held her sobbing beloved, tears moving slowly, silently down her own cheeks. She was always aware of Kitten, but her own numbing grief and an unreasonable, growing fear moved its claws through her body/mind. Julie was aware of some truth trying to make its way past the irrational emotions and feelings but whatever this truth was, it couldn't make itself coherent enough to be congruent with present reality, what ever that was.

How long has it been since I felt anything? Julie's mind meandered. *How long has it been since I cried? How very long has it been since I've known fear of any kind? Why now? Since I've been an attorney?... No! Even before... death is no stranger to me. Sometimes I felt something, sometimes I felt nothing, but the awareness of death as a part of life is there. Life is: death is.*

For the first time, death was too near. Death was too real. It brushed by her body and she felt its Presence. Was Death looking at her? Was that why she was so uneasy? Uneasy- HELL! She was stark raving terrified. Time to be honest with herself. She'd never been this delusory with herself before. The high tide of emotion was cresting. Still holding Kitten in one arm, her hand went to her face and tears washed away years of forgotten grief and pain. She wept for the distant thundering coming ever closer, naming her fear. She would sooner or later have to face it. She wept for the barrenness of life and the cruelty that prevented fulfillment, until the end, if then. She wept for the loss of the one true friend she ever had and the only unconditional acceptance from another human being she had ever known. She may never know Agape love and friendship again.

Together... they wept.

* * * *

Dee headed for the yellow pages as Penny slammed the door. "I want to know where she is and see for myself... vegetable my ass!" Dee gritted her teeth as enormous tears fell down her face.

"I'm in with you." Penny slung herself down on her bed, thinking of what would be the best, most natural and painless way to help Hazel. "Jimson, or hemlock," Penny said matter of factly, "I think Hazel said there was hemlock growing wild around here," Penny sat up and looked at Dee.

"Sh!..Yes, can you tell me if you have..." Dee began checking out the hospitals.

Penny went over in her mind what the different plants looked like. *What grows here in this region and where are they most likely found? What do I need to do to process them properly? If Hazel isn't dead, is there a possibility she's been given a certain plant usually grown on the islands or a certain snake venom? They would give the symptoms of death... but I'll have to see Hazel first and do some body psychics to know for sure. For damn sure I'll see to it Hazel is good and dead before she's buried. Not any of this in-between stuff. Hazel's not going to wake up and find herself buried alive.* Penny shuddered.

"We need to get Bri with us... If she's been poisoned by special means or locked up some other way," Penny pointed to her head, "then we might need all the help we can get. Bri is High-Priestess and always brings some ritual things with her."

Dee nodded her head, put her hand over the mouthpiece of the phone and said, "I bet Bri is two steps ahead of us, she wasn't out and out crying, so she doesn't believe this shit either." Dee tended to the phone again.

"Think I'll mosey on down to scout out the turf, so to speak... 'be in Bri's room or where ever she's at." Penny slid off the bed and out the door as Dee nodded acknowledgment.

* * * *

Chris squeezed Jo's hand as the elevator stopped on their floor. Finally able to assimilate what just happened and make some decision around it, Chris spoke, "Hazel is NOT dead. I would have known it. I would have felt it."

She thought about the morning she had a feeling to call Hazel...

she could have missed it with the two expirations... No! If it was Hazel expiring, she would have known. It might have been close... but no! She would have known. She might not have known with anyone else, but Chris would have known about Hazel. Chris shook her head. It could only mean, if what Jack said was true, Hazel must be trapped somewhere between life and death. Hazel wasn't fully alive and she wasn't fully dead.

Is Hazel frightened?... No. Not Hazel. Is Hazel wandering lost?... No. Hazel's lost and a stranger ANYWHERE for a short time. Hazel'd end up leading a parade, or something, wherever she is. Would Hazel want her body to be here, waiting for her, while she's somewhere else, indefinitely? Depends on how long 'indefinitely' is. They walked back to the room. Jo briefly looked at Chris. They didn't say anything. They didn't know what to say.

Before the "Gathering" Jo'd had a feeling of **Change**. She wasn't sure what it meant, but any other time she'd felt it; wrenching, powerful forces turned lives upside down, wrung them in knots, untied them and left those lives completely altered with no possibility of going back. She was not exactly afraid of these **Changes**, she had been through too many of them, but from one stability to the next were usually monumental upheavals in emotions, values, personas. The trick to surviving these **Changes** seemed to be learning to tread water, work as fast and as hard as you can to grow, hold on to something familiar, minimize the losses.

People lost jobs, homes, friends, themselves and replaced their whole lives and beingness with that which was so unlike what was before. Nothing was recognizable as the same. Jo had seen those able to make it and those who crashed and burned... most didn't die. One thing Jo learned in A.A. a long time ago, though she couldn't verbalize it then, was: Everything that happens in your life can be chosen to be used for your own upliftment-- to keep sober-- used as a challenge and opportunity-- to make the changes necessary... or... or you could crash and burn-- get drunk-- fade with their failures-- be unable to change or die. It sounded cruel in the face of some real tragedy and real life-twisting unfairness. It sounded heartless in the throes of unsurmountable pain, but it was true. Whatever the circumstances in your life, you choose how to deal with it. You may not have a lot of say as to what comes into your life or you may but what you do with it is your choice to make. As Dee said, "If you believe in something about yourself, there are no limits surrounding that thing, only possibilities." Jo reflected the same holds true in reverse: if you believe something negative about yourself, there are only limits and no possibilities. The choice of what to believe about yourself and what aspect of yourself to focus on, however, was still yours.

When Jo was diagnosed with multiple personality disorder, most people, even those who had known her for a long time, began to shun her. The only ones who would hang around her were the people who like to take advantage of mentally handicapped people. Although Jo was temporarily dysfunctional, she was not so permanently. Before or after integration, the average person refused to include her once they found out she was M.P.D. and the rapists of the truly handicapped couldn't quite take advantage of her, nor keep her quiet, so she was genuinely alone. She still had the choice of growing in the direction she wished. With a survivor's keenness for information gathering, she could compare the options and possibilities to her talents and limitations to move in a direction to her best advantage. It continued to work for her. She continued to grow and integrate.

If we were a different kind of being, we might be doomed to live with despair or success depending upon our early programming or genetic structure. As the beings we are, we can, at any time,

change our early programming, our diet, our beliefs, our actions,
and just about anything else in or about ourselves. We can
actually change our entire lives. We can do this for the better or
for the opposite, as we choose.

While it is never easy and most people give up long before the
changes take place, they can be made. Jo knew. She had made
some of those changes, usually with the aid of the **Change**, but
made them, she had.

Now that she had effectively managed to avoid the situation at
hand and escape for a few seconds in her mind, she began to feel
the loss of a person who had helped her see just what she had been
thinking about a moment ago.

A weight was beginning to descend in the pit of Jo's stomach and
was going to squeeze all the water in her body out through her
eyes. It would make the tears she just shed look like a bucket of
water thrown into the ocean. Hazel had also helped Jo to realize
emotions were the connector between life force and third
dimensional reality, between feelings and behavior. Emotions
translate between the two to provide direction, good sense and
healthy living. Jo certainly didn't want to squelch the emotions she
had, only be sure they would not immobilize her when she needed
to take action or provoke behavior that was inappropriate or not in
her best interest.

Chris was saying, "We'll find out where she is and just see for
ourselves what the situation is. When we get back to the room,
we'll call the hospitals... We'll say we're **ALL** her relatives. If she's
still around and able, we'll bring her back, or... or..." Tears were
starting for both of them in earnest. "We'll let her go."

The weight just hit bottom.

* * * *

Ollie and Bri were still leaning on each other when the elevator stopped at their floor. As they moved to get off the elevator, the only thing Ollie could think to say was,

"I... I... think I'll see if I can reach Michael again. I hope he's found a job and that's why I can't get a hold of him."

Bri just nodded her head. Her senses were suspended until she was sure, either way, what the situation was with Hazel. If she didn't know better, she would think she'd shifted to another time/space plane. Maybe that's where she needed to go to find out what was really going on. She considered for a moment and began assessing what she had with her in the way of ritual accoutrements. Bri knew she could count on Penny, Dee, maybe Jo, possibly Chris if she wasn't being a charge nurse/health practitioner. Julie and Kitten just didn't believe in this stuff, but maybe they'd lend their energies. Mona was out and probably Lea, if for no other reason, Lea was so intimidated by Mona. Lea's fear would make her vampire the energies. Bri didn't think Ollie could stand the energy drain psychically or physically, but could stand by. Bri didn't know about Libby and Judy- Judy, maybe yes,- but something was wrong with Libby. Her aura was a mess, mostly dark, but what was not dark was zinging about, arcing and popping everywhere, like pulling freshly dried towels apart on a cold, dry morning. Libby was so stressed she was projecting images which Bri saw as shadows overlaying and moving in the atmosphere.

Bri considered asking Libby if she wanted help grounding but it became apparent, grounding whatever it was, would only suppress it. If it was suppressed instead of dealt with, it was likely to come back and ambush Libby later on. At least Libby was rooming with the right woman. Judy was possibly the most competent therapist for people with that kind of aura disturbance Bri had ever met.

Bri wondered if Dee had brought her drum. What time was it now? Should they do it in Hazel's hospital room, here in the hotel, where the vehicle was found, or somewhere else? If they did it in Hazel's room, how much ceremony and ritual would be allowed? How many tools could they bring to the hospital? How much would be needed to prevent outside interference? Should they go to where the car was found? The same questions presented themselves as to tools and interference. Was Hazel hovering, attached to some place they could never know or guess the location of? If they couldn't connect with Hazel, could they speak with the trees, bushes or rocks in the vicinity where Hazel was found? Don't forget the car. They should try to connect with as many options as possible, she decided.

They would need all the information they could gather before taking any hasty actions. How much time would this take? How much time did they have? What kind of obstacles might be in the way? What kind of hazards might be encountered on 'the other road'? What kind of physical concerns were there? This was October in the Rockies. When they received some answers, what would Hazel want them to do? Bri was brought back by the stress in Ollie's voice. Ollie looked up at Bri bewildered.

"But he's got to be there. He's taking care of my apartment while I'm gone and making sure my check gets into the bank to cover the checks... Are you sure you've got the right apartment? I have a whole apartment full of furniture. It's not much but it's mine. I only owe on the TV. Yes. Yes. Could you check into it and call me back... Um.. Yes, alright, I'll call you. Yes you have my permission to go into the apartment. When do you want me to call back? Okay.... Tomorrow morning. Bye." Ollie hung up the phone. "They say Michael's not there and hasn't been there for a day or so. They said they saw him taking things out of my apartment and when they looked in the window, they didn't see anything in there."

"Who said that, Ollie?"

"My next door neighbors. They said they'll get the landlord to look in. I'll call back tomorrow sometime." Ollie didn't want to believe the picture forming in her mind. Not Michael. She'd spent her last moneys to get him a suit to interview with. She'd let him live in her home. She'd understood when he wasn't feeling well and couldn't contribute to the expenses and the everyday living things people had to do. She'd understood when he was too tired to touch her and belittled her. He'd promised to take care of everything while she was gone. There must be some good explanation she couldn't possibly think of right now. She tried to put it out of her mind and was confronted with another enigma.

"What happened to Hazel?" she asked Bri, "I didn't understand what her husband said. Ex-husband said. She was found somewhere? She's in the hospital and they don't know if she's alive or dead? How can that be? You have to be one or the other, don't you?"

Bri thought a minute. She didn't know the words to use to help Ollie understand. Neither had the technical medical vocabulary and Bri knew Ollie didn't have the metaphysical vocabulary.

"Maybe we can get Chris to explain it where we both understand it." Bri paused and asked carefully, "What are you going to do tomorrow if it's true?"

Ollie burst out in tears and sobbed. "I don't know, Bri. I just don't know.

Chapter 9

Libby held tightly onto the elevator rail. The only reason Judy looked up, identifying the terror on Libby's face, was a sense of not rightness she felt as she noticed Libby's white knuckled hands.

Judy was as stunned as the others hearing the news about Hazel. She and Hazel were friends on a soul level. They didn't have to communicate in the ordinary sense to be aware of each other and the wonderful warmth it always brought. Like a flash of a camera, suddenly, Judy remembered the morning-- *When was it?-- Yes, it was about two weeks...*

Libby moved Judy over. "Here, let that man out, Judy."

The elevator stopped, no one left, no one got in. Judy looked at Libby-- at the empty door-- at Libby again. She wasn't sure how to approach Libby. Judy looked at the door again, as if maybe she could have been wrong. The elevator continued. There had been no one but the two women on the elevator since they got on and they were almost to their floor.

Judy very cautiously studied Libby and said, "Libby. There's been no one on the elevator but us. The elevator stopped. No one got on or off." Libby still had a look of terror on her face. She was seeing something Judy did not see and was ready to bolt off the elevator as soon as it stopped, whether it was their floor or not. She looked at Judy as if she were trapped and Judy was blocking the only escape hatch.

"Libby. I won't hurt you. Won't you tell me why you look so scared?" Judy asked softly.

Libby looked at Judy then at the air in the middle of the elevator.

Libby looked at Judy as if Judy were a secret conspirator. The elevator stopped at their floor and Libby slinked out behind Judy, looking back at the closing elevator door.

Judy's mouth was moving as if she were saying something but Libby couldn't hear her because that strange man was laughing at her. Charles and her father, at least, stayed on the elevator, but that strange man... that strange man with the strange laugh. Libby shook her head and began to hear Judy's voice in what seemed like a mumble.

"Libby!! Please tell me what's wrong. I can't help you if I don't know what the situation is. I won't touch you... I won't hurt you, but Libby, you **must** speak!!."

Judy's voice sounded panicked as she quickstepped down the hall beside Libby.

"Where's our room, Judy?! Where's our room? He's gone and we need to get to the room before he comes back and knows where we're staying." Libby grabbed Judy's arm. Judy put her hand lightly over Libby's in a reassuring manner.

"Here, we're going the wrong way." Judy said and began turning them around, heading for their room, "When we get in the room, will you tell me what is frightening you?" Judy patted Libby's hand.

Libby turned toward Judy, stopped abruptly, jerked her hand away with trapped animal eyes, ready to lunge. Libby whispered, "You didn't see anything?"

"I just thought we'd talk about it better in the room." Judy looked directly but calmly into Libby's eyes, stood evenly on both feet and put her arms slowly, gently down by her sides, hands open to view, waiting for Libby to respond. Libby's breath began to lengthen but her eyes were still frightened and her body was ready for flight as she considered Judy's words.

"Yes, yes!" Libby said. She eyed Judy and evaluated, "Let's go to the room. We can talk there and maybe you'll have an idea what I can to do about this. There's no one to talk to since Rafael's gone and I don't know if I'd tell him anyway. He... I... well. I can't quite remember right this minute, but I'm sure it will come to me. The room." They walked quickly. "What happened to Hazel? I don't remember all that was said. That terrible man just kept laughing louder and louder and nobody seemed to notice or be bothered but me, so I couldn't very well tell him to leave if he wasn't bothering anybody else. Who was he with, anyway?"

They got into the room.

"Let's sit down." Judy guided them to chairs.

"Judy! Please don't look at me like I'm crazy!"

"You're upset, and I'm concerned, Libby. That's obvious. Look at yourself." Libby noticed for the first time how she was trembling and clenching Judy's arm. She let go of Judy's arm, sat down shakily, and looked at Judy perplexed.

"Are you able to tell me what you're upset about... besides Hazel?" Judy sat in the opposite chair with her hands evenly on the table and very concerned.

"Hazel! What happened to Hazel?" Libby seemed to just remember.

Judy remained composed. "Exactly what do you remember about

this afternoon? I'll fill you in on the rest," Judy was guessing. Libby took a deep breath and was obviously thinking. Judy noticed Libby's eyes would glaze over every now and then and her body would go very still, her breathing shallow. Finally Libby responded,

"Um... We were all in the room ready to begin the meeting... and... oh yes! We had this lovely lunch and a wonderful time talking and catching up," Libby smiled in memory, "Everyone wondered where Hazel was but we were all having such a good time... it doesn't seem like thirty years have gone by since we graduated from high school, twenty five since college...", she shook her head at memories, laughed a little, relaxed a little more.

"Then a girl and a man were at the door. I think Chris or someone said it was Hazel's daughter and husband... oh, that's right... ex-husband... I suppose Hazel will tell us about that when she gets here. Anyway, her daughter began telling us about why Hazel was late. Her car got stuck in the mountains and that's when that rude man started laughing. Who was he, Judy? Who was he with? Anyway, then I noticed Charles and my father were here and I thought 'that's impossible, my father died a while back'... I think."

Libby began to tense and grind her teeth visibly, looking to Judy for some kind of cue. Judy sat there thinking of how to respond to what she just heard and also trying to figure out what it meant and what she should do. Libby began getting more and more uneasy; her hand was beginning to tremble. "That's what you remember, isn't it? That's what happened, isn't it? Judy?"

Judy was finally able to speak, "Not only do people process tragedy differently, but even people seeing the same accident have different stories about what they saw. Frankly, I was paying attention to something I'd remembered about two weeks ago, a sound I'd heard early in the morning. No one else appeared to hear it. But to answer the question I think you're asking me...," Judy took a deep breath, "I did not see all the people you saw. The only man I saw was Hazel's husband in our room and I did not see anyone but us on the elevator."

Libby's blouse drummed as her body hammered the thunder in her heart. Judy gently took one of Libby's hands in hers, ready to release it if Libby saw it as a threat. Libby looked down at Judy's hand and could not help but wonder how much of this was real. Libby felt like she was being propelled through a tunnel and would fall if she made any movements of her own. People flashed in her mind tunnel. Scenes from some violent pornographic movie, with headless people doing things to her she didn't remember consenting to. Libby felt hideous pain, then a terrifying moment of pleasure alternating with a vision of a hotel room with Judy looking very concerned, holding what looked like her hand. Judy was saying something she couldn't hear. Libby's breathing was too noisy although she tried to keep her breath short and quiet. There were other noises and they sounded like they were coming closer, like an avalanche approaching. Libby frantically tried to make everything stop, her noisy breath, her pulsating heart. The terrible noise was going to make her head burst open any second.

Like a mountain exploding, fireworks burst inside her mind tunnel, then blackness. The black void wraithed forth a grid of images projecting what appeared to be a memory: there was Charles and three other men, whose faces she could see but whom she didn't recognize. They were doing disgusting things together and she was doing sickening, perverted things to them and she was smiling through the shame and the pain, then she was tied up and they were hurting her, and someone was filming this and... and... she was going to throw up.

Judy held a wastebasket while Libby purged the memories to the surface. Libby couldn't control her bladder and bowel functioning. It seemed every opening in her had something coming out, as memories flashed to expose themselves for her recognition. She didn't know whether to tell Judy or anyone, for that matter, what she was seeing in her head. If her body hadn't duplicated every bruise, every cut, every burn, every pain-- she knew she would have to believe these were hallucinations. The horror of anyone being able to do this to another human being was beyond comprehension. Surely she was just imagining this.

That's what her father said, "It's all in your head. You're just imagining it. You ought to be ashamed of yourself for saying..." There was a sinking feeling in the bottom of her stomach as hope died, protection died, self-integrity shattered, connection to humanness severed and aloneness shaped its egg around her.

Libby watched her spirit separate from herself and move away as she looked from her father's eyes to the man who had violated her. She saw his face, she watched him laugh. He was able to worm deep inside her, because he had been there. He saw her dirtiness, her shame. He saw her brief, disconnected moment of ecstasy after all the hurt. She couldn't be a good little girl, she couldn't be good like everyone else if she felt so good after that much pain and if she was so dirty and so bad then she probably deserved so much hurt. Libby knew she was so much badder because after he'd hurt her, he did something she couldn't see below her neck and she bunched up, went away for a moment and felt real good all of a sudden. She knew it was wrong and he said they'd say she was a bad girl if she told anyone. He said they'd laugh at her like he was doing, and make fun of her and know how dirty she was because she liked it. He said he really liked her and didn't want to stop making her feel good like that. She could really feel that he liked her because when she was close to him, there was something around him that surrounded her that made her feel like she was in a bathtub full of wonderful warm water and that warm water made the pain go away. And although she was aware of shame she couldn't feel it in that good feeling that surrounded her when she was near him. He slid his hand under her dress where she couldn't see and started doing something in her underpants that kinda felt tickley inside her belly and asked her if it felt good and did she want him to stop? He said after he hurt her he'd **always** make her feel real good, like that -- that he **really** *liked* her. But she didn't like it, but it felt good, but then it hurt and she didn't like the hurt. She was afraid of the hurt. Was that the way to keep that warm feeling and him liking her? She wanted him to like her. Maybe if he liked her more he wouldn't want to hurt her any more. But would he still want to make her feel good if he didn't hurt her? Even though she knew he liked her there was something else... in his eyes... that made her feel shame. The good feelings couldn't hide that thing in his eyes. She would have to stop looking in his eyes to keep the good feelings. The good feelings and his eyes-- they didn't go together. There was Charles laughing. He and the other three men were leaving, slapping themselves on the back and laughing at her. She wasn't able to move, though her mind was awake and aware of pain and relaxed muscles. Pain and relaxed muscles-- they didn't go together, not if you were normal, not if you were...

The tunnel collapsed and Libby was in the hotel room with Judy holding a basket in front of her. Judy was smoothing her back, talking low and calm, looking very worried.

"It's okay, we'll get this cleaned up in no time, don't worry. When you feel up to it, we'll go to the bathroom, you can shower off and get into some clean clothes. If you want, we can talk about it. Or, if you like, I can phone your therapist to call you. Would you like for me to call your therapist?"

Judy wiped Libby's mouth with a tissue. Libby shook her head "NO", and became aware of some uncomfortable wetness she was sitting on. She looked at the mess but was afraid to move, much less get up and go to the bathroom. She was shaky and too stunned to be ashamed. She also remembered what she had just remembered and tried to piece it into the rest of the experiences of her life. Anger began to burn... crackle and fester at this new awareness.

What does this mean? Is it real? Did this really happen? Can this happen again? How many times did it already happen? Why didn't I know about this before now? Is that why Charles acted so strangely, as if he didn't respect me anymore? Was this the reason? wondered Libby.

Libby tried to fit some congruity to all this and stay present with Judy. Libby tried to deflect Judy's questions until she could make some sense of it and name the rage arising in her.

The bathroom, Libby thought, *Clean. I've got to get clean. Can I ever be clean again?* The pain welled up in her and tears impelled release. Could all the tears in the world wash her clean? Sorrow vied with rage. She felt she might slip away-- to where? She looked at Judy.

If Judy had been one mark less concerned, one feeling less real, one hair less loving... Judy wasn't laughing and wouldn't make fun of what Libby would say. Judy wouldn't put Libby away or make her go away or leave because of the filth that would come out of her mouth if she told the truth. But what was the truth? In her mind she saw what she saw and she could start there. Maybe...

She would have to trust this woman in front of her. A woman who knew Libby more than thirty years and had never known-- *Hell! I didn't know it!* Libby could feel the tunnel closing around her. Libby knew if she didn't want to wander in the tunnel for the rest of her life, moving away from the laughing man, she would have to speak up. She would have to speak up through the laughter. Libby would have to speak up through the sneers and sniggering. Libby would have to speak up, now. **NOW**, out in the open, exposed, with the safety of the tunnel behind her.

To take this chance, Libby would have to **feel**; awaken the truth of the past... small... alone. The alternative was the safety of the tunnel... the prison of the tunnel. Fear was beating at Libby's body, shame was whipping her raw, flaying her: guilt was beginning to push her-- weigh her down -- down -- into the tunnel-- away from all...

NO!!...   NO!...   I want out of here!

"Judy!" Libby gasped and reached for her, "Judy... I remember... I think I remember... I saw... they did..." Libby was sobbing incoherently. Judy didn't laugh. Judy didn't tell her to straighten up and fly right. Judy didn't belittle her for acting like a baby. Judy put her arms around Libby, gently, safely and let her cry. As tears and words began to wash the fear and shame and pain out, rage was beginning to move in. *They did this to me! They really did this to me! If I don't do something about it, they'll get away with it! But what can I do? Charles said it, they were credible witnesses and what am I? If Rafael got on the stand, it would be all over but the crying... my crying... their laughing.*

No!... No! I won't let it happen. Not again. No! I'll kill them. One by one, slowly. Then they can do whatever they want to me after, but those four will never do it to me, or to any other woman again. They ought to give me a medal for it. Libby was collecting herself and beginning to quiet.

"You can't just go killing them." Judy whispered to her, as if she were reading Libby's mind, "You have a right to be angry, you have a right to be enraged and hurt, but taking their lives won't put you in a better position. There must be a better way."

"You know the way the system is set up," Libby spat out. '**They**' victimize you and if you speak up, you get victimized more. And if you don't speak up, '**They**' get away with it and you end up victimizing yourself. Judy, I'm a business woman. I don't like those odds. The only way to narrow the losses is to eliminate one of the debits. I've worked the good ol' boy system too long to not know when the odds are stacked against me."

Although Judy didn't show it, she was beginning to panic inside. She knew from experience, the overpowering rage of the first awareness of violation and injustice was usually tempered the more a person verbalized. Calm as Libby was now, Judy was concerned. It would have been much better for Libby to be screaming and acting out her rage. Libby certainly wasn't detached from the feelings and pain of the memory. Judy wondered if she should call for help. She was not Libby's therapist, she was her friend. But Judy was a therapist, an experienced therapist who was wondering if this was getting out of hand.

"Libby... why don't we clean you up and try to get some rest. We can call room service for food and clean towels and you can sleep on it. We've all been through one helluva day. Honestly, I'm not in the mood to be around a lot of people and after all the emotion you may feel a bit tired yourself." Judy said hopefully. Libby could feel herself begin to drain but wasn't quite ready to leave things unresolved.

"Look," Judy picked at straws, "If you don't come up with

something else by morning, the option to 'eliminate' them is still there. No matter what you decide to do, the option is always there. I just know you have a more intelligent and creative mind than to have only one option. You're too good at what you do. You're tired and can't think of the others right now. You don't have to act within the next thirty minutes. They will probably be around for a while, which gives you the advantage."

"But they'll be around" Libby hissed. Judy sighed.

"Whatever you do or don't do it can surely wait until morning, can't it? Maybe I'll be able to come up with some ideas that will help." Judy was exhausted. Libby remembered Judy's concern. Judy's sincere concern was the only thing allowing Libby to weigh what the woman said. Libby was truly beginning to wind down from emotions she hadn't permitted herself to feel in lifetimes. Her body was wrung out of energy and she was fading quickly. She might have just enough energy to clean up. She was just becoming aware of the sickening smell and was beginning to feel shame. Judy picked up on this right away.

"Let's see if we can get you into the shower before you collapse. I'll clean this up, don't you worry about it." Judy looked directly into Libby's apprehensive eyes, "This is not uncommon for what you've just been through. I see it all the time. It would be much worse if it didn't happen. The human body continues to amaze me in its wisdom." Judy emanated a gentle, loving kindness. Libby doubted the words... but she desperately wanted to believe Judy.

Chapter 10

A clear autumn morning in the Rockies is nothing short of spectacular. The aspens are in their most brilliant golds, reds and oranges. The pines are a variety of deep greens. The hillside brush patchworks the mountains in jewels of startling magentas and deep garnet reds, radiant sun and citrine yellows, pumpkin and amber oranges, and emerald and algae greens. Colors contrast with the bluest sky, the cleanest, crispest air, the clearest running waters to make you believe Deity's given the human race a chance to inhabit a small space in heaven.

Those crazy runners are out running all times of the year, even in the coldest part of winter, but in the autumn even the couch-potatoes take to the trails. Tourists come from all over the country to watch Mom dress up before She sleeps. You can even see an array of reds, yellows, and greens on the same tree at the same time. Nature's last attempt to motivate us to finish up what we need to do before it's time to slow down, be still for a while. And so it was on the second day of the "Gathering".

"Mona, did you look out the window?" Lea was as excited as a school girl.

"I saw." said Mona coming out of the bathroom. "I think I'll try to get the Cog to the Peak this morning and maybe hike down. It's much to beautiful to be indoors today."

Lea looked a little confused then remembered about Hazel. With the wind knocked out of her sails she said, "You're not going to the "Gathering" today at all?"

"Why should I? You know I can't stand all the emotionalism that's going to be going on because of Hazel. And it's not likely anything will be accomplished until all the endless possibilities surrounding Hazel are exhausted. I can't contribute anything constructive and I'm not about to waste this beautiful day being excessively maudlin over something I can't do anything about."

Mona could not express in words her own sense of loss surrounding Hazel and her true astonishment of these feelings. She needed time alone to process.

"You're going by yourself?" Lea asked sheepishly.

"Yes, Lea. Why don't you go to the "Gathering" and take notes so you can tell me what goes on, since I won't be there. That way I'll be informed if we really have a "Gathering" at all," the executive spoke.

"Sure, Mona." Lea answered with an accusing face that said her palatine protector was abandoning her to a pack of wolves. Mona strode out the door, leaving Lea staring after her.

* * * *

By the time Libby finally woke up-- maybe came to or came in for a landing was more like it-- Judy had taken her shower, been out for a vigorous walk, and had tea waiting for both of them.

Judy acknowledged Libby's apparent struggle to join humanity in Colorado Springs, which, between the altitude, time change, jet lag, exhaustion, and whatever went on last night, all working to keep Libby "away", was a courageous attempt on Libby's part. Libby felt she was in some kind of race, battling for control of her mind, with the time clock still going. Winner takes all.

"I got tea for both of us and figured if you wanted something else we could order it" Judy spoke more to confirm coherence than anything else.

Libby looked up, tested her body to see if it was ready for motion. It was not! Her mind checked vital functions. *Yep! Breathing, heart beat, eyes move. Will the body sit up? It is safe to test: There's a warm soft bed to fall back on if all efforts fail?* This was sounding like a NASA launch mission to the part of her who was observing all this. *Okay!... **Rise!** Wasn't that word used on the dead?!...* and Libby's body sat up. The room spun just for a second as she felt as if someone slammed her back into a body she'd been suspended painlessly and contentedly above.

"Tea is fine for now," Libby mumbled.

"We probably need to start getting downstairs, if we're going to be a part of whatever will go on today. I think you have time for a quick shower. You can get breakfast in the conference room. If you know what you want, I can order it. It'll be waiting for you when we get there," Judy offered.

Libby was trying to remember what was going on just before she was jolted back... back from where?... back to where? Which was real? This or the other?

"Hazel was speaking to me. I guess it was a dream? I don't know what it was or where I was. The last thing I remember, she said there would be two others to join me and not to lose hope... not to do anything... What was the word? Self-defeating... Self-something. Wholeness doesn't depend upon revenge... something like that." Libby looked like a person trying to examine the vistas in her own mind to find the rest of the dream puzzle, her feet dangling off the side of the bed. "Something about not sweeping the dirt floor of the house but going to a new level, a new direction ENTIRELY. She emphasized new direction over and over. Something like the stupid phrase about the glass half full or half empty... Oh wow! I'm rambling, but it seemed so important. Something about a story she wrote. I can't remember it all now... It was so clear just a minute ago..."

Libby shook her head, hoping the dream or the present reality would take dominance over her foggy mind. The battle was getting tiresome. *It's like being in a big stadium of talking people, not knowing what you're edgy about until the crowd quiets down. Whoever they are and however many there is, I wish they'd take it to a conference room or something so it would be quiet in here.* Libby frowned and jerked at the awareness that this was the first time she'd admitted to the noise in her head as a reality.

She wasn't sure what it meant or if she wanted to find out, unless it was something so common nobody would pay attention to it. She suspected that wouldn't be the case as she stumbled to the shower, trying to hurry against the protests her body was making.

* * * *

Julie and Kitten met Ollie and Bri on the elevator and exchanged morning pleasantries.

"Ollie, you look like you've taken Hazel's... What do we call it?" Kitten looked around for an answer, only to find shrugging shoulders.

"Well you look like you have taken it pretty hard." Ollie had the most hopeless look anyone could imagine coming from a human being.

"Ollie got other bad news this morning. She's leaving for home in a few hours." Bri said as she squeezed Ollie's hand and left it at that.

Julie and Kitten waited for Ollie to fill in the loud silence, which she did not. The elevator stopped to let Lea on. Greetings exchanged.

"Is Mona coming down later?" Julie asked. Lea looked a little uncomfortable.

"No. She scheduled something for this morning. Maybe she'll be here this afternoon." Lea shuffled and looked at the elevator floor. They looked at each other and no one commented on the lie. There was noticeable relief when the elevator stopped at the lobby. They headed for the conference room.

Penny, Dee, Jo and Chris were just coming in the front door. They had obviously been out doing something important, the way they had their heads together. Bri took one look and pretty well summed up the business they'd attended to.

"Did you get in to see her?" They gaped at each other and you'd think a sudden rain cloud gathered.

"They've got her hooked up to all kinds of instruments," was Penny's only comment, as tears began down her face. Dee was dry-eyed, but was the epitome of a volcano before eruption. She wasn't going to say anything just yet.

"I got her vitals and reports since she's been there," was Chris' comment, as if it was self evident what was to be next. Jo was in deep thought, following the footsteps of the others, evaluating the information gathered.

The entire party was stopped short by Hazel's daughter suddenly appearing. "Anya! What brings you here, dear?" Chris approached the young woman.

"I found what would have been my mother's contribution on the computer last night," the girl said softly, but clearly. "I thought it was important enough to bring here for you to do whatever you do at these things. I think my mother would have wanted that." Tears began.

"Yes, we think so too," one of the women said. "Would you like to read it or have one of us read it?" someone else asked as they began to gather in the room.

"It doesn't matter," Anya mumbled.

Libby and Judy walked in and Bri and Chris quietly filled them in. "Why don't you read it, Anya, since you're most familiar with it." Anya looked at eleven women, her mother's peers, took a deep breath, nodded her head, exhaled slowly, and began,

" *AND THE WIND CALLED MY NAME*

*"And we were **ALL** in the garden. It was late afternoon and the gentle breeze that blew across the land at this time of day, began as a soft dancing of the trees. Our home was called paradise, as we later learned. **ALL** was harmony, **ALL** was bliss. We communed with **ALL**, always, and there was no distance in space or time or form or feeling. We resided in **THE ALL** and **THE ALL** resided in us. We were aware, **ALL** was safe, **ALL** was nurturing and nourishing and transformation from one state to another was accomplished with no pain (as we have since come to know), with no challenge: simply a shift of attention, or thought as you might call it now. Days blended into nights blended into seasons into days into nights into seasons. We never had want for anything because **ALL** was ours simply by shifting attention. As I said, we were AWARE.*

*"I don't remember the exact time or place or space, but suddenly we were **ALL** aware of the wind calling our name.* **THE ALL** *spoke to **ALL**, although I can't explain how we knew **THE ALL** was "speaking" and how we knew we were "hearing", but* **THE ALL** *made a request of us.* **THE ALL** *"said",*

" 'Beloved, it is NOW, that I need to experience another AWARENESS of MYSELF. It is NOW, that I need to have knowledge of MYSELF as other than UNITY. It is through you, my beloved, that I can BE this experience. You are the most perfect creation for this. Through you, I have experienced bliss, ecstasy, unity of ALL. I would ask that you permit the illusions of separation and distancing. I ask the most profound experience of LOVE from ALL: a willing illusion of that which is other than GOOD, that which is other than LOVE, that which is other than ETERNAL, that which is other than LIFE, that which is other than an awareness of ALL. Do you LOVE enough to do this?'

"We considered. We reached into **THE ALLNESS** *of time and space and being. We could not remember anything like this in our experience. In the fullness of bliss, and ecstasy, and unity called LOVE we agreed. None knew, at that time, what it would be like. We had been LOVE forever.*

"So we turned our awareness and all of a sudden there was awareness of something other than what we had ever known before. There was an I and a YOU. There was a vague remembering of a time when there was no I or YOU but it was covered in a cloud. And as this illusion **BECAME***, also then, the solidification of a separate You and a separate I. We were still aware of how to turn our attentions but as we did, this time, things began to manifest.*

"Somewhere in "time" the separate You and the separate I began to move apart with our creations inbetween and we created DIFFERENCE. At first, DIFFERENCE was only that, just DIFFERENCE, one of the many experiences of **THE ALL**. *Then the polarization of the movement pulled us further apart, tearing our connectedness, and "created" PAIN.*

"With each shift of separate attention, the PAIN became greater and more intense and FEAR, CONFUSION, ANGER, DISILLUSIONMENT came into being. This lasted a long "time" before we were able to turn our attention to being less separated and solid. It was then that we all learned what true separation was. Many of us could not find the light that was our connection to **ALL** *and stop the illusion.*

"There was horror, terror, betrayal and pain as no one had known before. Our abandonment and longing to return to our **BEING** *at the garden caused the pain to crystallize and shatter and crystallize and move to places we had never been before. It caused us to know many things and to feel that which was other than bliss, that which was other than harmony, that which was other than unity and most painful of all, that which was other than LOVE.*

"After many turnings of attention, called "lifetimes", we forgot that we had ever been connected to anything at All. We lived with no awareness that there was LIGHT, LOVE, LIFE. We knew emptiness, aloneness, mistrust, unworthiness.

*"There were those that talked about love and light and life and claimed they knew how to acquire those things and touted their brightness everywhere. They called us **darkness** and tried to alter our paths and our being. They labeled us **bad** and **evil** and proclaimed our difference needed to be destroyed. I suppose they,*

too, forgot the origin of all.

"*So I accepted. I did many things in the name of evil. I murdered, I raped, I stole, I took away hope with the snap of a finger and each time I did, they were able to find their way home. Yet, I remained. So!... So... this will be my home, and I will make it MINE. If they do not like it, let them leave. If they complain too loudly, I'll help them leave in a manner that will see to it they don't want to come back. I don't need them or anyone else, least of all a so-called BEING that drops you, abandons you, plays with you, and if... if you survive, makes you come back without your consent.*

"*The only relief to pain and fear and being less than is creating more pain and fear to be able to take from others what you lack. When you can do that without being stopped you never do without again. Who needs anything outside this reality to create what you want- what you don't already have? Who needs any more than what reality provides, right now, anyway? Loneliness is an illusion that can easily be overcome by acquiring people around you. Money buys that, money buys all. Money is power, power over, power to get what you don't already have. Let those stupid enough or weak enough talk about all that other stuff. The stupid and the weak need to be controlled anyway. They want it! They crave it! So the kindest thing to do is to give it to them! They deserve what they get! They wouldn't know how to live out of slavery to something. Why not to me? Having to be stuck in this muck hole deserves some compensation since I am anathema to 'all'.*

"*So I lived and lived and lived. Each lifetime brought new powers, new ways to feed off pain and fear and chaos and anger. As I fed, the more I needed to feed as if I had no source of energy of my own. I guess I don't have any energy of my own. Oh! Well! There's enough here to feed on forever, there's plenty for me to stay alive.*

I can create enough fear, anxiety, pain, chaos, hatred to keep me alive for eternity. Look, over there... Watch this! Another one of those sickening sweetie love and light people loses hope and gives their energy to me. <u>TO ME!!</u> This could get boring it's so easy. Just what I like, an afternoon breeze after feeding. Prop my feet up, count my assets, I'm full... for now... What's that? What's that I hear? Great! Now I'm hallucinating!

"No... someone is calling my name. It sounds like the wind is calling my name. What's that? Either come out where I can really hear you or go away. I've heard you before, I think. How can you look like that? You're just wind. Oh! sure! I can tell how precious I am. Where were you when I needed you? Say, if I'm so precious why don't you lend me just a little of your energy?

"And **SHE** *looked at me, gently reached in and took this big black weight out of my chest.* **'We wish to thank you for all that you have done these many lifetimes. Without you, many would never have been able to complete their learning here and return home. We honor you for all that you are.'** **SHE** *said.*

"Oh yeah! and just what am I and if you honor me so much how's about a little to munch on while you're here! and I grabbed for **HER.** *My hand moved through air with no resistance.* **SHE** *looked at me and said,* **'It is time to awaken. The time is now. It is time to lift the illusion of darkness and time for you to see the light and brilliance that you are.'**

"As **SHE** *spoke,* **SHE** *removed the veils from the weight in* **HER** *hand one by one, until the final shroud was removed to reveal a ball of the brightest light I had ever seen. I became hungry and greedily said to* **HER,** *'Why don't you let me see that?'*

"SHE *replied so gently, it hurt,* **'Of course. It is yours. This is your light. You have always been connected, you have always been loved and cherished and united with ALL. You have always been in harmony. We honor you for maintaining the illusion for this long. It is time to release the illusion.'**

"As **SHE** *said that, awareness began to stir in me. Pain! Pain! I don't want this thing! I tried to smash it, it kept moving ever so slightly. Its softness and gentleness and power hurt. I fought to keep it from me.*

*"***SHE** *looked at me with compassion. I felt something that I realized I hadn't felt in many lifetimes... kindness. A gentle warmth swept over me and this light... my light, grew brighter. In agony, I was aware that I was not alone. There was* **SOMETHING** *that knew everything and all there was to know about me and LOVED me still. The womb of creation opened and its waters washed me clean, washed away the excruciating pain and left with me the knowingness that I had never been alone and had always been looked after and tended by the gentlest beings in the universe. I collapsed with my light in my hands, sobbing, as lifetimes of contribution, lifetimes of the most profound LOVE raced across my awareness, knowing that I gave. I gave willingly ALL, I gave lovingly ALL. I gave for* **THE ALL,** *I gave to* **THE ALL,** *and now with my light in my hands... myyyyy* **light**... *the illusion of separation is over. Joy!! Ecstasy!! I gave that* **I AM**.

"As all is balanced, this lifetime has been spent learning much about the nature I had lived for lifetimes by being on the other side. I no longer resent this, but in truth I cannot say I... like it. It is what it is. And my sibling spirit, I am before you, now, as you look at me with distaste. You wonder why I am in your Presence if I will not use what I have spent lifetimes learning with the power I have, for you surely will.

"Yes, the wind is calling your name. Yes, I have reached in and in my hand is a large black weight. You're welcome, I know you feel lighter... and, yes, I know it won't make a difference as to what you'll do to me, but as we speak, and as I remove the final shroud, please look at what is here.

"Of course you can have it. This is your light. **We wish to thank you for all that you have done these many lifetimes. Without you, many would never have been able to complete their learning here and return home. We honor you for all that you are. It is time to awaken. The time is now. It is time to lift the illusion of darkness and time for you to see the light and brilliance that you are. You have always been connected, you have always been loved and cherished and united with ALL. You have always been in harmony. We honor you for maintaining the illusion for this long.** *I am profoundly honored to be the one to tell you...* **It is time to release the illusion.**

The scream... the scream... I am familiar with the scream. I will not take advantage of your vulnerability, you know that. That is why I was uniquely chosen for this sacred task.... Yes, you can still do all that you could before, especially to me. The choice is still yours-- but you make the choice in full knowledge and consciousness. It is yours to make... And this is yours... I gently handed my sibling spirit the light, turned and silently, respectfully walked away."

Anya finished. She put the story on one of the tables, looked around the room, and decided there was nothing more to say. She represented her mother as best she could. She sat down before weak knees could betray her. The quiet enveloping the room made the young woman nervous. The women, finally, leaving a state of awe, looked at each other.

What did this mean? What did Hazel want them to do now? Did Hazel do something... "different" to herself?... or did someone else do "it" to her? With or without her permission? The questions became endless, after this reading.

Anya began to fidget, "I suppose... uh... you've been... been," She couldn't complete the sentence. The girl still wasn't sure what was going on or how to put into words something that reflected what she understood .

Penny was the first to speak up, "Yes, Anya. We went to the hospital this morning," she said gently and began to fit the crying young woman into her arms while her sweater mopped up Anya's tears.

Bri began to form some direction for the group. "Anya, would it be alright if Penny spoke to you and your father about your mother... what was going on before this happened?" Bri asked Anya, while she looked for Penny's approval. Penny nodded her head as she still enfolded the sobbing girl.

"I... a... suppose so." Anya looked bewildered. "I don't know much about how mother felt about... things. She took the breakup pretty hard. She just wasn't the same after it."

"Well, Penny will ask you some questions like who she was dating and what groups she was going to. By the way, was she going to a therapist?" Bri coached. The girl couldn't seem to focus on the questions. Bri seemed to overwhelm the girl.

"Bri! Can't you see the young woman is having a difficult time!" Penny chided as she held Anya close but nodded her understanding to Bri. Penny had this end covered.

Bri nodded back, "Well, I suppose you're right." She looked from Penny to Anya, "I'm sorry, Anya. Would you like Penny to be with you for a while?" Anya nodded her confirmation, and Penny and Anya went outside the room.

"We need someone to nosey around the hospital... Chris, that should probably be you?" Chris nodded acceptance.

"We need someone to go to the public library to check the newspapers and any other literature..." Dee raised her hand, Bri acknowledged.

"We need someone to find the site where Hazel was found and look around. Probably two would be better, if there is any rugged terrain. They said she was found in the mountains..." Julie and Kitten looked at each other and nodded to Bri. Bri acknowledged.

"We need someone to go to the police department..." They all looked for Jo's acceptance.

"Great Goddesses and Gods. I just can't get away from them!" Jo shook her head, the half-smirk on her face belying her chagrin and acceptance. They all briefly chuckled amidst the seriousness of the planning. They all looked at Ollie, Judy and Libby. Libby was alternating very pale and bright red, in varying degrees. Ollie just kept her head down.

"We really do need a few to stay here for contact and coordinating while I take Ollie to the airport. It looks like maybe you and Libby should stay here and keep the fort secure..." Bri spoke to Judy. Libby looked up, still apparently unaware of what was taking place, and Judy acknowledged for both of them. All of a sudden Lea became visible.

"I... I... I think maybe I'll go back home, too." Lea spoke half animated. Lea had faded to an almost non-presence and appeared reluctant to be visible again.

"Are you sure? There's certainly enough to do."

"Yeah, I'm sure. Nobody needs a cheerleader now. You **will** let me know what you find out, won't you? John's so lost without me, he's always so glad to see me when I get home from these things. Since we won't be having a real "Gathering" this year, I should probably get back... We won't be having a real "Gathering" this year, will we?" Lea said with a faint note of hope in her voice.

"No. We won't be having a regular "Gathering" this year."

"Will we ever have another "Gathering" again?" Lea looked at each of the women in the room as if this were the last performance of a long running hit show.

No one answered... no one had an answer. Lea turned, went to her room to pack and reschedule her departure.

"I'll check on Lea before I take Ollie to the airport. When I get back, I'll go walking the 'other roads' and see what I can see. Shall we meet for sharing after dinner sometime?" Bri looked at all, there was no dissent.

"What about Mona?"

Bri thought a moment and said, "What about Mona?"

No one answered. Each woman got up to do her part.

Chapter 11

Ollie and Bri took the elevator in silence. Ollie was grateful Bri didn't announce to the whole world what happened. Apparently, Michael had waited just long enough for Ollie to get out of town before he moved or hocked everything in the apartment.

Why? Why? It would be different if I had something of real value worth hocking or stealing. My entire worldly possessions, my life's fortunes, couldn't amount to more than a thousand or two. It's not like Michael would strike it rich. It's not like stealing from me or making me feel smaller than I am was going to gain him anything or pay off some big debt. Betraying me wouldn't make a dent in anyone's revenge plot. Shit! It couldn't even be counted as good practice for some imagined 'real bust'. Why?

After 'Why?'-- then what the hell was she going to do? She couldn't get her things out of hock. Her neighbors knew where Michael was because they had followed him, figuring he was up to something, but so what! She wasn't sure what the law would do. She already knew the law wasn't necessarily on the side of the victim, no matter what was written down.

For that matter, why am I going back in the first place? I have nothing left to go back to. What did Janice Joplin say... "Freedom's just another word for nothin' left to lose." Ollie was one of the freest people she knew.

"What are you going to do when you get back?" Bri asked, as if she were reading Ollie's mind. *So what if she's reading my mind.* Ollie just contemplated Bri's question, too overcome to cry, too depressed to be angry, too 'free' to believe it mattered.

"I don't know," Ollie replied when she could finally speak. "If I had a fairy Godmother, I'd have it all back in a flash and him turned into a toad. If I had any resources at all, I might have an idea what should be done. I'm empty, Bri. Completely empty and I'm not permitted to leave this life. I don't know what Hazel did or what was done to her, but I think I'd like to volunteer for the next expedition out. I always felt better after I talked to Hazel, like there was an idea that hadn't been thought yet, or something or someone would swoop down out of the sky and make it all better. Perhaps some big magic wand in the sky. All you'd have to do was find the right end, make a wish, and **Poof**! It would appear. I hate dealing with the system. I don't even know if I have the energy to this time... or if I want the energy. Bri, you're a witch. Can you wave your magic wand or pop your magic twanger, and make it better for me?" Ollie looked for one more ray of hope.

Bri thought carefully before she began to answer Ollie. "Ollie. I think there may possibly be a Cinderella inside every woman. Maybe inside every man. That Cinderella has to die to the idea there's a prince charming or fairy Godmother- or anyone for that matter- who will make it all better. She has to wake up and take responsibility for herself and her life. She has to know within herself, she is complete... a whole person... not a half person. Two half people have never made a whole person yet." Bri paused briefly to check Ollie's aura.

"Sure we have help, sure we coexist with others, and I grant you very few of us can live as sovereign, self-contained, self-sufficient islands. Part of every learning experience is learning to be in harmony with the beings around us or to move into spaces where we naturally harmonize with those around us. But each of us pays a price and reaps rewards based on what we are willing to do or not do. What we are willing to take or not take, what we are willing to hear or not hear, change or not change, see or not see. In this respect, there are no exceptions, Ollie, none. This is the same for me, as well as you, as well as all the people on the street we don't even know. What can or cannot be done about anything varies in the same way each snowflake is different." Bri continued walking as she talked. She hoped she was giving Ollie encouragement.

"Hazel gave me a poster once, which she said had a profound effect on her. She found it on a school counselor's desk. It said: NOT EVERYTHING THAT IS FACED CAN BE CHANGED, BUT NOTHING CAN BE CHANGED UNTIL IT IS FACED." Bri paused, "Ollie. It had a profound effect on me also. If Hazel stood for anything, it's there is no such thing as a hero. There's not going to be a Moses to lead us out of slavery. We can band together to be stronger but even a chain is only as strong as its weakest link. We can share, we can connect in many ways, we can network. We can cry and laugh together but the sovereign life force beats through individual hearts only."

They had been walking at a snail's pace towards the room, after they left the elevator. Once in the room Bri continued. "Ollie, when any of us stands naked between the worlds, really naked, what we have is ourselves. The rest is adornment that comes and goes. The adornment doesn't make the naked spirit more or less whatever it is. The naked spirit gets to choose the adornment it wishes to wear to express itself. Ollie, if you don't want this to continue to happen to you, you must do something really different. You must think, believe, do, live something different even if the physical reality doesn't catch up for a while.

"People can support us with their good will, kind thoughts and all those things. But the doing can only be done from a point of sovereignty. The mistakes incurred are sovereign mistakes. The corrections made, sovereign corrections. The benefits and misfortunes are simply carnal experience to our naked life force.

What we hang on to, what we focus on as being real is what continues to manifest in our lives. If you want to keep getting what you're getting, keep thinking and reacting and believing and focusing on what you're focusing on right now. If you truly want a change, stop! Right now. Stop!" Bri was as gentle as she could be.

"Think something different for you. Do something different for you. Believe something different for you and then act differently for you and see what happens. Do it long enough to see some kind of change. If you don't like the results, try something different and do the same process again until you see something different. Do it until you get something you like or want, or is just plain acceptable. With inertia, it will take a lot more energy to move in another direction then it will take to maintain the same course or lifestyle. A lot more energy. These simple words are not so simple put into practice, but compare all the alternatives and see what you come up with." Bri knew from personal experience how hard change could be.

"Our commencement, when we graduated from high-- school wasn't only because we were beginning a new phase of life, it was also because we were receiving our diplomas. We completed something to enable us to begin this new journey, hopefully. Let this be your commencement to a new way of living. You received your diploma when you got the news over he phone. You've made a thorough study. You have learned, in **depth**, what poverty is. You've graduated magna cum laude. Let this experience enable you to never have to go back to the same thing, ever again." Bri finished as they got into the car for the airport.

Something was visibly beginning to shift in Ollie though she said not a single word. Bri left her to her thoughts and changes.

* * * *

"Chris!" Julie called.

"Wait up! Julie and I will take you to the hospital. We want to talk to you anyway," said Kitten, as they ran to catch up to Chris.

Chris stopped and turned around with a warm smile on her face. "Thanks. I could use the lift."

They got to Kitten's car and Julie spoke, "We'll go to this little coffee shop we found and have a cup of coffee. If it's alright with you?"

Chris looked puzzled. Julie was doing some strange hand-jive, pointing to her ears and mouth, then to the car and shaking her head "No". Julie pointed somewhere outside the car, shook her head "Yes". *Can I teach her to sign in five easy lessons in five easy minutes?* Chris wondered.

Chris did, however, recognize they weren't going to speak about whatever Julie and Kitten wanted to speak about right now. Julie casually talked about the weather being mild and warm for this time in Colorado; how the trees were beautiful and maybe they'd go into the mountains for a ride a little later; what did she think about needing to take extra clothes this time of year; any good eating places in the mountains; is there skiing now? Chris just kept quite or grunted occasionally, with an "Oh!", appropriately placed, every now and then. It did not take long to get to the coffee shop in downtown Colorado Springs.

"You'd think a city this size would have turn lights and get rid of the damnable parking meters. If a street is important enough to have a traffic signal, it's important enough to have a turn light!" Kitten snapped out, sounding very annoyed, "Neither condition is very friendly or hospitable. In Texas we know how to show our visitors we want them to return with their money!"

Julie and Chris just looked at Kitten and smiled. They went in, got their coffees, and sat down in a quiet spot. Julie and Kitten looked at each other and squirmed a bit. Chris took the lead.

"Well, you obviously don't want to talk about the weather because you did a thorough job of it in the car, and you obviously didn't want to talk about the important issue in the car, that's what we're here for." Chris' eyebrows rose to await the answer.

Julie flushed, Kitten picked at her cuticle and found something terribly interesting in her cup of coffee, nudged Julie under the table.

"I don't know exactly where to begin but we thought we might talk to you because of... um... well..." Julie shifted and sat up straight like the attorney she is, looked Chris in the eye, and spoke, "Both of us had a funny feeling before we started for the "Gathering" this time. We were especially looking forward to seeing Hazel because she was the only one who knew." Julie paused.

Chris knew her line, "Knew what?"

"Knew about Julie and me." Kitten pushed on over the quiet. Silence. Chris looked at both of them and waited with an expectant look on her face.

"Kitten and I have been lovers now for about seven years. I wanted to go away with Kitten right after this "Gathering" or as soon as I could clean up my responsibilities to Kitten's husband and retire. When we left Texas, we both knew something wasn't right. The Duke had us monitored from the time we left. We think he has the car bugged. We don't know if he knows about us or not. Hazel was the only one to know about us, so we thought."

"Whatever happened to Hazel, we think it might have something to do with Duke and the 'good ol boy' system. Hazel would have helped us with her connections in foreign countries. I've already switched over my bank accounts to foreign banks and deposited the majority in the same banks as Mona. Mona and I talked at the last "Gathering" about finances and the necessary discreet concealment methods, shall we say, of investing anonymously. The Duke doesn't like giving up what he believes is his, especially to a woman."

"So, Mona knows?" asked Chris. Kitten put her hand on Julie's and they looked lovingly at each other.

"No. She only knows I want to retire quietly. But I don't think Kitten should go back now. If the Duke knows or suspects about us, it's just a matter of time. His time. Kitten'll be there unsuspecting, or just waiting for the same thing to happen to her that happened to Hazel. We can't prove anything, so there's no use going to the police. Besides, he'd have Kitten locked up and put on thorazine, biding his time till he was ready. I'm sure you know it's been done enough with uppity, upper class women who didn't know their place, and not a soul to protest or object." Julie looked at Chris. Chris nodded her knowledge of such things.

"I appreciate your telling me this." Chris thought as she spoke, "I'll be especially careful investigating the circumstances surrounding Hazel's 'condition' in case there's a connection. But you seem to have more on your mind than just warning me to be careful and investigate deeper?" Julie and Kitten both took a deep breath and looked at each other as if they were jumping off a cliff.

"When we go to the site where Hazel was found, after we snoop around we're going to have an accident on the way home." Julie said matter-of-factly. Chris snapped her head up to look at the two of them.

"I've had it planned for a long time financially," Julie said. "We were waiting for the right time. We thought maybe after I retired would be the right time but Kitten can't go back after Hazel's whatever-it-is. I'm not sure I want to be within such close range of the Duke myself. So we virtually need to die so we can live out our lives together."

"What exactly do you want me to do?" Chris asked not quite believing what she was hearing.

"We'd like for you to hold on to these papers, passports, and such until we return to you to pick them up. As I say, we've planned this for quite a while. After we come back to give you our report, we'll have to keep moving for a while, but we both like to travel. Kitten believes we'll only have a short time before the Duke finds us and really completes the job, but I'm willing to take my chances. I figure if we can keep quiet enough, stay out of his way and the sight of his playmates, the Duke can still look good. He might let us be. He's first of all a business man. He's had Kitten's replacement picked out since the girl was old enough to bleed. You know: old enough to bleed, old enough to slaughter. Kitten is getting past child bearing. He'd have to figure out what to do with her pretty soon anyway. I figure if we provide an easy solution that won't even be questioned, he'll have his mind on other things and he might not want to take the time to look closer."

Kitten hung her head to the truth of Julie's words. Julie squeezed her hand and desperately wanted to put her arm around her beloved. They didn't dare in such an open place. The only comfort they could show each other, now, was the comfort appropriate to extend to mutually grieving friends. Julie continued, "What we would ask is unless you see the cold dead bodies, don't believe we're really gone and give these things over to The Duke. There will probably be news teams and other media to cover the demise of a rich Texan's wife and brood mare, but that will pass quickly. He'll want to get on with the new 'little woman' and start her poppin' those critters out. We'll leave it up to you whether or not to inform the group or who exactly to inform. We'll contact you when the time is right." They looked at each other again, "If by some chance you do see the bodies after all," Kitten took in a swift breath, Julie continued, "we'd like you to give these things over to Mona."

"Mona?" Chris raised an eyebrow in question.

"Yes. She's the one who made this even remotely possible with her financial wizardry."

Chris took some time to think about it as they drank their coffees. Chris finally agreed to do it. They drove Chris to the hospital and moseyed on down to the library to find out where Hazel's car had been found. They met Dee, exchanged information, got a map and started on their way. The sun was high and bright as they left the library.

"It's a good day, as the Native Americans would say." Julie stopped to put on her sunglasses, look at her beloved, and take a deep breath. They were on their way.

* * * *

Bri got back from the airport to the hotel a little after lunch time. She hadn't had breakfast or lunch and her body was making a commotion in the vicinity of her tummy. She walked into the hotel restaurant and saw Judy there.

"Mind if I join you?" Judy looked up, put on a strained smile, waved her hand for Bri to sit down.

"You look a little frazzled around the edges." Bri was evaluating Judy's presence. Judy gave a weak nod, put down her eating utensil.

"I just left Libby upstairs, hopefully sleeping. I wouldn't know how to explain what she or I have been going through." Judy paused. Bri ordered and waited for the staff to leave the vicinity before looking at Judy to continue.

"From what I can gather, shortly before the "Gathering", Libby was gang raped by an unidentified number of men in positions of authority. Something similar happened to her when she was a child.

"Hazel's uncertain situation, not to mention the car accident a while back, triggered memories of both incidents. She's been processing ever since."

Judy took a bite of her food and continued. "Last night the only option Libby had was to kill them all and let whatever would happen to her, happen to her. She said this morning Hazel came to her in a dream, told her two people would join her and help her to take care of the situation. Hazel said to Libby that the situation was bigger and more complex than she could know now. Its roots were in money and power, but to hang in there. She's been 'remembering' all day. I'm not sure what to do. I'm Libby's friend in this situation, not her therapist, but I'm quickly approaching the 'Let's get some help!' point. As long as she's not hell bent on murder, I don't have to involve anyone else." Judy hesitated a moment to decide which direction to go in now.

"She's not bonded with her therapist and the type of bonding she would need to process this kind of thing just doesn't develop over night. I won't turn her out to the wolves, but I'm not sure where to go from here. With the exception of wanting to commit murder, she's not being harmful to herself or others. Frankly, after what she's told me so far, I'm not sure murder isn't the proper solution. I wouldn't know who to confide in outside our "Gathering" group, and the only person who might have a clue about a direction to go in is in limbo somewhere between life and death." The tension of the last two days snapped like an overstretched rubberband and Judy sobbed her release. Bri moved closer and gently smoothed Judy's back as she cried her grief. Bri motioned the waitress to just put her food down and leave. When Judy finally wept the tension of these last two days away, she dried her tears, moved over and began picking at her meal.

"Feel better?"

"I feel foolish crying like this in public." Judy blew her nose, got out fresh tissues and wiped off her face. "I'm glad you were here though." Judy blew her nose again. "I'd hate to do this, here, all by myself. They'd come to take me away and I'd probably go." Judy still sniffled a little and gave a little laugh. They ate their meal in relative quiet, sharing the comfort of presence. After they finished eating, Bri spoke.

"I hate to bring this up right now, but I'm going to need someone with me while I travel the 'other roads'. I don't know how deep I'll have to go or what it will take to come back. I don't think I'll need any chemical aides but I'd like the reassurance of a trusted friend's presence to monitor my life signs."

"What do you mean?" Judy was puzzled and concerned.

"Well, when you do this kind of traveling, it's not uncommon to forget to breathe or swallow for a while, and the body gets so relaxed, it's not uncommon to have a significant temperature drop. It's good to know there is someone close by to help your body remember to breathe or have a hot cup of tea waiting. It's always reassuring to know if you begin choking, there's someone to help you till you return to your body," Bri said lightly, as if this were the most common thing in the world.

Judy was not only confused but frankly more than a little worried. What did Bri mean, 'till you return to your body'? Where was **she** going that her body wasn't, and why would her body's functions stop? What if Judy did something wrong and Bri couldn't 'find' her body or her way back from this 'other road' or where ever it was she was going? Bri must be joking. Bri always had a strange sense of humor.

"I don't think we ought to leave Libby alone that long, though. It's a bit of a dilemma," Bri was saying. "Some people get frightened watching if they haven't done it themselves." Judy just looked at Bri with an 'Is that so?' look on her face as Bri continued. "And if Libby's processing that heavily, she might find herself on the 'Roads' with me. She probably would be scared out of her wits. But I think it's a chance we have to take, right now, if you're up to it?"

Judy had no earthly idea what Bri had been talking about but she had some vision of Bri's ghost running around the room frantically trying to find Bri's body and Libby shrieking out of control trying to catch the ghost. Judy didn't know if she was up to it.

"What if both of you need help at the same time?" Judy offered.

"I thought about it and I think we may need to take our chances if one of the group doesn't get back soon." Just then, Dee walked in.

"I got all the information I could about what happened from media sources, so I came back to see if I could help with anything else." Dee stated, as she sat down. Bri and Judy looked at each other and grinned.

* * * *

With the sun shining brightly, the air at ten thousand feet is so crackling clear, every solitary molecule invites the human spirit to ascend and merge into the atmosphere with each second. The aspens were turning and all of nature sang the last and most beautiful colors of the living. As the lovers drove through the Colorado autumn mountains, each thought how easy it would be to forget their mission.

It would be easy to forget everything and everyone but the Mother's reminder of the magnificence She creates within us and around us. It is also easy to forget this grandeur is precursor of the necrosis to come. The splendor, as well as the moribund silence, is an evocation of that which passes, of that which is eternal. Life is ever-constant change and balance. "It would be easy to believe Hazel would choose to crossover in a place like this." Kitten said in awe, "When it's my time, if it could be in a place like this... if there's a heaven... it would be easy to reach it from here." Julie looked at her a little apprehensively.

"What's the matter?" Kitten spoke as she put her hand on Julie's thigh, "You've been so contemplative, you're missing the high in 'Rocky Mountain High, Colorado'. Here we are, surrounded by the most breathtaking sight in the universe... Well, this part of the West!... and you don't even seem to notice more than you would on the subway. What's going on in the beautiful, intelligent head of yours?"

"I don't really know. You know, I don't place much value in intuition or feelings not based on concrete evidence... but..." Julie was trying to express an irrational feeling in rational terms, "But... I've had this feeling something is trying to get my attention. I don't know what it is or how it's trying to get my attention. Whatever it is, it seems to be very important. It seems to be somewhat urgent. And this all sounds stupid because I can't point to what **it** is. I can't say it's a voice in my head. I can't say it's some kind of vision or clairvoyance. I can't say it's some kind of telepathy... but it feels like some kind of warning. About what? I don't know. Probably indigestion or altitude sickness... something. I can't seem to shake it."

Kitten nodded her head, keeping her eyes on the winding road. "I'll have to get the brakes checked when we get back, they're getting soggy."

Julie was about to tell Kitten to slow down when there was a pop. When Kitten tried to put on the brakes, the pedal went all the way to the floor. The steering wheel wasn't steering the car any longer and, had it not been for the fact Kitten was already going slowly to drink in the beauty of the meandering road they were on, the car would have dropped off the edge of the mountain going too fast to do anything about the sudden calamity. Julie saw what was happening and before the car left the road had both safety belts undone.

She screamed at Kitten's quiescent panic to open the door and jump. Kitten froze, white knuckles seized to the steering wheel, nostrils flaring, eyes hypnotized to a windshield revealing only open sky as they rolled off the side of the mountain. Julie reached past Kitten, opened the door, wrenched Kitten's hands from the steering wheel and pushed Kitten out. The car collided with the ground, jolting Julie nearly senseless. Her head hit the roof. The rest of her body parts compressed in unnatural positions, molded by the car's dash and accessories.

Just as the car was about to take flight down again, Julie opened her door, threw herself out, bounced on the ground, and watched the car burst into flames. All went void as the shock wave of the exploding car knocked Julie out.

Kitten came back to awareness as she bounced on the ground, twisting and rolling wildly downhill. Momentum increased as the mountain's slope increased her velocity. Brambles and branches gouging and puncturing- tearing at her flesh- couldn't disguise the meaning of the exploding car. Her beloved, her reason to live, Kitten's life was in that car. The pain inflicted on her body offered a distracting relief compared to the pain in her heart and mind. Nothing mattered anymore. The tunnel called to her and she gratefully began walking toward the light.

* * * *

Neither Julie or Kitten saw the man with the strange eyes smiling from atop the roadway ledge the car had gone off. But as Chance would have it, he had not seen Kitten thrown from the car and the angle he was observing from did not allow him to see Julie's escape. All he saw was the car bursting into flames, as he had planned. He was reassured there would be nothing identifiable in what was left of the vehicle. Although the arid landscape would support a forest fire of momentous proportions, he seemed satisfied the valley would contain the fire and still destroy what evidence there might be floating around that could imply something other than an accident.

Synchronistically, he did **not** see Mona, on a nearby trail. She was hiking her way back down from the morning Cog journey up to the top of Pikes Peak. She'd spent most of the time examining her feelings of loss surrounding Hazel. She went back through the years and tried to figure out how this had happened without her conscious approval. She was a mile or so away, now, watching the whole terrible scene through her highpowered binoculars, panic rising as she recognized the car.

The same serendipity finding Mona on this particular trail this day, arranged conditions so Mona did see Kitten thrown from the car and Julie's escape. In the time it takes for a camera to flash, Mona realized the women in that car were more to her than "net profits and capital gains". These were her Sisters.

Hazel's loss pushed home the possibility of losing the entire "Gathering". Through the years, they had become her family. Each woman had her own distinct value, even the women she had formerly thought of as "virtual losers". Through the years she had bonded with each woman so that she would feel a sense of loss no matter which woman left. It had happened so naturally, it escaped her conscious awareness.

Now, her family needed her. She stopped to think: could she hope to get there before the entire canyon was ablaze? She wondered what in the hell she could possibly do, and what it would be like getting caught in a roasting forest fire. She saw through her binoculars the car had dropped only a few pieces of burning debris in the canyon and their fire was not catching on the dry tinder as one might expect.

Maybe... If these conditions hold till I can get there. If there aren't any unbreachable obstacles on the way and I don't break a leg or get roasted. She knew the man would be gone by the time she got there. She might possibly get Kitten and/or Julie to relative safety before all hell broke loose, if they were alive. If it was none of the above, her heart sank and her stomach flopped; it looked like she had a way to safety regardless, via the road or the trail. She was sure, carried by the impetus of self-preservation, she could make it up the hill or back to the trail to safety.

She looked up at the high noon sun, checked the sky for clouds, marked the direction of the wind both where she was and on the side of the mountain where the accident occurred. If all went well, she could get the women to relative safety, drive her car back to get them to medical attention... If everything went well...

"What the hell! No guts; no glory. I've done about everything else. Time to put all my survival training to work." Mona spoke out loud to no one. She could hear the trepidation in her own voice. She put her fear and loss aside and cut out toward the accident scene at a quick pace.

Chapter 12

It was dark before the women began gathering together. Bri looked drained and pale. She wasn't able to keep the contents of her stomach where it belonged since she had come back from the 'other road'. Libby was a bit anxious but had managed to get some rest and get back some big chunks of her life. Judy was wondering how much of this was real? Is she really in a strange dream? Judy couldn't keep the unsurety off her face. Jo looked as if someone had just puked on her and she was trying to ignore it. Chris was restless and dissatisfied with the gaps that made her profession an 'art'. Dee was available for anything adventurous after what she had just seen, heard, and, quite frankly, just participated in. Penny was thoughtful, putting together all the information she had gathered from the family.

Julie and Kitten's absence was noticed by all, with an added mysterious twist of Mona's room registration still being concurrent with Mona's truancy during the last twelve to eighteen hours.

 "Well... Do we want to begin processing the information we have now or wait for a while longer to see if Julie or Kitten show up?" Dee asked enthusiastically. The rest exchanged looks with each other a little less enthusiastically, but seemed to agree to begin and fill in the latecomers when they arrived.

Dee volunteered first. "I looked in the local papers, all two of them, scanned the videos of the news for the days before and after Hazel was discovered. It was mentioned and forgotten with no meaningful details. Typical media thing. Sports and the latest sensationalism keep the masses addictively fixated, quiet, unthinking. Why get upset with reality-- there are no big deals! What could you do about it anyway? They found an unidentified car and an unidentified woman dead in it. Then they realized she wasn't dead and didn't know what she was. Very untidy!

"No one would commit to **how** they knew she wasn't dead or who found out or to exactly what she was, but whatever she was, was pending test results and notification of next of kin. Of course, we can't have the experts not having sure facts and immediate answers or leaving unresolved problems for the paying public, so it was dropped. Not another word, but they'll keep us informed. Don't call us, we'll call you. I have dates and times and other published data if you're interested or if we need it later." Dee's report finished, she looked around expectantly for the next woman ready to give her report. She didn't have to wait long.

Penny and Jo started together, Jo amicably continued. "The police did not want to be cooperative at all, especially to a total stranger and with the confidentiality act. It's amazing how people clam up with a stranger but make them your friend and they'll speak all kinds of little nothings to fill you in and catch you up. Prison slave labor doesn't have to keep secrets if they don't want to and won't if they like you. Drunk survival training 101!..." Jo said as an aside, then continued. "Anyway, the officials nearly bungled it by putting her in the morgue. They had the scalpels out, the blood sucking equipment ready, until someone noticed she wasn't quite as blue as she should be, nor was she quite as cold. There was some other indicator but no one I spoke with knew the exact medical terminology or what it meant. So they wheeled out a few sturdy pieces of equipment measuring brain waves, heart beat, blood pressure, temperature and the like which led to some blood tests I can't remember the names of, and couldn't pronounce if I did. These tests put the scalpels on hold, and revealed she wasn't quite dead. So, the dilemma: do they kill her and settle it? Do they put her on life support? What does the family want, if they can find a family? If she comes to; what is the likelihood she'll come to with any brains left or the ability to function? And, oh my! We have more than a cadaver to work on, wouldn't that be interesting? The test results are so close, the difference between dead and what she is, is a technicality. Which leaves an interesting legal impasse. If she's not dead, and she's not alive: what is she, and what are her rights?"

Jo paused to look at her notes. "Next we have the possibility of administered evil doings, which forensics, I must say, did what appears to be an excellent job and to be notably commended. No obvious anything in or on the skin, blood, internal organs, brain, intestinal tract, hair, in or under nails, teeth, orifices, anywhere. That includes poisons, bacteria, viruses, all forms of parasites, bugs of any kind known, unnatural or incompatible chemicals of any kind known. Samples were also sent to the center that tests for everything, twice. Nothing in the area of foul play or any other kind of play. The question of what state is she in, and why, remains unanswered. According to reports, the site where she was found held nothing unusual. Again, no evidence of perpetrated misdeeds. The automobile was in excellent condition with nothing to suggest why she was there, what she was doing there, or what happened there. The site itself was well traveled by runners, joggers, and trail people so the likelihood of her being found this time of year was extremely good. If she were in the woods to be away from everything, there were better spots. There were no notes, books, records, or any other kind of evidence pointing to why she was there. If by some chance there was treachery, there would have been better spots to leave her. Conclusion: Don't have a clue." Jo's report was ended, leaving the room pensively silent.

Penny finally broke the silence, "Chris, why don't you continue from here?" Chris looked up and nodded.

"I can't really add too much to that. Vitals, lab tests, observations, remain the same as when she was brought in. There were several attempts to jumpstart her into being either more active or ceasing all evidence of life altogether with no change in either direction. There was one thing however. On several mornings, somewhere between about four a.m. and eight a.m., the machines show a minor brain activity increase. Lab work for those days show minor chemistry changes. It would have gone unnoticed except for a very sharp aide. There's not been any change in the last week or so, not even when we were in the room. When I got back to the hotel, the same aide left a message for me. The same changes occurring only early in the morning prior, occurred sometime this afternoon, then stopped again." Bri looked up sharply on that one but didn't say anything as yet.

Penny had been trying to fit her information into the information already offered and decided to just put it out. "Well, according to Hazel's daughter, Anya, her mother had been a little depressed lately. Her mother began to get 'political' by joining some women's organizations, some church organizations, and other activities. Although she was happy with her people involvement, she was apparently getting a picture of the political environment which didn't match any information she grew up with. She and the ex were friends but not intimate. No significant others, which the daughter attributes as the cause of her mother's moodiness. She said her mother didn't even seem interested in dating. Hazel answered some of the classified singles advertisements and wasn't too impressed. Anya said it was like her mother didn't know what she wanted anymore and wasn't finding 'it' where ever she was searching for 'it'.

"Jack said there was nothing but friendship between them, although he would have liked more. He, too, noticed Hazel becoming more depressed and moody. He said something knocked the wind out of her sails and she seemed to be just drifting. Even though the divorce was her idea, he was sure it had something to do with the depression. Possibly, the onset of menopause was taking its toll but not enough to make her do anything more than contemplate more. Which might be an explanation of why she was found where she was, but not what happened to her. He said there could be a remote possibility of deception. Hazel never looked for evil and it naturally avoided her because of how she was. There was a possibility that with the onset of this depression she was vulnerable, not looking, and something swooped in to take advantage where it couldn't get near her any other time. Makes sense to me but still feels like something's missing. Without questioning the people of the organizations she was in, we have no way of knowing if any of those could be a factor. Neither Anya nor Jack had any opinions either way, other than what I've already mentioned. As near as anyone could tell, her habits hadn't changed, her patterns for eating, sleeping, paying bills, exercising, dressing, et cetera were the same. Her social life slowed down to nearly nil compared to when Jack dated her before they were married, but she filled the time with the organizations she'd joined. Not that dating was less important but she allotted time for the other important things in her life as well as dating."

They were all summing this information with the pieces received before and looked at Bri. Bri hesitated, thinking which was the best way to speak about her information, causing the least confusion and argument.

"It seems the 'other roads' are being well traveled as of late," Bri began slowly, "I did make contact... To put it abruptly, but as gently as I can... Hazel's requested we go on with our lives and loves. She said there would be three of us who would need our help and silent shelter. She could not tell me much more because there is much still unresolved; which could affect things yet to be. She did say one strange thing for Chris..." Chris was attentive as Bri elaborated, "Let's see... she said to be sure and get this right...

She loves the idea of a parade but don't forget to... something... I couldn't quite make it out, but my guess would be: it would have to do with being 'in' a parade rather than just 'looking' at one all the time. Oh, yes! She said something about listening to Mona. It didn't make any sense to me, but she began going where I couldn't go and I was being pushed to move or get off the road." Bri ended her part to more confused looks from everyone but Chris, who was sitting there with her mouth hanging open, in comical surprise.

Each woman was summing the information in her own way, each trying to make sense out of the information in a way to draw some conclusions and formulate some plan of action or inaction as the case may be. There was almost telepathic agreement to hold any final conclusions until they heard from Julie and Kitten, and, by the way, where were they?

Dee said, "I'll go to the front desk and see if there are any messages for any of us from them." There was only one message to Bri, from Ollie. It was short and sweet:

"To make a long, tiresome story short. Michael was in jail, posted bond off the money he got from my things. WILL PURSUE AND PROSECUTE. Hazel's poster is right. Thanks much, Ollie." Bri had to smile, but decided not to say anything to the rest until she gained Ollie's permission.

The women stayed and talked till early morning. They decided to leave a message for Mona, Julie and Kitten to contact Bri when they got in, if they felt up to it. The women decided to go to their rooms reluctantly, and meet at daylight. All of them were feeling the altitude a little. This wasn't fun anymore and was far too much of the kind of excitement they had never counted on. Coupled with the jet lag and the emotionally charged events, the women were ready to pick up their baseball bats and gloves and go home. They might have done just that, too, if it were anyone else but Hazel... their cherished Hazel.

* * * *

Somewhere between two and four in the morning, Chris heard a knock on the door. She looked over to see if Jo had come to bed, but the bed was empty. *She must have stayed up talking to Bri and forgot her key,* she thought. "Ugh!" She got out of bed to open the door only half awake, body protesting and demanding she not move from the bed. Locked in a test of wills, her hand opened the door, slamming her mind awake to the sight of a burned, exhausted, dirty, bleeding and scratched Mona.

"Chris, can you come with me, please?" was all the executive said.

Years on emergency and obstetrics pumped Chris' body and brain into action. Towels for cleaning were the only emergency supplies in the room, except for a small emergency kit. Chris spun around, found them, grabbed them, as Mona slumped in the doorway, then followed the nearly dead woman at a maddeningly slow pace. Instinctively, Chris knew Mona's slow pace could only mean a real disaster had happened. Chris was sure that whatever supplies she had would be inadequate for the apparent crisis she was walking into.

They walked into Mona's room; Chris realized her instinct could not have prepared her for the overwhelming shock. The devastating reality of a broken, half living, half recognizable Julie and Kitten made the life force in her threaten to leap all boundaries to succor them back to health. *My Sisters, my Spirit Sisters...* but Chris was one of the best in the country: R.N., Nurse Practitioner Chris stepped forward. Chris began mental evaluation:

They need Ringer's, i.v., stat, (where to begin, oh my broken Sisters) bleeding's dried, caked, no apparent compound fractures,

214

but not to eliminate possibilities. 1.) Julie: breathing shallow, nails and possibly mouth blue, possible rib puncture, fracture likely, nose bleed dried, wound possible bruise on face, possible fracture or concussion, hand dangling, likely fractured, ankle swollen, likely fracture, possible sprain, not disjointed, must look at her eyes. Is she unconscious or exhausted sleep? Blood on back of head, face swollen, contusion right temple (NO! It can't be, sweet Sister!).

"Mona, we need an ambulance. All of you need to be in a hospital. I don't have what I need to take care of you," Chris spoke as she continued to evaluate. Mona attempted to stop Chris from getting near the phone but could only manage a distressed "No! No!"

2.) Kitten: arm fractured two places, knee disjointed, swollen, blood and vomit around mouth, bloody clothes, but dried, possible internal hemorrhage, nails good color, no blood from ears or nose, color good otherwise, asleep or unconscious? Breathing okay, (Oh! Her beautiful face, her beautiful gentle face, so mangled. Oh, Dear Lady! Please Dear Lady!). 3.) Mona: conscious, scratches, bruises, possible hypothermia with so few clothes,... Chris' physical evaluation took only a few heartbeats as is the way with the finely trained, and expertly tested, sharpened by crisis seasoning. *The best trained and most intelligent minds can function poorly in trauma, I have to ask, in case there's something not obvious.*

"Mona?" Chris said in a well-trained, calm, low-pitched, monotone, "Why didn't you call an ambulance and go to the hospital or flag the police?" She not only listened for the answer but observed as Mona spoke.

"Couldn't. He would know they weren't dead. Called my personal physician. She's on her Leer, with equipment... MUST NOT!...

MUST NOT! call any... outside. Someone tried to **KILL** them. Not even husband!" Mona could only get this much out with the last of her energy. She dropped her head back in exhaustion.

Chris began examining all their eyes for reactivity. *What to do? They need emergency treatment now, not hours from now. At least they're in a warm room. It looks like hypothermia's set in on all three. Blankets. Bri and Jo! Clean water on the outside to help better evaluate, a little warm water on the inside for the conscious. If Mona's coherent...*

All she could do was clean them up, keep them warm, and make them as comfortable as possible without moving them too much. They couldn't have anything internally except a little warm water. She shook her head as she called Bri's room. Mona's head snapped up, ready to move if necessary, to protect her charges.

"I'm calling Bri and Jo." Mona returned to her former collapsed position. *Whether or not Mona's accurate, she's ready to defend the belief Julie and Kitten are in danger, even in her extreme fatigue,* noted Chris.

Bri answered the phone in a fog. *Her and Jo what? Who is this?* "**Wake up!**" said the voice. *Oh... this is a dream then..* Bri was about to hang up the phone and doze off again, but someone kept calling her name. "This is Chris? Chris who?" She definitely must be dreaming, "...emergency... Julie and.. JULIE!" Her mind snapped to but her body was planets behind.

"Right, Chris! Jo just slept in Ollie's bed. She's zonked out... Yeah. I'll see if I can wake her and we'll be right down. What room is it again? Okay, I got it. No... I won't go back to sleep, but no guarantees about Jo. Do you want Penny, Dee and the others? I'll get as many as I can. Okay. Bye... Jo! **Jo**! Wake up, Jo- Julie, Kitten and Mona are hurt. **Wake up, Jo**."

Jo resisted awareness until Bri mentioned Julie, Kitten and Mona. It looked like her sleeping mind was evaluating the last statement and gestalted the necessity of coming to a conscious awareness level. Her body didn't move as her eyes flickered open, wondering where she was and why she was coming to when it was obvious to her body she should still be sleeping. *Hurt... someone is hurt*. Jo turned her head to look at Bri who was now getting dressed. Bri didn't stop what she was doing as she spoke, "We need to go to Mona's room. Mona, Julie and Kitten are hurt. We need to call the others but we must not let anyone outside our circle know what's happened."

Jo made it to a sitting position, "Why? What's the matter?"

"I don't know all the details. Chris was a little vague, but apparently they need our help. I think to get them to the hospital. Can you call the others and get them down there, pronto?" Jo felt as if she were looking out a window or mirror or maybe looking out from a tunnel. She watched Bri grab towels and zip to the door.

"Do you want the others to bring towels too?" It suddenly occurred to Jo: *If they are that bad, shouldn't they be on their way to the hospital and why aren't they already there... why are they here?* "Why aren't they in a hospital, already?" Jo queried.

"I don't know. Can you manage by yourself okay?"

"Sure." A few more details and Bri was out the door.

Jo did an excellent job and within a very short time all the women left were in Mona's room, following Chris' directives or getting ready to leave for the airport. Getting the doctor and the equipment into the hotel was not a problem at all. *"Everyone knows"* conferences have specialists all the time. *"Everyone knows"* when a bunch of women get together health, welfare and social concerns will be priority topics of discussion!

Getting everything into Mona's hotel room required some ingenuity-- no problem-- they were women. Women have had to be ingenious forever, especially the last seven to ten thousand years, since the takeover of the partnership societies by the dominator societies. As the women watched the competent doctor and nurse practitioner work, they saw first hand why it is good to pay the very best very well. Mona knew how to do that and retained the best on her personal staff. They found out Julie had a punctured lung caused by broken ribs, in addition to broken bones, lacerations, contusions, and a concussion. Kitten was a little better off, but not by much, and Mona was ready to kick ass after a warm bed, a couple of hours sleep, a hot meal and a workout. The injured women were temporarily bandaged, realigned, put together and made as comfortable as possible in the small hotel room.

It didn't take much discussion to decided they would have to finish the "Gathering" elsewhere, in an out of the way place, for Kitten and Julie to heal. Everyone except Judy would be able to stay after making arrangements with business', significant others, etc. Judy promised to speak with Libby every day if necessary and to keep in contact.

After some discussion, they decided Hazel's situation and what happened to Kitten and Julie were no mere accidents. If someone was watching the group or if any more of them were going to be targets after they got home; it might not be a good idea to expose the location of Julie and Kitten with regular phone calls, for as long as they could manage. The motive for this dirty deed and the person or persons involved had not yet been discovered, nor how many of those present might also be targeted.

Stealth would be their only advantage now. They used their networks to get a very private, very secure place in the Colorado Rockies before the snows. They paid the hotel for the entire reserved period, even though they had several days they would not use. As a matter of fact, the weather stayed uncommonly warm as they quietly moved everyone to the new location. It was just what they all needed to recover from the trauma and find out more details.

They all wished they could move Hazel there, even if not to recover, to be with them when she moved on. To keep close tabs on Hazel, they would surely expose where they were immediately. Julie and Kitten needed time for recovery. They hoped they hadn't expose themselves already in the move and personal arrangements. No sense pushing Fate. This change in venue would be okay with spouses and significant others while the week planned for was not fulfilled. Afterwards personal logistics could get sticky, but not unmanageable.

Competent medical staff and security would be hired. Mona could take care of those details. Between Penny, Dee, Jo, Chris, Bri, Mona and maybe Libby, one of them could be there all the time until the two women recovered sufficiently to move to a more secure hiding place. Even if the snows set in, there would be a way to keep them safe.

Perhaps the trickiest part would be making sure temporary agencies didn't, inadvertently, hire the killer or killers. They would watch carefully all substitutes for regular employees once they were sure of the staff they chose. What is known can be planned for, what is unknown would have to be dealt with at the moment of occurrence. One could only hope if and when an emergency situation happened, 'it' was taken into account in the planning considerations, dealt with, and 'all' be enough. Fortunately, with the amassed brainpower of these women, not much was left to chance. Serendipity would play hell to try and edge in with these players.

Chapter 13

The Chalet was warm, well stocked, out of the way, but near enough to modern services and people if the need arose. Fuel, snowmobiles, and other survival equipment were checked. Medical staff and security personnel would begin the coming Monday. Mona's doctor would stay until then, with Chris to assist. Medical provisions were secured for almost any kind of emergency. Love and friendship intensified and sharpened the planning for the safety of their Spirit Sisters to a caliber sufficient to dim the efforts of even the most paranoid Survivalist. Only then could the protecting mother lions begin to decipher and sum the events so far.

What they were finding out did not appear to mesh congruently. They had details, facts, events that did not seem to relate with each other until, by sheer coincidence, Penny mentioned one man's name. Hazel's political organization was steadfastly opposed to him getting into office. Libby's head snapped up with a vile, reproachful look on her face and venom in her voice as she related details of 'business dealings' this man was involved in, making 'Love Canal' look banal. Although she never met the man personally, the name sent up red flags all over the place.

Libby's manner and attitude still reflected the energy drain and rage brought about by the sudden emergence of horrific memories of past and present events she was still dealing with. But she was able to contribute to the current plannings with her 'Sisters' while holding a segment of her mind for planning retribution to those who harmed her personally. What Libby was processing involved a certain amount of disconnection and disassociation between survivor memories and present reality but most of the time Libby functioned adequately in present reality, her mind doing something like a time-share with the information coming to her consciousness. Jo understood as no one else there could. She and

Libby began to develop a very special relationship, with Jo being able to extend to Libby the benefit of her own recovery.

Next, Mona remembered this name in association with a group of investors Kitten's husband was listed as a member of. The group's broker had approached Mona... oh... several years back, for her to join. Some investigation at the time linked them to a radical, international political group believing in one world government at any cost, with a select few to govern, none of them women. Currently this group was rooting toward financial, political, bio-psycho-social control of the entire world at a noteworthy pace. They advocated different education for men and women with only a few men receiving higher education. They proposed an educational curriculum that would be as the few leaders of the group decided, keeping the masses ignorant, strong of body, weak of mind, void of consciousness. Women and children were to be educated for use in the home. Men were to do all other tasks and these leaders would control and manipulate the tension the masses lived under, much as Hitler tried to do in WWII. Those who would not readily comply and be reasonable would be subject to, as Hitler said, "the weapon which most readily conquers reason: terror and violence".

Mona knew their arguments in favor of this ideology and did not necessarily disagree with the premise. *It certainly is true most people would rather someone else be responsible for making decisions in and governing their lives. Look at how few people vote and fewer care to investigate the validity of the voting and legislative systems. Guess they'll have 'time' after they're in concentration camps. In short, only a few care to think anyway.* It's their method of solutions Mona wasn't exactly in favor of.

Mona had joined the organization to keep up with their progress and frankly, it was in the best interest of good business, then. She knew the level she was placed in the 'investment group' barely kept her privy to the most basic plannings and movements. Mona heard about most of the events after they happened, but with her mind it was not too difficult to make some accurate predictions or put the right information into the computer. Mona also noticed there were no women in certain upper level groups and was told she would not be permitted in these groups or be on any boards controlling policy. She would be assigned where she would be if she wanted to participate in the investment group at all.

She noticed the same exclusion to access on the international computer information systems. Fewer women were being permitted access to certain levels of the computer Bulletin Board Services, known as BBS's, with a few sysop's appearing to twist government regulations to fit their own agendas. The starting of women's BBS's was certainly monitored closely. Mona was remembering those lost files and the trouble she all of a sudden had with her computer while hooked up to certain BBS's.

Mona couldn't help conjecturing a guess that this radical group had something to do with access and dissemination of information. Maybe they had something to do with hiring policies, certain government contractors and large corporation policy, as well. *Worth looking into!* Mona had been told by several sources in some of the organizations she networked with that attitudes within social services and a whole host of agencies, private and governmental, recently seemed to have changed their positions on how they will serve the public. It's easier to notice change the more one travels and easier to compare change with areas that this new 'position' hasn't filtered into yet. And wasn't there a big stink recently about some agency controlling subliminals not only in the field of video but something about a resonant sound affecting certain populations in a certain way? *Ah, the computer!* Mona permitted herself a brief moment of wandering,

As a tool, it can be most helpful but someday, dependence on it will even make the Illuminati bend the knee. Succumbing to the allure of an easier, softer way could mean demise even for the elite. The mind/ body is anesthetized by modern convenience. Lulled by the token power of easy and fast accomplishment, the work and discipline required in the past to obtain gradual, less precise results, is a lot less appealing.

If there were a species of beings feeding off pure energy, it would be advantageous to keep the world 'brain dead' or in an agitated state of fear, anger, chaos, and confusion. What energy the people of the world had would be used to ward off crisis rather than to think of better things. Thinking requires more energy than doing. The world would have less overall power to oppose control, leaving the energy consumption/ calorific value ratio a little lopsided, in favor of unused, usable calories floating around and more energy to feed off of. The tension between brain anabolism and catabolism, if it is amplified in the direction of peak synaptic and cellular performance, exacts a high energy price to maintain. The oxidation/reduction rate is much too efficient to leave much residue to munch on. Hmmm. Could this be a possible explanation for the strong opposition of people taking charge of their own lives? Maybe people would naturally choose a way of living designed to uplift themselves rather than create adipose energy? Is there a possible connection?

As remote as it was, the name Hazel's political group opposed was the only apparent connection between Hazel, Julie and Kitten. If, in fact, there was a connection, Mona was linked defacto, both for her wealth and power, and because she had regular, periodic communication with her Sisters who had been apparent victims. Mona was now beginning to believe Hazel had been victim to something, but what on earth for? Hazel was well liked around the world, but as far as Hazel being a threat to anyone, even if she could, she probably wouldn't harm anyone. Something was missing. Computer. Mona needed to link onto her mainframe, search some databases and do some actuarying. Could she do all this without alerting this group, if there was such conspiring. *Is paranoia communicable*, she wondered? They all followed her as she went to the phone and made the arrangements.

"Get anything?" Dee asked, ready for something exciting.

"I don't know for sure. Some of the names mentioned in the general conversation I recognize from different organizations. If I recognize them, then I am a possible link. I want to see what other links they have to each other. Each of us seems to have a piece of something and I want to see what these pieces have in common, if anything. My mind keeps going back to one of the 'investment groups' I belong to. Maybe several, but I don't have all the information I need here, to make any valid suppositions we could take off on. We'll see what the computer comes up with and then what we can come up with. But for right now, I'm ready to break after I've input the data. Anybody else?"

Kitten and Julie were put in the same room, with the beds pushed together so they could be near each other without disturbing the other's rest. More often than not, even under sedation, when they were able to be sedated, the lovers were found holding hands, linking the space between their traumas, creating a healing space of love.

Kitten and Julie's 'accident' was all over the news. The Duke, the bereaving widower was taking it well. The entourage he had around to shield him from the mean media during his time of trial and sorrow included a darlin' little girl in her late teens, a friend of the family, and the Duke's rock of support. She went with him everywhere so he wouldn't have to face all those memories and familiar places alone. It was purely coincidental she was a younger clone version of Kitten, purely coincidental. They all had bets as to when he'd be taking her to the preacher.

Kitten and Julie were not permitted anywhere near a TV or any other kind of news media by the sister lionesses, especially after what Julie had told Chris. Mona did, however, take care of Julie's accumulated assets to the specifications handed down to Chris, and then through her own network wiped out any trace of Julie's capital and assets with the same skill that made Mona's fortune truly her own.

It appeared to the world, Julie, Esq. had died somewhat impoverished but owing no one. Poor dear, that Julie. Apparently no head for finances. Hell of a good lawyer, but not practical where money was concerned. There had mysteriously come to life in the world, however, a financially secure but not conspicuously rich middle-aged woman not too many people had ever or were ever likely to notice. Imagine! She looks *just like Julie*, may heaven rest her soul, **used** to. You know how middle-aged women tend to have the same look, with an ordinary name like Barbara-or-something. This Barbara-or-something would probably be able to live comfortably the rest of her life with her dearest friend and companion, whom she's known since high-school. Both spinster women, you know, more like sisters than real sisters. Not an exciting life or anything like that but middle-aged women didn't need much excitement, you know. The twilight years should be peaceful... retreating... preparing the way for the journey to heaven for the good.

Mona told Julie and Kitten what she had done and how she had done it, when they were able to sit up and eat. The story made both of them smile, followed by raspberries, hoots and one last comment to the report, "Gag!!" Julie and Kitten's recuperation seemed to take off after that.

No one told them about the man with the strange eyes, yet. It could wait until they were on their feet. With them being in a safe and nurturing environment, where they didn't have to pretend what they were to each other, it didn't look as if recuperation would be long. Julie and Kitten, both, knew this time together was a small reprieve from ordinary living seldom granted. They used it wisely and cherished this time. They had felt Death's breath on their necks and heard Death's scythe-song singing their names in whispers too close to their ears. Life caromed off the near death experience with an intensity bordering ferocity. They were alive and together. The rest they would work out. No one told Julie about her replacement or the newest information they received on the man's political leanings.

The computer helped acquire data and collate information that under normal circumstances would not correlate as apparently as it did now. Within the last twenty-four months an alarming number of female CEO's had had accidents, litigations, rare, unmanageable, debilitating diseases, stress related disorders, breakdowns, and other situations very effectively removing them from the business world. These women weren't necessarily in the same bracket as Mona. Mona owned her own international business, and her accumulated wealth put her leagues apart from most American business. But they were easily in the same bracket as Julie and Libby.

It was beginning to look like a business cleansing seen only in wars designed for ethnic cleansing. Mona turned the computer to the world wide political scene to gather more of the same kind of information. They waited for results.

Bones, cuts and bruises would take longer to heal than Julie and Kitten's spirits. In spite of that, the next week found Julie and Kitten up and part of the brainstorming. They added enough new information to begin putting a larger picture together. Between the brilliant minds and the computer, the puzzle was taking a sinister shape. Access to Mona's database added dimensions that were frightening. The arenas were political and financial. The circus appeared to be world domination, but by whom?... The good ole boys? The Illuminati? Some other of the scads of radical dominator groups? Looked at with a computer and the right data, patterns of war, poverty, the intentional and manipulated generation of fear, anger, hatred, confusion took on new meaning.

Controlled dissemination of information and subliminals, food and medical supplies, birth control, commodities, natural resources, and financial underwriting were used as sources of power. Murder was not generally relegated to the practice arena, it was usually performed somewhere in the substantial threat arena. What about Hazel had posed a threat? In fact, looking at the group and what just happened, the questions needing an answer were: what, about Julie, Kitten, Hazel and Libby formed a substantial threat? Libby had to be included because of the trauma she recently went through and her financial bracket.

Mona didn't flaunt her money, assets, financial acumen or prowess. She kept a low profile, which could sharpen her skills from time to time, having so much tangible solvency. She loved the game and she was a paragon sublime, a virtuoso playing the instrument of world trade. But her successes could not go entirely unnoticed. She was asked to join the exclusive 'investment group'. What anyone knew about her true worth was reflected in the significantly leaner grouping she'd been assigned to associate with. The act would not tell them a lot about her, her parameters for value were her own, but it did tell her about their values and database on her. Why wasn't she considered a substantial threat? Or was she? Mona would go over her amassed fortune again, maybe convert some to gold now and rearrange a few accounts to be sure she still controlled and could access what belonged to her.

Want to know about your competitor? Get him to talk about you. Go so far as to provoke him into being angry with you and speaking about you. The information can be quite revealing. Let a person tell you the worst of what he would do to an enemy and he reveals to you what he fears most. Let your opponent do his dirtiest to you and you now have the secrets of his soul. It is amazing what those who hate you can teach you, if you will let them, Mona reflected.

The only thing out of all the data even implying a threat was an organization supporting the political candidate with the shady business dealings. They went over it at length. The organization didn't seem to pose what would be called a substantial threat. Maybe this linked to something else, linking to something else, etc. They would have to dig below the carefully manicured surface if they were to find Theseus' clew.

Libby went to lie down for a bit. Penny went walking with Dee and Bri. Chris made sure Julie and Kitten were comfortable and then rested herself. Jo went off by herself. Mona wanted some answers about this candidate and the organization after the break. Mona called one of her offices and assigned her secretary the job of getting as much information about the man, the office, and his playmates as possible. She would probably have the information by morning.

We shall see what we shall see, Mona thought, and got up to do her workout. *Move that body! Work that body! Your body's gonna loovvvvvve this!!*

* * * *

The women took care of their individual businesses, personal routines, and plans for the coming week. Once Kitten and Julie fully recovered, they would have to assume permanent disguises, find a place to live and plan their lives in such a manner having the least contact possible with anyone from their pasts. No one could avoid fortuitous meetings, but they both had employees whose habits, families and preferences were known. These situations could be avoided and only ignorance or carelessness could jeopardize their future happiness together. So careful planning about their future was added to the list of brainstorming. Likewise, each woman there could not avoid her connection to Kitten and Julie. They had to plan a course of possible action, linking them all, in case the 'lovers' arranged demise was not going to be an isolated incident. How would they be alerted if someone were trying to pick them off one by one? What would be the signs? How would family and friends fit into the big picture? If they wanted to reverse the tables, what would they have to take into consideration to be able to do the same to someone else? What needed changing to stop the direction this trend was taking? What qualities made them targets in the first place? What in their daily routines posed hazards- what posed asset? What could be avoided and what not? What kind of defense or offense, as the case may be, could be used to assist a paranoia free life? "Fear based in fact is not paranoia", as Thaddeus Golas says in <u>Lazy Man's Guide To Enlightenment</u>, so what could be done to live a fear free life. Especially since Kitten's and Julie's near death experience, they were all acutely aware that no one stood up her real date with death, but they all insisted on living life to its fullest until then.

A little planning now could avoid the tedium of dealing later with unpleasant or threatening situations that take time and energy away from enjoying the moment. So, safeguards, checkpoints, cross reference standards were added to the brainstorming as well as how to inform the others who already left. The intensity of prior events added elements of awareness and encompassment that would not have been as keen or clear. Factors ordinarily relegated unimportant, or entirely overlooked, took on new perspectives. What was usually relegated to paranoia went through intense interrogation and evaluation only the sharpness of the moment could accentuate.

They would be no one's victim nor live under an edict of fear. Their bodies and minds cried out with a savage ferocity at any kind of slavery, subliminal or otherwise. Like the ancient Celts, they would live free people or die fighting for it. They were becoming aware this ideology was surfacing as the radix encouraging momentum to a new kind of rebellion. They would no longer be a part of a system that required, for simple survival, that people allow themselves to be victimized by others, or must victimize themselves for the pleasure of onlookers. The vitality of Roman dominance ideology hadn't died; it had simply gone to a masquerade party and kept changing costumes. Looking at an overview of the news, Rome did seem to conquer the world with its values still giving nourishment to a few and sucking the life force out of the many, especially from women and children. Not until recently was prosperity truly within hand's-reach view to many: it was being squashed, again, by a few extremists.

In less than two weeks, a transmutation was taking place in the "Gathering" group, whose effects were yet to be evaluated. The impact these nine women and their networks could create could start a mass, systemic evolution. None of them doubted one woman can do much. They all had either read about or talked to Muriel Siebert, Mme. Curie, White Buffalo Calf Woman, Bev Francis, Helen Keller and Anne Sullivan, Monica Sjöö and Barbara Mor, Rosa Parks, Elizabeth I, Elizabeth Cady Stanton, Vigdis

Finnbogadótir, Babe Didrikson, Jacqueline Cochran, Henrietta Szold, Susan B. Anthony, Riane Eisler, Simone de Beauvior, Aphra Behn, Devaki Jain and Peggy Antrobus, Golda Meir, Naomi Wolff, Gloria Steinem, Mary Baker Eddy, Sojourner Truth, Corazón Aquino, to name a few out of the hundreds of thousands that have impacted humankind.

They played with the threads of the awesome potential of a united womanhood woven into the world tapestry. Imagine what women together can do... women sharing and utilizing **ALL** their diverse and varied talents together, all over the world. Imagine women and men all over the world working together to enhance life, instead of destroying it. Imagine a world where people naturally assume responsibility for themselves and the earth they live on and naturally choose life enhancement in its whole spectrum. All of them couldn't help but dream for the future.

For the present, it was becoming obvious from the data coming in that successful women were being targeted for destruction. In the past, everyone who reached a certain society level had the same values. The Old Guard saw to that. Those who didn't have the same values never moved from the lowest ranks of society. With the rapid advance of technology, the aging of the Old Guard, the vibration level of the planet changing, and a few other things, those relegated to stand watch over the social lines were watching other things and a few undesirables got past who would never have been let through. At the time it was happening, it didn't look so bad to the Old Guard. One or two were okay; they proved valuable when they were made examples of to the elite who were questioning the Old Guard. Soon the Old Guard figured that, as with cockroaches, when you see one you probably have an infestation somewhere. The babyboomers as a generation classification were beginning to change the world. Now it would take a lot of time and trouble for the Old Guard to clean this mess up and get back to business as usual. They would have to use the present crop of teenagers to help them. They were the easiest to dupe, influence, and control through drugs and media.

As every advancing aggressor has known since well before the Romans, women and children are the easiest targets. So too, this Old Guard appeared to be calling first blood on successful women. If these women weren't entirely loony with the conclusions deduced from the information they were gathering, they needed to initiate some kind of world wide response putting an end to the destruction of human equality and the bondage of women and children. Women and children were still being raped, pillaged, starved, and put into slavery under the guise of patriotism. The majority of women in the world still did not have control over their own bodies, nor access to adequate education, medicine, and financial resources but they had hope.

Someone, or a group of someones, was trying to take away the progress that had been made, little as it was, in the last 100 years or so. **They**, whoever **'They'** were, needed to be stopped and stopped by the women of the world. But how? Female doctors, scientists, professors, engineers, and attorney's had to compromise their Woman Way to achieve success, hoping that once they were in these positions they could make the changes necessary. They were beginning to succeed.

Women were becoming Head of State- there were 15 women Heads of State in the world, now- as well as entrepreneurs, politicians, lawmakers, writers, and earth healers around the world and now there seemed to be a small group gaining momentum that would make these women into nothing more than higher paid slaves. This group sought to crush these successful few and vaporize the hope these courageous women gave their Sisters.

"We need some kind of common ground we can link to," thought Jo out loud. "We need a common bond that we, as women, hold the strings to."

"Sure we do," chimed Dee. "But what do the women in the United States have in common with the women in Turkey, or Iran, or Africa, or South America? We bitch about our lives, but compared to our Sisters in other countries, we have it pretty damn good!"

"But the same thing happened to Libby that's been happening on a daily routine basis to women all over the world," dared Penny gently, "on a much larger scale and accepted as merely cultural custom."

Libby perked up at Penny's comment and replied, "Maybe... maybe it's time to really see our connection to our Sisters, since there are those who're hell bent on pointing it out, and see what we can do about it together! I'm sure there are many men who are ready for a new paradigm too." They all nodded their agreement.

"We've been playing by the rules forever and each time we come close to succeeding or near an equal position, we are stopped in our tracks," Bri put in.

"Seems to me... we've followed the rules and now it's time we start making the rules. We don't justify these rules. We don't explain them. We just live them." Jo looked up.

"Wait a minute! Who's making all these 'rules'?" Penny looked concerned.

"We are... and every other person who believes it's time for a new paradigm, as Libby put it," Dee challenged.

"Dee's right!" Jo responded, "If dominators can divide and conquer, partners can unite and change. If it's a good day to die, then how much more is it a good day to live?... If people have been afraid to look at their shadow sides, they have equally not looked at and been responsible to their own light. Change can be brought about by more than destruction." Jo paused a moment to think. "Remodeling, the Woman Way, encompasses change as well constancy. The same fire and water and air that erode the earth makes the pottery and bricks that contain it."

These women didn't necessarily want to destroy what is, although they were not afraid of that method. They wanted to change or modify the way it is. Something along the lines of balance. They also did not want to ignore the seriousness of the situation.

"Instead of picking apart what's bad, holding it up for view while the good lies rotting, let the bad fertilize the growing ground. Hold up what's good and see what we can make out of that. Both are needed for balance, but value goes to what's focused on and given attention to, not what's cast aside and taken for granted," said Bri.

"Yes! Focus is the fertile ground, desire to change is the seed, but it's action that causes germination. Endurance, steadfastness, the willingness to change what doesn't work and the patience discipline requires is what nourishes the seed to grow," added Dee.

They instinctively knew they had to incorporate all these qualities, not the few they liked, to accomplish their tasks. If they were to be successful in their journey to change, they needed to plan and anticipate each stage of the process. If any group could do it, they could.

"You know, it bothers me that this group... me and ya'll... have somehow ignored the fact that men have been victims and women have been perpetrators. All I'm hearin' is woe is woman, an' all because of those nasty men!" Kitten slid in cautiously.

"We haven't ignored it! But how many women have you heard of participating in the ethnic cleansing of Bosnia by raping every *male* between the ages of four and four hundred?" Libby stabbed.

"In this country, alone, eighty five percent of the females have been or will be raped sometime in their lives," exclaimed Chris. "The figure goes up to ninety something percent when you include the world. How many of those females were or will be raped by women? Ninety something percent of all violent crimes are perpetrated by men and out of those crimes at least seventy five percent were committed against women and children, in America alone. We are talking about at least sixty percent of the world... the entire world population being traumatized in this day and age, 1995. Today!"

"Wait a minute!" Jo pursed her lips as she spoke. "My own mother raped me before I could tell you what happened in words and there were women involved in the physical torture I remember. I'm nearly fifty years old. None of those involved in my mental reprogramming were the slightest bit concerned I wouldn't 'remember'... until recently in therapy, that my sister is my daughter. She's nearly thirty five or six and still doesn't know. The ones who wiped out my memory on that one were male *and* female. Both my mother and my father not only knew but permitted it! Frankly I haven't seen a whole lot of so-called humanity from either gender... wherever I've been. And the little nurturing I have received has been from *both* genders."

"While we're in the territory," Chris chimed in, "even though the numbers are rising in America, how many women steal by breaking and entering or any other kind of violence? How many women work hard most of their lives only to have some male take away, consume, or totally wreck all she's worked hard for because she won't hand over the profits of her labor? Just the other day I saw on TV, a fourteen-year-old black girl in South Africa was beaten so severely by her own brother, he broke her nose and cheek bones and generally smashed her face because he thought she spoke to him in a manner he didn't care for. In my neck of the woods he'd be ridiculed as a coward. The same show said that domestic violence is the number one problem in Africa, in Mexico, the U.S., South America and I didn't catch the rest. The police won't do anything and the mothers don't seem to know what to do."

"I still say it's up to women to make the changes and set the direction. The female of all species brings life into the world. We, the female of our species, must set the value on life and protect that value," Bri moved in.

"Women have the power to **not** bring life into the world, if they choose not to," Chris voiced, "Even if a woman is forced to have sex or be fertilized, she can choose **not** to carry that life within her body. Women of the world could choose not to bring forth new life for a year -- or two years -- or five years."

The room stopped. As if each woman was confronted face on with an unfathomable, catastrophically powerful, personally alterative heresy too overwhelming to be comprehended or considered seriously immediately. The remark was totally bypassed in the present conversation, but Chris knew her Sisters heard her comment and would reason and deliberate the idea when they felt appropriate.

Bri's hesitant pause was seconds as her mind seemed to take in Chris' comment, shelf it and continue what she was saying "One ritual we did with the Unitarian Church where I live was a Yule Celebration that their Men's Group put on. There was a father-daughter team that told their version of manhood. They were both touching as the older man explained the changes he had to go through to be different than his father and still love and respect the man who raised him. The daughter told of the frustration of the young men on the college campus she was attending and how these young men want to shout out loud to the women they pass on campus, 'Please don't be afraid of me! I didn't hurt you! I won't hurt you! I'm not that kind of man!' Especially, to every woman who cringes from them in fear as they pass on the street.

"One of men in my Circle cries when he realizes that each act of violence, both mental and physical, takes away the credit and acknowledgment of ten years of progress that he and his men's group have made on themselves. There are fifty-year-old men in his group that take pride-- take pride-- that they have never been in a fight with another person other than a war in which they thought they were protecting those they loved. Where do those gentle souls go for answers? How do they convince those violent young men who can't feel secure in their manhood without keeping women and children in some imaginary place below them there is truly another way? The far right is consciously changing and manipulating native cultural histories around the world, to their own interpretation, and getting a few natives to agree with them..."

"The far right?" questioned Mona.

"Yes," said Bri, "the far right. I won't honor them in the same terms I do the good, religious Christian friends I have that I love and who love me. Although I'm Pagan, I've read Christian scripture and I don't recall anywhere Jesus advocating deceit, out-and-out lying and murder to convert non-believers. That's what the far right is advocating and beginning to do."

"I have to add to this too!" Kitten pushed in, "There are many women who just take and take and expect to give nothing in return. I think we all know a few of them! And there are many men who nurture and provide for their partners. A man can be just as crushed when a judge takes all he's worked for and awards it to a woman who's been home tending the fires as a woman who hands over to some male leech what she's worked hard for..." Kitten was cut off.

"Are you saying a homemaker doesn't have equal value to a person who works outside the home?!" Dee spoke up heatedly.

"How many women have lowered their values to give men a chance to be equal, hoping men would rise only to find they themselves sunk lower than they could imagine?" Libby asked.

"What do you mean, Libby?" asked Mona gently.

"How many secretaries, students and production workers have done their boss's work hoping for a better position or recognition only to have that boss hire another man and pay him more to fill the position. To put the frosting on the cake, she then has to train the new man, who most likely will do an inferior job that she will be expected to clean up. Why isn't this seen as rape? Why is this perpetration of lies about who's doing the actual work, getting paid for it, and getting credit for it so acceptable the world around? Why have women not only allowed this to happen but also insisted it be that way?" Libby replied.

"Hey! What about all the times all of us have had to tread lightly and hide our intelligence, our organizational skills or any other accomplishments to save the face and ego of the particular male we were in the company of? We had to lower our own standards and come down to his level so he could 'feel' equal or superior. What's wrong with that picture? I say let's stop acting like they're unable to learn the way we did. Let's let them know our egos are just as important to us as theirs are to them. Let's stop treating them like they're inferior." Julie finally contributed.

The room began to buzz now.

"How many men have ever needed pimps?" cried one woman. "How many men have needed laws to receive equal pay for equal-- sometimes exceptional-- work done?" exclaimed another.

"Wait right here, just one minute! Seems to me Blacks, Mexicans and a whole host of other minorities have needed laws throughout recent history, if you please," Texas was heard from again.

"Sure they've needed laws," Dee pushed in, "but let's look at the over-all wages between minority males and minority females. The males still make more than the females, even for the same job. And with all these laws, what has the minority male done for the minority female to equalize the wages or opportunities? How many emergency rooms still receive an inordinate number of minority women and children, victims of domestic violence? How many minority women can't take time off from their many jobs to even register for welfare? Out of all the women in the United States, minority females have worked the hardest, gained the least for all of current time. They are still working and not getting recognized, in this of all countries! **This is intolerable!**"

The room threatened to resonate apart as the voices got louder and more intense. "Does a man have to have his wife's permission, in writing, to have a vasectomy? A woman must have someone's permission to have her tubes tied or a hysterectomy and in some states to even get birth control of any kind!" Chris shouted.

"Maybe that's not such a bad idea. How do you know the schmuck isn't running around on her?" Julie added her two cents. The room was a caldron of bubbling stew, with each woman releasing the contents of her hidden agendas, unspoken ideas, untested theories, personal prejudices and areas of expertise.

Mona, however, sat quietly observing and listening very carefully. Outside of the computer reports, she hadn't much to contribute, yet. When Mona finally spoke, she still needed more information, "Why don't we wait until all the computer reports are in and maybe tape the next session so we don't lose valuable ideas?"

The women stopped.

Libby spoke first, "Maybe we should go over what we just discussed and put it on tape now. I think we've covered a lot of ground and we don't need to re-invent the wheel every time we get a good debate going."

They came to resolution and agreement on what they'd been discussing and decided it was time to do something personal. Each woman had her own balances figured out so each pursued her own preference.

* * * *

After the computer reports were in, Libby recognized one of the photographs as one of the men who raped her. Julie recognized another as someone in the judicial system. Mona recognized still another in one of her investment groups, all connected to the political scene. A big picture was forming of a different kind of ethnic cleansing. They knew their lives had been a training ground for this moment and time. Training was over, no more dress rehearsal. They were ready for opening night.

They hadn't left the main living room for several days now. They had their meals served there, they cat-napped there, they left the john door open to be able to continue thought and talk. The energy built up from time to time almost made the heater unnecessary. They were cookin', excuse the pun.

Someone would come up with an idea aspecting one area. They would grill the issue (not the person), break it down, build it up, turn it over, bake it and set it down to return to later after it cooled. Their efforts were achieving amazing results but they needed a cohesive facet, an element common to everything they wanted to set in motion or stop the motion of, without interrupting the process. They needed a common surface joining all the individual avenues without becoming the avenue, something like the bus in a computer system. There must be something common to all people, especially women that could be used as a lever and some common source of power to make the changes necessary. The tension of highly charged, kinetic energy filled the air.

Mona was sitting side angle to her computer, the TV was on without the volume. The morning news was on between the commercials. There was a particularly attractive commercial on. Even without the sound, this commercial got across its point and did it well enough to draw in the senses. Books, data sheets of information that shared doodling, and an old novel lay on the floor next to her feet, amid newspapers, magazines and crumpled scraps of paper. Just about all the resources they'd used were now occupying the same room they were and, any moment, would probably start vying for territory.

We need to do something about this, thought Mona. She kept looking around the room. Things began catching her eye, demanding she notice. She would try to go back to concentration on the issues and the room itself kept calling her back, over and over, from one object to another. *What is it? What are they trying to tell me?* Over and over, object to object. The telephone, the TV, the computer print outs, the doodling, the TV, the books, the computer screen, the magazines, the TV. Then it happened -- the satori.

"I've got it." Mona put down her pen, "I've got the glue. Actually I've got the how, what, why, where, and when. The how is media! All media! We write articles. We develop programs. We have TV spots. We write books for long term effects. We write, produce, and market a film, we set up a BBS, we connect around the world. We make music, we do workshops, lectures, offer courses, get the whole damn world involved to use the skills they have for creating and making changes."

The group gave full attention to Mona. They were all curious what the 'what' would be.

"What are we going to do all this communicating about?" Libby opened.

"Libby! You collaborate with Julie and Kitten to write a magazine article about your rape experiences and how all rapes connect politically into controlling systems. We'll make an award winning 60 minute documentary of it. We can do it in such a way all the characters are damn well, well known without being libelous, but we get the point across. We expose every single one of them and their methods, and give you and the love birds a chance for justice without having to victimize yourselves to get it. We don't let any of them get away with anything!! Plus with the exposure, people in similar positions can prepare themselves to take counter measures." Mona was beginning to get excited.

"Next we **show** what needs to be changed, really changed. So there's no misunderstanding we mean business, we make a list of demands that consider women and children first. We don't keep the same system, use a different name, different personnel, and different rhetoric only to find out no real change has taken place. We outline what changes need to take place and how to accomplish it with time blocks, checking for accomplishment. We point out the indicators of success, the symptoms of ineffectiveness with step-by-step strategy for getting back on target, and we do it in two hours or so. Most people's attention spans are directly related to their seating or bladder capacity, which ever comes first. People are more than ready for a change- a world wide change- but they don't know how to bring it about without destroying the world with it. The baby and the bath water thing." The executive was brainstorming.

"I agree we need a standard to measure progress," stated Libby, "The thing I most vehemently disagreed with while I was talking to Judy was the idea of forgiveness. It seems the idea of forgiveness is equated to: 'Oh! If she's forgiven me, it must not have been that bad. I guess if I do it again it won't be so bad and she'll forgive me again.' Then it eventually turns out to be: 'Well if this isn't so bad and she keeps forgiving me, exactly where is she going to draw the line and say it's too much to forgive.' Then there's an endless focus to try to counteract the next perpetration and so on and so on so that your whole life is consumed in 'What will he do next?', instead of being able to live a productive life. I'm not advocating not forgiving as a focus for getting even but there does need to be a way to say we mean business without having to spend every waking minute making sure everyone's doing the right thing or having to execute justice in place of making progress and really living life. I've seen it over and over in my offices with the women I employ. If they get an award that is justified, they have to spend the next twenty years trying to collect it. If they're able to collect it, it's usually not worth the effort they've put into it, but if they don't hold these perpetrators accountable, the perpetrators figure it's alright to continue to perpetrate."

"I agree with Libby!" Julie added to the conversation at this point. "I've talked to my colleagues and their clients and it seems we need to develop something that can't be mistaken for wimping out or being able to wear us down into submission again. It seems groups of people have done this before and if this Old Guard lets them have a minor victory here and there, all too soon the world is back to business as usual, some profiting enough to keep quiet about the leaders of the movement being dealt with when the hoopla is quieted down by the masses. Something like 'Everything must be fine now: we can go back to sleep... everyone's belly is full and there are no bombs for now. Don't see anything wrong now!' type of mentality. What I wonder about is if we get it going, will the Old Guard wait us out, deal with us later and return everything to the same old stuff with worse penalties for traitors? Will we all try to rest on our laurels, so to speak? We, the women of the world, in a very big generalized statement would much rather work and live than war and strategize for war. When we all go back to work, will they wait just long enough so that it's almost impossible for us to take time off again to keep the change going? How willing are the women of the world to be ready for that kind of change?"

"Yeah! I think the women of the world are ready for a change. They're tired of begging for their lives and the lives of their children in the face of so much abundance," Jo shook her head in acknowledgment. "Besides making the change, I think they're ready to make it a permanent change. But how do we do it? How many generations before it's a permanent change?"

"We use all our resources to open the doors, motivate and train them to more action and less talk, we turn this incident we experienced and every tragic event that happens into an initiator of change. We make it the best possible thing that could have happened and show others how to do it too." Mona looked around the room at women who were beginning to glow with the same fire burning inside her, "We lay out our demands for change with its timeframe, then we prepare to back it up."

"Back it up how?" came several voices.

"Not <u>how</u>? We're still on <u>what</u>?" Mona grinned at 'If she doesn't get to the point!...' faces.

"Look! I know the women of the world and many good men of the world are ready to stop seeing their children starve to death. They're ready to stop seeing their children raped and murdered and being compelled to kill others while a select few feast. But you're talkin' about the whole world." Kitten was lost in amazement.

"I agree with Kitten," Chris was truly surprised. "I believe the women of the world are ready to stop seeing their daughters raped and their sons killed and some anonymous male making decisions about their bodies, their lives and loves... But the entire world! Maybe we could start here and in a few decades..."

"Why not the world?" Bri looked up and got a letter out of her brief. "My friend Lisa just got back from the Women's Conference in Beijing. Listen to what she wrote me... Let's see... Here! 'In twenty years some countries of the world will have a surplus of young men to access for military needs. Will we see an increase of the trafficking of women, sexual tourism, and enforced prostitution to meet their needs? Who will respond to the women who survived and lacked the medical and educational opportunities their male counterparts had because of their gender? Who will address these young women's psychological and emotional disorders related to such powerlessness?' I ask you, can we or any other woman afford to focus locally and wait? I don't think so. I think we've waited too long now.

"There's no magic wand and no fairy God-mother. If there's going to be any changes we have to do it and we have to do it **NOW**. None of us got to vote by waiting for the world leaders to magically release our equality into the wind! Most of the successful people I know didn't wait for others, somewhere in the future, to make the conditions right to do what they needed to do to start the ball rolling. They made the conditions right in their present.

"How many of you can picture a world where your precious daughters cannot get a safe abortion if they need it? How many of you can picture a world where your precious granddaughter must marry. Must marry and possibly be second or forth or whatever wife and be tied down by you, her relatives, to have her clitoris cut out with a used razor or gouged out by a broken piece of glass so her husband can receive pleasure from her without fear she will receive pleasure and run around on him? Will **you** wield the knife? Will **you** hold her down and force her legs to remain open? Will **you** tie the rope around her legs or maybe put the egg and sugar mixture on her bleeding labia? Or perhaps you think this should be a father's ritual rite to be performed on your newborn granddaughter. This is happening globally, daily, where women have no say and even in this country as a 'cultural rite'. Will **you** watch as your precious daughter and granddaughter are stoned to death when your granddaughter is raped and your daughter is accused of not raising her girl-child right because the child **allowed** herself to be **raped**? This very thing happened not too long ago. Or perhaps you'd rather go back to minimum wage because that's all a woman deserves? Will you continue to write the thesis, make the discoveries, invent the cures, do the work and have the credit and money given to the head male? Would you like never being able to own anything again, not having a say in your government, your education, your medical treatment, where and when you travel and are free to move, who you marry, who enters your body, when and where you may live, when you must die and be considered nothing but chattel **again**?"

The room's very space stopped movement to take in what was just said... To feel the impact of each fact brought forward. What seemed like a sonic boom cudgeled the silence.

"It's all too clear! We don't have a few decades anymore. We begin by getting Hazel's address book from the family. We notify all her key people around the world what happened to Hazel and what we've found out. The computer information and statistics speak for themselves. All of us are in a position right now to have all we've worked hard for taken away from us. So do many successful women around the world stand a chance of losing the edge we've worked so hard to gain. As one group or one country it won't work but together... We stop the world!" Mona tossed the words of evolution to them.

The room's buzz threatened to become a roar.

"It's simple." Mona shouted over the roar, "There's not one single woman in the entire world who doesn't work at something, who doesn't contribute something. We make sure we have what's needed for at least a month or so... world wide, I'm talking about... And we stop the world. We go on strike!

"Factory workers don't go to work, housewives don't cook except for children, they don't buy at the market. Those who work at arms factories make sure important pieces are missing, keys can't be found, computer passwords are no longer valid, manufacturing equipment already in use finds it's way to the repair shops, airline reservations turn up missing, important files can't be found, every office worker, every female technician, transportation worker, hospital worker, consumer does her part! No woman goes to work and tries to assure her job can't be done by anyone else... for one week, around the world... the first time. We threaten to continue until our demands are met.

"Imagine no paperwork generated for a week. Imagine no nursing care for a week. Imagine no production for one week. Imagine no buying for a week! Imagine all the things that women do, not being done for a week! At least sixty to seventy percent of the work done all over the world is done by women. Without the menial as well as the profound work that women do being done; the world will come to a screeching halt. Why we haven't exercised our majority before now, I don't know. It must be an all-or-nothing thing: women who have must share with women who don't have for at least a week. We'll have to stick together as we've never done before. We show what power is without shedding blood. Even if **'they'** kill **us**: they can't make us produce. We've already been through the 'there are some things worse than death' training.

"I've been plagued with a feeling, if we don't do it soon there won't be future generations to do it for... What do you think? I think it will work. We'll all have to do lots of work. There's work for everybody and the only reward will be getting people off their asses, making decisions, making choices, taking risks in areas they never have before. In short, disrupting comfortability and causing creative chaos, making the changes happen. I think it's the only way to make the changes begin instead of talking about it and accomplishing nothing.

"We encourage everyone to speak up. We encourage everyone to write a book, make a movie, write a song, paint a little of reality, photograph what's happening in their neighborhood, get on the school board, run for mayor, do a documentary series that will be shown in the public schools. We open the gates and help 'em through while we keep to our timeframe to stop the world. Instead of 'Stop the world and let me off', the battle cry is: 'Stop the world and give it back!' What do you say?"

They were all thinking. They were all trying to match their individual and combined skills to Mona's idea. They were trying to recall people, places, names of key people that just might be able to help make the shift. The world!

The doubt of dreams began shifting to the possibility of action. Mona looked into faces quickening with the reality of an idea whose time had come to happen. Was it possible? Would the outcome outweigh the sacrifice? What were the chances this would amount to a lot of nothing after the suffering dies down? Mona said one last thing.

"The Bumblebee flies."

The room was beginning to glow with the energy they were raising. Like a champagne bottle being opened, their voices, almost in unison, created a bang of discharging energy.

"Yes we can!"... "I think we can do it!"... "It just might work!"... "I can see it happening!"... "I think it's crazy but I feel it can happen!"... "I can hear it already!"... "Sure we can!. We can do it!"

The first time block they set was for Winter Solstice. It was a day commonly recognized all over the world. Julie and Kitten went to live near Libby to begin the magazine article and documentary film script. There was a lot to work out. Julie and Kitten were especially supportive by guiding Libby's writing efforts to keep her focused. Libby began intensive therapy and had to sell much of her business, to the delight of her former attorney and the 'boys'. Libby's therapy would be long and at times all-consuming.

The healing process Libby had to go through wasn't for the fainthearted. But the process, as with many of the recovering processes, would enable her to stop self-defeating behaviors and her writing would keep her connected to the rest of the world with the aid of Julie and Kitten. Jo kept in touch. No recovery process begins with changing everything in the world around the person, hoping like hell they'll change with it: Libby had to fix herself first. Libby found out the whole process of recovery, when worked correctly, is designed to reintegrate the person, bringing their talents and services into the world to whatever degree is possible. It is not intended to have a person contemplating her own naval, processing forever. There is balance.

Although Libby might still want to kill those Good Ol' Boys slowly, perhaps the article and the documentary, if she stayed focused, could do Justice that a murder or a torrid court battle couldn't. Libby didn't defend herself or make excuses. The 'boys' figured she was defeated for good; she didn't bother to correct them. She wasn't using any of the methods or tactics they expected her to use or were familiar with. She delighted in showing the statistics and other facts to her women's groups.

Mona was one of the pivot points and kept operating business as usual" while assisting where needed as all around world courier-troubleshooter, main support and cheering section.

Penny, Dee, and Jo, artists that they were, jumped feet first into politics, theater, workshops, church groups, started new groups, computer networking, all while maintaining regular contact to keep updated and focused.

Ollie went to live in Bri's city and began intensive training and therapy for self-empowerment. She had a long range goal of not only learning to do it for herself but developing the skills to teach it to others that were in the same position as she once was.

Her healing, too, was going to take some time. First she would have to identify the problem, extract and examine the values surrounding the problem, desensitize her feelings (not eliminate them), develop new values and boundaries, then design, consciously, new behaviors that were appropriate to her. This process involved testing ideas, making mistakes, making corrections, sometimes ad nauseam. Luckily, the training involved in the making of a High Priestess is similar to many of the recovery processes so Bri, could lend a little more in the way of support for Ollie through the rough times.

Bri was another focal point and kept a fairly low profile, while devoting much attention to reinforcing Ollie's positive direction. Bri provided lots of encouragement and emotional support, and probably most important of all, she was there to witness Ollie's progress and applaud. Bri gathered and disseminated information throughout the spectrum of their endeavors. Enlisting Ollie's aid, they especially networked with existing women's political, financial, and professional organizations. This enabled Ollie to do some reality testing in a fairly safe environment while she was making the changes in herself.

Chris started getting political and encouraged Lea to do the same. Lea was perfect for politics and was enticed by the theatrics aspect and the lure of far away places in the international political scene. They shared the BBS networking.

Judy began to write, teach and publish works surrounding her research and the solutions she was finding. She gave lectures throughout the country. She kept close contact and encouraged Libby and Ollie every chance she could. Occasionally she would approach Lea, but Lea wasn't ready to go any farther than the fun of politics, yet. So Judy let that be.

The Internet was popping to the tune "Yes I Can!" and "The Bumblebee Flies!" Apparently women world-wide had already thought of these same ideas and were unsure how to put these ideas into motion. One BBS read "It is time for the Awakening. The time to Awaken is NOW!"

Every evolution, as every revolution, has its martyrs and this one was no exception. Women were burned in India. The Middle East, South America, and Africa did much worse as the news got out. Women all over the world were received into emergency rooms, morgues, cemeteries, jails. Women were shot in groups by firing squads. They were poisoned, gassed, stoned, tortured, excommunicated all over the world. The more force exerted to compel the women back to their inferior status, the more women and men began to join the resistance. The factories, schools, hospitals, offices, and markets of the world began to slump.

Like an ant who's found an abundant food source and sends its message back to the hungry colony, this small group of women worked relentlessly with only one focus propelling their every movement, every second of every day. In the same way a single dandelion seed flower becomes a garden of dandelions, the women and the men of the world ready for change passed the word and prepared for Winter Solstice.

Finally the plan was ready for full implementation. It was Winter Solstice, the longest night of the year. Traditionally pagans and other peoples celebrated the return of the sun and the conquering of light over darkness. The originators gathered together in Hazel's hospital room. They wanted to be near the woman who had inspired them and lived her life as a free woman. Hazel taught them *Change is inevitable: The direction of change is a choice and the responsibility of everyone.* The TV was on with only males visible.

"Women of the World are on strike today!" they said. "Demands for change involving politics, corporate policy, military policy, agriculture, and ecology are being made all over the world to affect change for humanity and earth. The demands and the threatened strike do not... I repeat, do not appear frivolous. Compromise negotiations are being arranged... We go to our anchor man... Tom, what do you see as the reason for..."

"Compromise??!!" someone in the room spat out.
"Frivolous?" someone started laughing.
"Did he really have a question about our reasons?" another asked incredulously.

Just then the hospital's electricity blinked a few times and went off. The TV died. The machines died. The emergency system began to hummm. The emergency system, however, failed on Hazel's floor. The women held their breath in reverent silence. Hazel's heart monitors stopped. The respirator stopped. Kidney, blood pressure, and other life support systems ceased...

Somewhere... for only a brief moment... the sound of a brass band and a big drum clapping out a duple-metered, syncopated, promenade melody floated in the air.

EPILOGUE

They all supported and encouraged each other, especially during the difficult times every evolution has. There is never only one way! Evolution has never been easy.

THERE ARE MANY WAYS TO MAKE POSITIVE CHANGE.

Everyone gets to participate and bring in their best.

What about you, you say?

Oh!... No?...

What about who?

Hazel? Well, she asked, most lovingly, what you were doing to participate in The Change, then she said something about a parade...

THE END